HEROINE

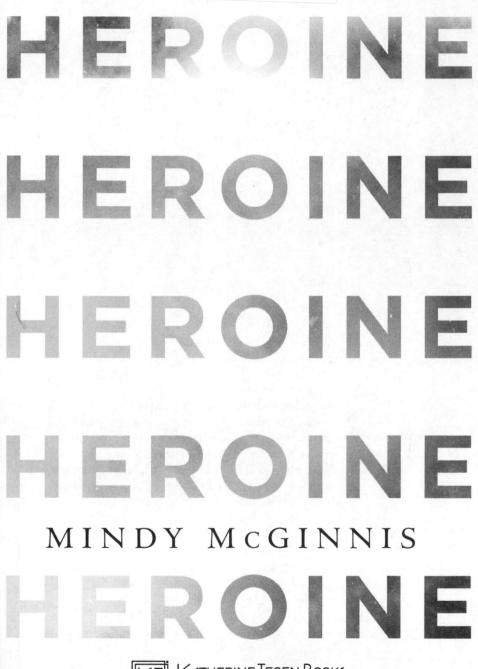

HEROINE

HEROINE

HEROINE

HEROINE

MINDY McGINNIS

HEROINE

KATHERINE TEGEN BOOKS
An Imprint of HarperCollins Publishers

Katherine Tegen Books is an imprint of HarperCollins Publishers.

Heroine

Library of Congress Control Number: 2018939881
ISBN 978-0-06-284719-5

Typography by Erin Fitzsimmons
19 20 21 22 23   PC/LSCH   10 9 8 7 6 5 4 3 2 1
❖
First Edition

For Paige—
I love to watch you play.

This book contains realistic depictions of opioid use.
Recovered and recovering addicts should proceed with caution.

PROLOGUE

When I wake up, all my friends are dead.

I don't know when they stopped breathing, or how long I slept while they dropped off one by one. Josie's basement is a windowless place where time does not matter, the lights set low. She's sprawled across a couch, lips gone gray underneath the plumping lip gloss she uses to cover the fact that she's started shredding them with her teeth, devouring herself with need when there's no needle in reach.

I try to get up, my hip refusing to carry me in the pivotal moment when I rise. I bump into the coffee table, sending a syringe rolling onto the floor.

Shit.

"Josie?" I say, putting my fingers to her wrist.

I don't know how to find a pulse, don't know what fingers I'm supposed to be using or if I'm touching her in the right place. I try the side of her neck, but get nothing, her skin cool.

It's expensive skin, the kind that's never had too much sun or been too dry. Josie's never had calluses on her palms like mine, and she paid to have the one scar on her body lasered away. Me, I'm a map of pain, needle pricks you could connect all over my skin to make constellations named things like Agony and Writhing Woman, all of them converging to form a supernova at my hip, one that pulses and breathes, on the verge of imploding into a black hole.

Even the fingernails I'm pressing against Josie's throat have dirt under them, tiny grains I've carried with me since this afternoon from behind home plate. I can still feel the sun on my back from where it baked in, now trying to seep out, escape the darkness of this cave and the dead inside it.

I am thinking the same.

I check Derrick and Luther, but they're gone. I curl my fingers with Luther's, our knuckle bones near each other one last time, the closest we'll ever get to a conversation about *us*, and what that word could have meant. I sneak up the stairs as if afraid I will wake them, the dose in my blood keeping me calm as I go out the back door. In the yard I move under the cover of trees that I doubt Josie ever climbed as a child, though I would have taught her how if I'd known her then. Instead I met her later, and the only thing she learned from me is how to find a vein.

I start my car but keep the lights off as I back out of the driveway, not turning them on until I'm out of the cul-de-sac. It's dark and I'm driving exactly the speed limit, because I am a good girl. I am a student athlete and the catcher for an undefeated softball team and a senior who needs to get a good night's sleep before her last league game.

I did not just watch my friends die.

I did not leave their bodies cooling in a basement.

I am not an addict.

CHAPTER ONE

accident: *a sudden and unexpected event, usually of unfortunate character*

A car crash does not happen in slow motion, like in the movies. It happens like this:

I'm talking to Carolina about the guy she likes, picking apart everything he said to her, every inch of body language that has been displayed for her benefit. I'm breaking it down for her, because while she's beautiful and smart and tough and perfect, she's also the only Puerto Rican for about a hundred miles and doesn't think it's possible that the quarterback would be into her instead of some white girl.

"Last week he said something funny at lunch and everybody busted out laughing, but you were the one he looked at," I tell Carolina.

"So?" she says, hands curled around the pizza boxes on her lap.

"So out of our entire table of football players and cheerleaders, Aaron looks at the softball pitcher to see if she thinks he's funny," I say, braking for a turn that can be nasty on freezing nights, like this one.

"He is funny," she concedes, spinning her class ring on her finger. "I think I even saw your lips twitch."

"Maybe," I say. "But I'm not the one he likes."

"People like you," Carolina insists, an old conversation that we've been having ever since I befriended the only other girl at recess who didn't have someone to play with. We were two loners then: her the kid whose skin wasn't the same color as everyone else's, me the one who never knew quite what to say, hesitating a little too long whenever I was asked to join in. The novelty of Carolina's race wore off, her smile overcoming any reservation the other kids had.

Me, I don't smile much.

"*Like* is a strong word," I tell her.

"Fine," she says, reaching for her phone to change the music. "But they're definitely in awe of you, and that counts for something."

That's no lie. My classmates have been in awe of me ever since a badly aimed kickball sent our gym teacher to his knees in second grade. But that admiration never warmed into friendship, just high fives and first pick in gym class.

I'll take it.

"The team loves you." Carolina isn't letting it go.

The team does love me. We've spent our summers together: sweat-soaked hair tucked behind our ears, wet towels on our necks when the Ohio afternoons shot past one hundred degrees. We grew up that way, back-woods girls knocking down bigger—and supposedly better—teams until even the city paper started sending out reporters to cover us, dirty kids with Capri Suns in our hands, arms draped over each other's shoulders.

We love each other, yeah. Even if most of the time they don't know what to make of their catcher, and our conversations tend to focus on one thing only.

"Maybe if you tried talking to them about some-thing other than softball," Carolina wonders aloud, her thoughts following mine, like always.

I consider that for a second. "I guess I could talk to them about basketball."

My friend busts out laughing. "Ay, Dios mío," she says, wiping tears from her eyes. "I'll know you're put-ting effort into it when you start talking to them about volleyball."

"Volleyball," I say, rolling my eyes, which brings another peal of laughter from Carolina, her head thrown back, neck highlighted way too much by the oncoming car that's brighting us. I flick my lights at them.

Then I'm not driving a car anymore.

I'm lying in a field, surrounded by frost and glass and corn stubble and the constant *tick-tick-tick* of a motor cooling. I stare at the sky, trying to figure out what just happened.

There's been a car accident, and I was in it. Actually, I seem to have sailed over it, out and above, to land face-down in snow and dirt, both of which are in my mouth. I don't understand, but I do know that Carolina was beside me and now she's not. Which means she's still in there somewhere, with exploded airbags and twisted metal and broken glass and all the things that make my car suddenly converge into sharp edges and crushing weight, a trap I escaped.

I'm going to save her, going to make it still matter that Aaron most definitely is into her, and probably won't be shy about it after this. I'm going to stand up and get my friend, pull her out of the wreckage, and see her in one piece, because that's the only allowable ending to this. I'm going to do these things, but when I try to come to my feet, I collapse.

My legs have a job, and have always done it without question, so I can't get my head around the fact that I've lost the ability to stand up. I spit out a mouthful of snow—the first snow, one my grandfather would have called a sugar snow, the perfect time to go tap the maple trees for their syrup. It doesn't taste like sugar though; it tastes like blood and dirt.

I try to get up again, and there's panic in my movement this time, more urgency rather than just a learned behavior—the art of standing. I've got one leg underneath me and am considering the other when the lights approach, red and blue mixing into purple as they slice across the field. It makes everything oddly beautiful and accentuates the lazy spin of my tires, treads pointing to the sky. Glass sprays from the passenger window, glistening like snow as Carolina kicks at it, and then crawls out, screaming my name.

I'm balancing on one knee, teeth gritted so tightly in concentration I can't answer her. I get up on one leg and tell the other to follow, but it simply won't. I go over again, my bad leg at an odd angle from my hip, one that shouldn't be possible.

My bad leg . . . why would I call it that?

It's not a good thought, one that seems to float separately from the world I just came from, the warm interior of my car, music playing from Carolina's phone, and the smell of the pizza. I don't know how I went from there to here, from somewhere I was happy to a place where I can't stand up.

"Mickey!" Carolina calls again, and this time I answer. She comes to my side, backlit by swirls of light, the chaos that we are so intimately a part of removed from us for the moment. It's quiet out here where I landed, which is a good thing because I don't have the strength to be loud.

"Mickey?" She says my name again, this time as a question.

Carolina kneels and I notice she's holding one arm like a baby, cradling it to her chest with the other, like it needs to be taken care of.

"Your arm," I say, but she shakes her head.

"Your leg," she says, and I shake my head too, because we both want to believe we still live in a world where we're whole. No one can tell us otherwise. Not yet.

A beam of clean, white light breaks toward us, a paramedic shouting when he spots us.

"Ladies?" he calls. "Are you injured?"

Carolina wipes a tear from her face as she looks down at me. She takes a deep breath and it hitches, stuck in her lungs, refusing to release.

"Yes," she calls back.

And just like that, everything changes.

CHAPTER TWO

communicate: *to make known information, thoughts, or feelings to another*

I'm not good with words.

They don't come to me fast and strong, like they do for Carolina, who switches effortlessly between Spanish and English, choosing whichever suits her meaning best. She can do that, plus inflect emotion into whatever she's saying, her body moving with her voice to the extent that when we were kids I always knew what she was saying, even if I didn't recognize the words. Now I'm close to fluent in Spanish, years spent around the Galarza dinner table giving me a mastery of my best friend's first language, as well as my own.

Technically.

In my mind I know what I want to say in either

language, but even though the space between my brain and my mouth is a short one, the words never get there. Just like on the playground, the pure joy at being asked to join with the other kids never made it to my lips. So they would walk away, whatever I was going to say coming out moments too late.

It's like that now, with nurses and doctors hovering over me, the strobes of emergency vehicles replaced with the harsh glare of hospital lights. They're asking questions—*What happened? Where does it hurt? Can you tell us your name?* And, as always, I've got nothing. I stare at them, willing the words to make the journey to my mouth so that I can communicate. But when they finally do, what pops out isn't an answer for them. Instead it's a question of my own, the only one that matters.

"Is Carolina okay?"

Two nurses glance at each other, one of them running a scissors up the leg of my jeans, shredding what's left of the bloody denim.

"Carolina Galarza," I repeat. "She came in with me. Her arm . . ."

I trail off, thankful for once that my thoughts don't make the leap out into public without first being examined. The truth is that Carolina probably is *okay,* according to their metric of the word. These people deal with ripped skin and exposed organs, patients who roll into the emergency room already dead, or halfway there. I can't expect them to understand that the arm she was cradling is supposed to take us to state in the spring, flinging fastballs from the mound that most girls in the county can't get a bat around quick enough to touch.

And if that doesn't happen, nothing is *okay*.

"Galarza?" a male voice behind me repeats. The medics put a brace on my head and neck before they loaded me into the ambulance, so I can't turn to see him. But we've definitely got a connection, because the next thing he says is, "The pitcher?"

"Yeah." I grab onto this word, spoken in a language I know. The language of sports. "Five no-hitters last season," I add, pride for my friend seeping out of me as fast as my blood is. We're moving now, the lights above going past in a series of bright rectangles.

"You play too?" He's still talking, and the other nurses have fallen silent, letting this conversation happen since these are the only words I can find right now.

"Catcher," I say.

"Shit," he says. "You're Mickey Catalan?"

I'm used to it by now. Pretty much everyone in our town knows each other, but with the softball girls it goes past our names and faces to our jersey numbers and stats. I've got a weekly engagement with Big Ed at the market for a Monday-morning analysis of our team's performance, and it's not unusual to have long conversations with people who stop me while I'm getting gas to ask about our last game. I don't always know their names but I can usually place their faces.

Like, Guy Who Always Brings His Wiener Dog, and Woman with Victoria's Secret Umbrella, and Elderly Couple in Matching Scooters. Now I can add Emergency Room Nurse to that list, if I ever get a glimpse of his face.

"Yeah, I'm Mickey Catalan," I say, addressing a spot of perforated ceiling tile above my head.

He doesn't answer, and I know why.

Our first-string pitcher just walked into the ER cradling her throwing arm, followed by the catcher, who wasn't walking at all. They might as well skip the X-ray entirely, because I saw, even though the medics did their best to distract me.

I saw my hip, the whole thing, exposed to the snow and dirt and all kinds of stuff that the insides of people aren't ever supposed to touch. I don't have to be a doctor to know that it wasn't right, the pieces of me that work together separated, bones that knit to each other in the womb no longer touching.

There's one word I learned a long time ago that never had trouble making it to my mouth, one I've relied on enough to get a formal warning from the umpire last season. I say it now, with feeling.

"Fuck."

CHAPTER THREE

trauma: *a wound or injury directly produced by causes external to the body*

I wake up somewhere else. I know I'm not in the local hospital because the ceiling doesn't have water stains, and the lights aren't bare fluorescents. I try to talk, but everything has dried together—my tongue to the roof of my mouth, my lips to each other. I finally put enough energy into it, the girl who once deadlifted the quarterback focusing all her might into opening her mouth.

My lips come apart with a dry smacking sound and I suck in air, rib cage protesting, everything groaning into motion like a car with a half-dead battery during a deep freeze.

"Thirsty?" someone asks.

I nod, and a nurse puts a cup in front of me. I raise

my arm to take it but she shoos me away, putting the
straw in my mouth, like I'm a baby. I'm not too proud
though, not right now. Not with no idea what's under
these hospital sheets or where I am or why I can't feel
my right leg at all. The nurse turns away and I risk a
glance.

It's still there. I swallow what's left of my last drink
of water, letting it wash the tears that were threatening
to overflow back down my throat, ice water mixing with
warm salt.

"Why can't I feel my leg?" I ask, while the nurse wraps
a blood pressure cuff around my arm. She takes a second, noting my vitals and writing them onto a chart
before answering.

"You just came out of surgery," she says. "You'll be
groggy from the anesthesia. Swelling can interfere with
feeling as well, and you have quite a bit."

I'll say. I might have been relieved when I saw that
there was still a shape beneath my sheet where my leg is
supposed to be, but the fact that it's twice the size of my
other one can't be good.

I want to ask when it will be normal again, when I'll
be able to walk, how Carolina is doing, why my mom
and dad aren't here, and where is here, anyway? I want
to ask all these things, but they're backed up, tripping
over each other in my head. They must show in my face

though, because the nurse puts her hand on my arm and smiles at me.

"Your surgeon will be in to talk to you soon," she says.

My surgeon. Someone whose face I haven't seen and whose name I don't know but who's been wrist-deep in my body, and is intimately familiar with parts of me *I* haven't even seen. Except for that one glance, which I could have lived without.

"When?" I ask.

She's saved from answering when a man walks in, his green scrubs telling me this is the guy I'm waiting on. He introduces himself as Dr. Singh, then takes my chart from the nurse.

"Catalan," he says. "That Italian?"

"I don't know," I say, partly because it's true, partly because it's the last thing I care about right now.

"Catalan . . . Catalan . . . ," he repeats, sitting on the rolling chair. "Seems like I've heard the name."

"My mom's an ob-gyn," I tell him, realizing I must not be too far from home if she's delivered babies in this hospital.

"Annette Catalan?" I've got his attention now, his eyes on me instead of a chart about me. "You're her daughter?"

"Well, I'm adopted," I say. Mom told me a long time

ago I don't have to say it like it's a bad thing, or even say it at all. But I've always felt like I need to explain how I'm the daughter of a small, cheery blonde.

"Where is my mom?" I ask, and he looks to the nurse.

"On the way," she says.

"You were flown in to Mercy General from county," Dr. Singh says. "With injuries like yours it's important that surgery happens as quickly as possible to improve your chances of recovery. I'm sorry that your mom couldn't be here—"

"Recovery?" I repeat, interrupting him to grab onto that word. "How long? Softball conditioning starts in March."

"Well, let's see . . ." His eyes are back on the chart again, but I know he's stalling.

I may not show my emotions, but that doesn't mean I can't see everyone else's. I know Dr. Singh isn't going to tell me anything I want to hear, just as surely as I know that Aaron is in love with Carolina, and has probably called her twenty times already. I can picture her clumsily texting with her left hand, propped up in a hospital bed like mine. I wonder if there's a doctor with her as well, and if he's pulling X-rays out of a folder, illustrations in the story about how her life just changed.

"You sustained serious damage to your right hip," Dr. Singh says, holding them up to the light.

It's not the first time I've seen my bones. I can still spot the fracture on my right femur from when Royalwood's catcher—who is built like a brick shithouse—landed on me when I slid into home during summer league when I was twelve. I heard the crack on impact, but the ump called me safe. I lay in the dirt for a second, relishing the cheering before everyone realized I wasn't getting up.

My coccyx is crooked from being broken twice, once when I fell off Nancy Waggoner's horse, and again when it was my turn to be taken out at the plate by a runner. I held on to the ball even though I had literally broken my ass, and she was out. We won that game, too, and all the girls signed the doughnut pillow I had to sit on for a month.

But those old injuries are nothing compared to this.

"We put three screws in your hip," my surgeon says, but he hardly needs to explain. I can see them, denser than my bones, so clearly defined that the threading even stands out. I grit my teeth together, remembering the time I helped Dad put up drywall, particles flying in my face as I drilled in screws. How much bone dust is on the floor of that operating room? How much of me was left behind when I was wheeled out, and can my leg still work with what remains?

I want to ask but I don't get the chance because Mom

comes barreling in. She's wearing pajamas and her hair is a disaster, but she plucks the X-rays from Dr. Singh's hand like someone with authority, holding them up to the light.

I didn't cry when I landed in the field, mouth full of blood. I didn't cry when they separated me from Carolina, or when I saw the meat of my leg, red and raw underneath the antiseptic lights of the ambulance. I didn't cry when I woke up lost and alone, wondering if I was still in one piece.

But I cry now. I cry when Mom's face falls at the sight of those screws, her mouth turning down the way it did last year right before she told me about the divorce. I cry because the pain has begun, a fiery hand clasping onto my hip that burns right through whatever they gave me to stop it. The nurse notices and puts a button in my hand, curling my fingers around it.

"For the pain," she says.

I push it. I push it until the pain is dull and the room is fuzzy. I push it until I can't tell Mom's voice from the doctor's. I push it until I'm floating and can't hear words like *options*, *therapy*, and *graft*. I push it because I can't be here right now, and that button is the only way I can leave.

CHAPTER FOUR

family: *a household, including parents, children;*
a fundamental unit in the organization of society;
any network of linked persons different from but
equal to the above

Dad gets it.

He shows up a few hours later with questions about recovery times, physical therapy requirements, insurance coverage, and future mobility. He's looking at this problem the same way he does anything else: something that can be controlled once enough data has been accumulated. Mom might be able to look at my X-rays and see what's been done and what needs to happen, but Dad is the one making phone calls, marking up a calendar with appointments so far in the future that I'll be a year older when I show up to them.

My life has been reorganized into time measurements called *weight-bearing.*

"Okay, Mickey," Dad says, his chair pulled up next to my hospital bed. "Here's what we're looking at. For eight weeks you're just healing—that's your job, nothing else. Toe touch to the floor for balance but that's all, got it?"

"Got it," I say, trying to sound obedient. But my eyes are scanning the calendar he put in front of me, and eight weeks eats up a lot of time between now and March, when conditioning begins.

"So I can't put any weight on it before that?"

Dad glances down at his notes, then back at the calendar resting on my legs. "Partial weight-bearing starts *after* eight weeks if you're on track with physical therapy, but you'll still need crutches. So you can walk on it then."

"Then," I say, flipping the calendar to February and pointing to the third week. "So when am I fine? When do I not need crutches? When can I walk? When can I *run?*"

"Um . . ." Dad looks at his notes again. "Full weight-bearing is allowed at twelve weeks."

I count forward, flipping to March. Softball conditioning starts on the fifteenth, right around my eleventh week of recovery. Able to bear my own weight, but that might be about all. Dad's eyes trace my finger, hovering over where I'd marked *Conditioning!* on the fifteenth in red marker.

"That's not good enough," I tell him.

"It's close, Mickey. Best-case scenario you sit out a few games at the beginning of the season."

Our best-case scenario doesn't sound good to me.

"It's a long way out, Mickey," Mom says. "And we've got you scheduled with the best people in their field. Your therapists will get you on your feet as fast as they can."

"Don't let me forget," Dad says, turning to her. "I've got to call back the office in Westerville . . ."

I let them fade out, the reality of the calendar and my broken body and what it's going to take to fix it overwhelming me. Mom found the right doctors, the best therapists, then handed it off to Dad, the two of them working like the team they used to be. I watch them from my haze, wondering again how this could have fallen apart, or if the little smile hovering on Mom's lips makes Dad think about how things used to be. Then Devra walks in the door, pregnant belly preceding her, and Mom's smile is gone, any camaraderie that had been resurfacing between my parents disappearing.

Dad's second wife is closer to my age than his, but that's not why Mom's face goes into a hard, polite mask that carries no trace of kindness. It's not professional curiosity that draws her eyes to Devra's belly, either. The baby growing in there is something she couldn't give Dad, the jokes about an ob-gyn who can't get pregnant going stale a few years into their marriage, and ending altogether once they couldn't be said without bitterness. Dad liked to say that I was cheaper and came with less paperwork, but Mom always flinched more than laughed whenever he trotted that line out.

I give Devra the smile I've practiced for her. Much like Mom's, it's tight and small, enough that she can't complain to Dad that we're rude. She told me to call her "Devra" when we met, not "Mom," since the idea of being a parent to a teenager was a little *whoa* to her. I'm fine with our arrangement, finding the idea of having yet a third person in the world who can lay claim to being my mom even more *whoa* than she does.

"Mickey, I'm so sorry," Devra says, coming right for my bedside.

"I'm all right," I tell her, even though technically she didn't ask.

"She's a tough kid," Mom says, and it's true. Right now I couldn't be more glad that it's the first thing that comes to mind when people think of me. Being pretty or smart or nice is all well and good, but none of those things can get me through what's coming.

"That's my girl," Dad says, and while there's a lot of pride in his voice, the nagging voice inside my head reminds me that technically, I'm not. Mom has been able to deal with the divorce, but she's nowhere near forgiveness yet. Me, I understood all along.

Dad loves me, and thinks of me as his kid, but I knew there was a pocket in his heart that wondered what his biological child would look like, be like, act like. It's the same way I feel when I think about my real parents, out there somewhere. I love Mom and Dad, but that doesn't stop me from scanning the bleachers at games occasionally, wondering if that one person I can't place might be my birth mom, keeping tabs on me.

Carolina laughed when I told her that at school one day, pointing to the statue of our school's mascot outside the front doors. "For all we know that's your mom *and* your dad," she said, climbing the base until she was nose to nose with the stone Spartan to give it a closer inspection.

"Yep," she declared. "The facial expression isn't changing and it looks vaguely irritated. Definitely your people."

"Dad," I ask suddenly, "is Catalan Italian?"

"Um . . ." Dad glances at Mom, making Devra bristle. "I think it's Spanish, maybe? Why?"

I don't know why. It was a thought that had been

floating in my head since Dr. Singh asked me, and whatever is in my IV pushed the question out of my mouth before I had a chance to consider if it was worth asking. Is this how normal people work? Do they just say what they're thinking as soon as it occurs to them?

I shudder at the thought. Devra misreads it, pulling the blanket up to my chin. Now it's Mom's turn to bristle, and I'm trying to decide whether to thank my stepmom when a doctor comes in, one I haven't seen before.

"Mickey, I'm Brad, Dr. Singh's PA," he says, introducing himself to me first, which I appreciate.

Introductions happen all around, made somewhat awkward when the doctor assumes that Devra is my older sister. Mom manages to turn a laugh into a fake cough, but I'm pretty sure the tears in her eyes once the fit passes are real.

"I'm here to talk you through what rehabilitation is going to be like," Brad says. "Remember playing with these?"

He pulls a Barbie out of his scrub pocket, and I narrow my eyes at him, because no, I definitely don't remember that.

"When you had your accident, your hip came out of the socket entirely." He snaps the leg off the Barbie, and all the adults in the room wince. Not me. I saw the real thing.

He goes on to explain the screws now holding my leg in place, the multiple fractures, and what that will mean for future mobility. Mom drops the names of the physical therapy place I'll be going to, and Dad recites the appointments that are already scheduled. Brad nods his approval and says it sounds like I'm in the best possible hands, but all I can think about is the calendar Dad showed me, grid lines like a ladder laid out for me to climb.

If I can get my leg up that high.

CHAPTER FIVE

friend: *someone for whom the bearer feels affection or*
esteem

I don't see Carolina until I'm home five days later.

Mom insisted on keeping the hospital visitors to "family only," which earned her a side-eye from Devra, who had set up camp in the reclining chair next to my bed, the better to compare the aches and pains of late pregnancy to the trauma of having my leg torn out of its socket. Mom gave Dad enough hard stares to render him the one incapable of having children, but apparently he counts his new wife as *family*, because she stayed.

Carolina is in my room five minutes after I get home, trailing the outfielders behind her. They're all named Bella, an unfortunate side effect of their mothers being overly involved in the *Twilight* thing a while back. On the team we keep it simple by calling them Left, Right, and Center.

I'm surprised to see the Bellas. Our friendships are like muscles you use occasionally to make sure they're still there in the off-season, but don't pay serious attention to until training starts. On the field we'll slap each other's asses and chest-bump and scream unintelligibly into each other's faces during a victory yell, but in the hallways we keep it to an up-nod and reminders about the next practice. It's like running into your teacher in the grocery store and trying to make small talk; I'm only comfortable with these people when we're all wearing jerseys.

Now they're in my room, carefully arranging themselves on my bed so as not to disrupt the pile of pillows my right foot is resting on. Carolina shrugs as if to say, *deal with it.*

"How you feeling?" we ask each other at the same time.

"I'll live," Carolina says, pointing to her cast. "It's a nondisplaced fracture, which they said is a positive thing. Six to eight weeks and I'm good."

It's the beginning of January now. If Carolina is out of her cast that soon, she'll be rebuilding muscles in her arm by February while I'm still tooling around on crutches.

"My doctor said if all goes well I should be back at it in time for conditioning," Carolina goes on, breaking my concentration.

"Good," I say, and hope I don't sound bitter. I don't need a calendar in front of me to know that she's going to be throwing fire from the mound while I try to balance on a weak leg behind the plate.

"Yeah, she'll be good to go as long as Aaron stops doing everything for her," Center says. Her voice drops into a deep mimic. "Oh, let me get that door for you. I'll return your lunch tray. Maybe I'll carry you to class. Can I rub your back? How about your vagina?"

"Shut it," Carolina says, but she's blushing, and the swat she delivers to Bella Center's upper arm has a little more force to it than necessary.

"What about you?" Bella Left asks, her eyes straying to the walker next to my bed. Mom and Dad put a lot of money into my rehab, but the walker they grabbed at Goodwill. It's got a strip of duct tape around one leg, declaring it the property of Helen W. I don't know what became of Helen W. that she didn't need the walker anymore, but I'm guessing it's not because she suddenly became young and spry again.

"I'll be ready," I say, which is total bullshit. Dr. Singh had cautioned me about setting realistic goals, and Mom had repeated his words after my first physical therapy appointment, which left me dripping sweat and swallowing back vomit. The truth is it feels like the screws holding me together are on fire, my hip melting into them rather than growing. But my teammates don't need to know the truth.

"I'll be good for conditioning," I lie.

Dad said our best-case scenario had me *almost* fully healed by then. So I just have to be better than best.

"Really?" Bella Center's whole face lights up, like the idea of me on my feet is the best thing she's heard since Westwood's shortstop got pregnant.

"Yeah," I tell her. "If I keep up with the physical therapy, I should be all right."

I'm probably never going to be all right again, is what my therapist actually told me. I'll probably be stiff as hell whenever I get up for the rest of my life, and will wear my teeth down to nubs from gritting them whenever I sit down. But I've been stiff before and have spent most of my life gritting my teeth, so whatever.

"When can you come back to school?" Carolina asks. "Not that I don't love hauling your homework over here."

"Next week," I tell her, smiling. "My physical therapist said they want to make sure I'm confident on the crutches, and my family doctor has to sign off. And you do love bringing me my homework."

"Yeah," she agrees. "It feels awesome on my arm."

"Damn," Bella Right says, spotting the lineup of

orange bottles on my dresser. "That's some serious pills, girl." She picks up one, reading the label.

"Oxy." She whistles. "Nice."

"For real?" Bella Left asks, reaching over my stomach for the bottle. She takes it from Bella Right, shaking the little white tabs inside. I keep the leftover smile on my face pasted on.

I pop one of those twenty minutes before I need to get up, relying on the warm fuzziness it provides to push me through the pain and get me on my feet. I couldn't even get a shower if it wasn't for the Oxy, and my teammates tossing the bottle around like a scuffed-up softball sets me a little on edge.

"You could get some serious cash for these," Bella Left says, eyeing my dresser. "Like, maybe even a new car."

"I have a new car," I tell her.

"Shit, I don't," Bella Center says, swiping the bottle out of Left's hand. A scuffle ensues, ending when Center gives Left a titty twister that makes even me cringe, and I've still got some Oxy in my veins.

"Ouch!" Left yells, kicking Bella Center off her from where they landed on the floor. "I definitely need an Oxy after that."

"You don't need shit," Carolina says, grabbing the bottle. "Except maybe a better bra."

"With two different cup sizes, after the swelling."

Bella Left winces, adjusting herself.

"Whatever," Center says, giving Bella Left an arm up from the floor. "I didn't even have a good grip on it."

"All I'm saying is, at a dollar a milligram—"

"Dollar a milligram?" Carolina interrupts. "Somebody's been watching *NCIS* again."

"I have not," Left says, but she goes bright red, glancing between the four of us. "I do *not* watch *NCIS*."

"Sure, you're just in the room when your grandma does," Center teases.

"Can't leave." Right shakes her head, in mock sympathy.

"Stuck catching up on season fourteen," Carolina says.

"*Fifteen*," Left corrects, then catches herself. "Dammit, you guys."

Right shrieks with laughter, ducking when Left chucks a pillow at her. Insults and bad words are being tossed back and forth, everyone forgetting that I'm injured. I could almost forget too, except Carolina put my Oxy back on the nightstand, where anyone could get it. I grab it when nobody's looking, and push it under my pillow.

I don't need a new car.

I don't need a dollar per milligram.

I need the Oxy.

CHAPTER SIX

pain: *an uneasy sensation in the body, from slight discomfort to extreme distress, proceeding from a derangement of functions, disease, or injury by violence*

When I was six Mom put me in dance lessons. It didn't go well.

She dressed me in a leotard and tutu, walked me into a room full of mirrors, warm-up bars, and other little girls. Our teacher came in, a sharp-faced woman whose body was perpetually tense, the gray hairs on her head scraped into a bun so tight her eyebrows were always in a state of surprise. She sat us down and told us how dance would teach us self-control, endurance, and character. She told us we only get one life.

"Pick one thing," she said, a bony finger up in the air. "Pick one thing, and do it well."

I picked softball.

Physical therapy reminds me of that dance studio, mirrors everywhere, parallel bars, and watercoolers with paper cups that can't even begin to hold the drink I need by the time I'm done. What's different is the view, and the smell. This room is not full of little girls with shiny barrettes in their hair, and it doesn't smell like baby powder. I'm the youngest person here by at least two decades, and there's more than sweat coming out of some of the other patients.

"Okay, Mickey. Let's swing that foot around," Kyleigh says, using the word *let's* as if there's more than one person in charge of moving my leg.

There's not. It's just me.

I'm white-knuckling the parallel bars, sweat already trickling down the staircase of my spine and a touch of snot dribbling out of my nose to rest in the divot above my lip. My brain tells my right leg it's time to move now, but the signal hasn't quite made the journey when my brain recants, half panicked at the pain it knows will come. The result is a lot of sweating and anticipation, with very little forward movement.

"You just going to hang there?"

That's Jolene, my therapist. She's the bad cop. Kyleigh—her student in training—is the good cop: all positive reinforcement, sips of water, and pats on the back. Jolene tells me to use the bars or get out of the way, asks me if that's all I've got, or says she's seen more effort out of octogenarians.

It's an effective mix.

They remind me of Coach Mattix, who can make every girl feel like she's the reason why we won the game, but also has no problem specifically saying whose fault it is that we lost. I want Kyleigh to be proud of me and I want to get to the end of these bars so that I can kick Jolene in the teeth, I don't care which leg I have to use.

I make it.

I pitch forward at the end, nearly landing on my face if not for Jolene. She catches me, a mix of snot and tears left behind on her shirt as she eases me into a wheelchair. Normally I would refuse it, but my good leg is shaky and weak, and my bad one feels like the night sky on the Fourth of July.

I sink into the chair and Mom comes over, hands balled into fists at her side. I know she wants to wipe my face, push my hair out of my eyes, hold my head up for me because right now all it wants to do is loll to the side. But I told her at the beginning of this that there will be no fussing, or I'll make her stay in the waiting room. She can watch women push other human beings out of their vaginas and stay calm; she's got it in her to watch me walk ten feet without getting emotional about it.

"Good work, Mickey," she says instead. "You look strong."

I don't. There are enough mirrors in here for me to know that. I look like a toddler, off-balance and awkward, complete with runny nose.

"How do you feel?"

I can feel the screws, three points of hot agony drilled right into my bones.

Grandpa taught me how to manage pain, with logic first and a good dose of storytelling later. He was a farmer, years of sun and wind making his skin as tough as the baseball glove I found in the barn, my first one. His scars were numerous, a story for each one: fire, chainsaw, a tear along his jawbone where a tree branch touched his molars.

I was helping him stack a wood cord when I was eight, anxious to make him proud, working against the sun that would set soon, taking with it the burning heat of summer, and our light as well. I was stacking like he taught me, making cradles with one layer for the next one, when my hand skidded along the surface of a piece of dry hickory.

There was pain, bright and hot, but more than anything I felt confusion, not knowing what had happened. I wish I hadn't looked, hadn't seen the thick splinter that ran underneath my fingernail, all the way to the white half moon at the bottom. I couldn't speak, it hurt so badly, only held up my hand to show Grandpa, who stacked two more pieces before reacting.

"Well," he finally said, pushing back his hat to wipe the sweat from his forehead. "You gonna pull that out or am I?"

It was a logical question, the next step that took the focus away from the pain. I remember biting down on that splinter, pulling it out with my teeth and spitting it onto the ground, leaving behind a tiny, bleeding valley under my fingernail. Grandpa drove into town and bought me ice cream, a Band-Aid he'd found in the glove box of the truck not quite making everything better, but coming damn close.

Sometimes I wonder what he thought as he lay in the ditch last year, that same truck a wreck of metal beside him. I bet anything he thought about the next steps, what needed to happen, rather than what had just occurred.

Sometimes I think of the screws in my hip as massive splinters, digging in as the bone grows around them. And I grit my teeth, and I take the next step.

Carolina is waiting for me when we get home, Mom's face lighting up at the sight of her car in the driveway. I'm glad she's there too, but I brace myself against the inspection I know is coming as I push Helen W. in front of me through the front door.

"Damn," Carolina says. "You're pale."

I'm always a washed-up mess after physical therapy, hair grimy with sweat, bright-red exertion spots on my cheeks. I lower myself onto the couch next to my friend, trying to keep a straight face as I do. Carolina lets out a low whistle.

"Seriously, girl. You're so white right now I bet you can't even remember a word of Spanish."

"¡Mámame el bicho!" I say.

"Sólo los insultos, veo," she says, shaking her head. "Basic."

"Whatever."

I get my leg up onto the coffee table, edging aside a pile of my schoolwork Carolina brought with her. I used the holiday break to catch up on everything I missed while I was flat on my back, with IVs in my arms. But January brought a flurry of assignments, along with the snow. There are a few hours of work in front of me, at least. From the kitchen, I hear the click of Mom turning on the stove, the rattle of pans as she pulls together something for dinner.

"You should stay," I tell Carolina. "Eat with us. We can do homework and Netflix."

Usually, I wouldn't even ask. It would just be assumed

that she's going to stay with me, dirty plates on the floor and background noise from the TV as we work. Now though, she checks her phone before agreeing.

Aaron, really?

"Yeah, I can do that," she says, and I relax, the tension that radiates from my leg letting loose a little in my jaw.

"So are you guys a thing now, or what?"

"Define *thing*."

Normally I'd kick her for the uncalled-for smart-ass move, but I don't have the energy left after therapy. Plus, they took her cast off and she's graduated to a simple brace, pulled tight against the thinness of her once powerful forearm. Kicking her feels like a bad idea.

"*Thing*," I say, "mutual adoration between two people, exclusive to one another, typically annoying to those around them."

It was supposed to come out light, like when I told her to suck my dick in Spanish. Instead the words sound hard, all my pain going into them.

"Sorry," I say immediately. "I didn't mean that."

But I'm not the kind of person who just says things, and Carolina knows it. She shrugs off the dig, but the corner of her mouth is turned down, and I wish I would've kicked her instead.

"Then yeah, I guess we are a thing," she says, eyes on her phone and not me.

"Mickey, you need anything?" Mom yells from the kitchen.

"No," I tell her, struggling to my feet and leaning heavily on Helen W. "Gonna go to the bathroom."

Truth is, I don't have to pee. But if I ask Mom to bring me my Oxy she's going to get the little line in between her eyebrows that shows up when she doesn't like something. I saw it the other day when I took one a few hours ahead of when I was supposed to.

We eat in front of the TV, Mom hovering to take our plates and move our books, until I finally tell her that between the two of us we can manage. Even once she's gone there's stale air between me and Carolina, and I'm not one to fill silence with empty talk. Carolina and I have always been able to be quiet together, still highly aware of one another and close in our silence. That's missing tonight, and when she says she's got to get home, I don't argue, even though I know there are still a few hours left before her curfew.

Back in my room, I shake the bottle the way Bella Left did, but the noise is way different than it was then. There are only a few pills left, and more than a week before I'm technically supposed to run out.

I've been telling myself that there's a difference

between *want* and *need*. That I need the Oxy in order to get through physical therapy. I can tell my muscles to move forward, order bones to be arranged in a certain way, but if my brain balks at the pain, nothing happens. The Oxy does its job, wrapping my mind in a warm cocoon, reassuring me that everything is going to be okay.

But lately I've noticed a deeper thought, one that slumbers below the warmth, so buried that it took me a while to find it, unwrap it, and realize what it was telling me. With the Oxy working I can push myself during therapy, but always there's a comfortable fallback, the acceptance that even if everything isn't going to be okay . . . I'll be fine. The Oxy doesn't just take the pain away, it wraps up all my nervous what ifs and I can'ts and says—*screw it*.

And I do *need* that, right now, after seeing Carolina's arm out of the cast. She didn't mention it, and I didn't ask, but she's healing well. She surreptitiously flexed while we worked, putting her pencil down to do a few exercises. She'll be ready for conditioning in two months, and I can't leave my bed without Helen W. leading the way.

I shake the bottle again and count what's left inside. If the one thing that defines me is about to be taken away, I *need* to not care, to be able to say screw it. I've been biting my second pill in half, telling myself I don't need two, but one isn't doing the trick anymore when it's time to get some sleep.

Tonight I take two.

CHAPTER SEVEN

static: *resting; acting without motion or progression—or— producing charges of electricity*

Today someone else decides whether I'm allowed to move on. The words I say in a little room with teddy-bear wallpaper determine if I can go back to school, drive a car, and use crutches instead of a walker. This ten-minute appointment is all that stands between me and a semblance of a normal life.

Mom wanted to be here, but there's a baby on the way in the hospital next door, one that she's watched grow over the past nine months, carefully monitoring someone else's life, charting the course that will lead to a moment she'll never experience herself. She'll be there to catch the baby, the first person to touch this new human being, her own type of maternal claim that will follow hundreds of people for the rest of their lives.

It never gets old for her, the way Christmas or birth-days start to get stale once you hit a certain age. The miracle of new life always lights Mom up from the inside out, and even her concern for me couldn't eclipse that when her cell phone vibrated on the kitchen table moments before we were supposed to leave for my appointment.

"I'll get Dad to drive me," I told her, as I watched her weigh the sight of me leaning on Helen W. against the need of her patient, a battered, brittle-edged life against an unmarked one about to begin.

"You sure?" she asked, but she was already zipping her coat.

Turned out Dad was in a meeting, but he was more than happy to pass the request along to Devra, who seems to take it as a sign that we're bonding. Apparently one of her New Year's resolutions was to improve her relationship with me, something Dad let me know as if it were a great compliment. She's in the waiting room right now, searching for Kohl's coupons on her phone so we can go shopping for new school clothes if the doctor green-lights me to go back.

There's a tap on the door, as if I live in this tiny space rather than being a visitor. Dr. Ferriman comes in, a guy I've talked to about concussions and infected pimples, muscle pulls and my poor abused coccyx. My doctor has seen more of my skin than any male, ever, and always in a detached, clinical approach that made everything normal, his eyes assessing me the same way I determine the arc of my throw to second to pick off a runner.

So why is my smile tight when I greet him? Why is the heel of my foot nervously tapping against the edge of the metal table? Why is my paper gown fluttering along with the beat of my anxious heart?

It's not because I lie right away—replying with the standard "fine" when he asks how I'm feeling. It's not because of the flare of pain that pulls all language away from me when he rotates my leg. And it's not because of the small pause before he agrees that I can return to school on crutches as long as I promise to practice good self-care. It's because this appointment is almost over and I haven't done what I need to do yet.

I need to ask for more Oxy, and I don't know how.

There are many reasons for this. The first is that I'm not good at asking for help. When I was nine my chest of drawers toppled over onto me and instead of yelling for Mom or Dad I wiggled around until I could get a decent leg press on it and got it up off me. I was partly worried about getting in trouble for climbing it in the first place—which I was doing in order to swat a fly that had landed on the ceiling and had taunted me from there. But I was also embarrassed at being conquered by an inanimate object, something that today feels more insulting than that lazy fly had years ago, a dark blot against the white ceiling.

Dr. Ferriman is already up and off his stool, writing a pass for me to return to classes and a prescription for crutches. I'm looking at that pad and willing him to flip to a new page and write *OxyContin*, when I realize he's not going to do that unless I ask.

So, screw it.

I have to say this right though, have to use the correct words and have the perfect expression in order to be what I am: a girl who needs a boost to get through the day. Not someone who likes the way the mattress sinks underneath her at night, the coolness of the sheets contrasting with the emanating warmth from the rush. Not someone who took another pill even though the pain was gone, but she hadn't quite fallen asleep yet and wanted to recapture weightlessness just a little while longer. Not someone who felt a jolt of panic when she popped the top off her last bottle yesterday, only to find it empty.

I can't be that girl. I have to be Mickey Catalan, who is beating the shit out of herself so that she can get back into the game, and just needs Oxy for a stepping-stone.

"So can I get something for the pain?"

It's out before I think too hard about the words like I usually do. A blurt that is so against who I am as a human being that even my doctor is surprised, hand still on the half-open door as I lean against Helen W., all my weight on my arms.

"Let me see." He taps away at the tablet he carries with him, pulling the door shut against the curious glance of an older woman in the hallway who overheard my question, her attention drawn away from her phone.

"We don't normally prescribe that strong of a pain-killer for long after surgery. And it looks like the prescription you already have shouldn't run out for another two weeks," Dr. Ferriman says.

"Oh wow," I say. "That's . . . weird."

Softball doesn't require a lot of lying. I don't have the skills for this.

Dr. Ferriman makes the same face I saw when I came in with a cracked tailbone—again. It's concern. And because I've spent so much time breaking myself and coming here to be healed, there's a personal edge to it that I doubt all his patients get.

While that makes him a good person and a great doctor, it's not what I need right now. I don't need him caring, worrying, or overthinking this. What I need is for him to act like what he is—an overworked man with a lobby full of sick kids and irritated parents waiting on him. I need him to be in a hurry to move me along, to give me what I want in order to make it happen. But of course Mom would have never chosen a pediatrician like that. Instead I've got one of the best, most conscientious people on earth.

And I'm sure as shit not getting any more Oxy.

I reach past him, opening the door myself and pushing Helen W. out into the hallway. "A bottle probably rolled off my dresser," I say. "I'm always bumping into things. Not so good with a walker, you know."

I laugh, a loud, forced sound that makes a baby being weighed on a scale start crying. The mom gives me a dirty look as I hobble past the scale, and I mutter a quick apology as I squeeze around the woman who overheard me asking for more Oxy, her hand now protectively cupped under the elbow of an even older woman who is inching down the hallway with a cane. I'm moving Helen W. as fast as I can, building up a static charge from the cheap carpet that's going to give me a zing next time I touch metal.

"Mickey," Dr. Ferriman calls after me, but I'm in public now. He can't say anything about Oxy, or even the prescription for crutches that I've got crushed in one hand, without infringing on my patient rights. And I doubt he's going to chase me down and pull me into a side room for a private talk.

I white-knuckle Helen W. all the way into the waiting room to find Devra nowhere in sight. My phone vibrates in my hoodie pocket with a text, telling me she went next door to grab us both coffees and that she'll meet me in the car. I feel oddly abandoned, left alone waiting for the elevator. I jab the down button, bringing with it a static zap that I can actually see, an explosion at the tip of my finger to match the one in my leg.

"Goddammit, Helen," I say.

And to my embarrassment, I start to cry.

I'm good at a few things.

Softball. Spanish. And I can eat a whole pizza by myself.

Up until the accident that was about it. Now I can add that I'm really good at pretending everything is okay while I balance on one leg, fold up a walker, shove it into a car, and get into the passenger seat. I'm usually capable of going through the process without crying or dropping anything. But today I do both, my phone slipping from my pocket to land in melting slush. I'm mopping the last tears away with my sleeve—*why am I crying so much?*—when another hand grabs my phone before I do.

"You okay, darlin'?"

Even people who care about me don't call me by anything other than my name, and *darlin'* isn't exactly a word that's used to describe me, anyway. But she says it just right, with a little twang that comes from south of the river and isn't affected at all, like she's not just asking to be polite, but because she actually cares what my answer is.

It is the woman from the hallway, the one who overheard me asking if I could get something for the pain. I blush, feeling my cheeks turn even redder under the tears they're so unaccustomed to. I'm about to tell her that I'm fine, the word half formed and my lips ready to deliver them out of habit more than truthfulness, when she stops me cold.

"When was your last one?" she asks.

"Excuse me?"

"Oxy? I heard you ask the doc for something, and I'm guessing you didn't get it. But that's not the only reason you're crying. You've got the shakes. And . . ." She puts her palm on my forehead, her skin cool and paper-thin against my sweaty brow. "You're running a low-grade fever. You're going through withdrawal, hon."

She takes her hand away, the smell of old-lady perfume lingering near my nose.

"*You're* going through withdrawal," I shoot back, which isn't clever or accurate, but I've never been good at conversation with strangers.

"No, because I *got* my prescription," she says, holding

it up. "Or Betsy's, really. But you don't care where it comes from, do you?"

It's just the right thing to say to make me shut up and listen. And she knows it.

"Here," she says, unzipping her massive purse, which has three photographs of what I assume are her grand-kids slipped into plastic pockets on the side. Her arm disappears inside the purse up to her elbow, reemerging with a little white pill, which she puts into my hand, folding my fingers around it.

"First one's free because you're breaking my heart," she says. "After that it's a dollar a milligram. Dosages start at ten, but I'm betting you already knew that."

She's kept my phone, and now her fingers tap over the screen way faster than I expected as she adds her number.

"Call me when you need more," she says, handing my phone over. I accept it numbly, but not with the hand holding the pill. That I pulled back reflexively, like a dog that's had too many treats taken away before they got to eat them.

She picks her way through the slush of the parking lot to get behind the wheel of a white van with the name of the county's senior citizen program on the side. I can see the outline of a few bald heads inside, and one with a healthy poof of hair, probably the lady with the cane.

I'm not quick enough to stop the driver with my questions, anything I had to say lost in a cloud of exhaust as she starts the van up and pulls away.

I scroll through my phone to look for the new contact, jumping in surprise when Devra opens the driver's door, steam rising from two cups of coffee.

"Good news?" she asks.

I close my fist tight around the little white pill, sweaty in my palm.

"Real good," I confirm, showing her my prescription for crutches. She squeals and tries to high-five me, but misses.

Right now, I know a few things for sure.

I'm going to slip this Oxy, throwing it back as soon as Devra's not looking. I'm going to call this woman— Edith—who is apparently now my pill supplier.

Also, Bella Left *definitely* watches *NCIS*.

CHAPTER EIGHT

punishment: *any pain, suffering, or loss inflicted on a person because of a crime or offense*

I can feel the screws. Both ends.

The threaded tips are growing into my bones, which is what they are supposed to do. This was explained to me by the PA, who snapped a Barbie's leg off after talking me through my X-rays, the tip of an expensive pen from his coat pocket tracing the path of titanium under my skin. I knew about that, was told that bone and screw would meld together, creating a new version of Mickey Catalan that may not be better, but would— hopefully—be serviceable.

It's the heads of the screws that I'm stuck on now. Literally.

I'm soaking in a hot bath, the water scalding my body

a bright pink the moment I step in, gingerly lowering myself. My right hand keeps dropping to my hip, probing the point of pain, fingers digging down between what's left of my muscle and tendon to find those alien parts that now keep me in one piece. Mickey Catalan, the most unlikely doll in the world.

I hear Dad's voice in my head the second I press my thumb against the first screw, a terse reminder—"don't pick." Adolescence isn't nice to anyone, but my preteen years were vicious, rendering me taller and broader than the boys, and granting me the bulge of breasts at a time when everyone found them embarrassing instead of interesting. I also inherited from somewhere in my DNA zits that were more like mountain ranges than pimples.

Dad always insisted I was a *force*. He knew better than to call me cute, and rather than telling me that I would grow into my looks, he found ways to compliment me that weren't lies. "You've got great teeth," or, "Some girls would kill for that hair." And yeah, both of those things were true, but then a never-ending vat of oil opened somewhere deep inside me.

"Don't pick" became the words he said to me the most, whenever he caught me leaning over the bathroom counter, inspecting yet another eruption. Or when I flipped down the passenger's seat visor right after practice to get a better idea of what it was that had begun to make its way into my peripheral vision an hour earlier.

He'd turn off the bathroom light or flick the visor back up, warning me that acne goes away eventually but scars last forever.

Like I didn't already know about scars.

We don't talk about my birth parents. I don't remember much from before the age of three, but there are some marks on my body that I don't have stories for, and no memory of who put them there. Someone, at some point, taught me that punishment was how bad things were corrected. Mom told me once that not long after they got me she found me smacking a bloody scrape on my knee, telling it to go away.

I know better now. But it still makes its own kind of sense.

I hate these screws in my leg, the same way I hated those swelling pimples. And even though the rational part of me knows perfectly well that the reasons why I don't get them anymore are because of some visits to a dermatologist and expensive treatments, there's a small part that thinks maybe they're gone because I beat them. Because I pinched and popped and dug and made them hurt so bad they decided not to come back.

So, yeah, I know it's not helping, but there's a weird satisfaction in feeling around deep inside my leg, past the bruises left behind from the last exploration, to find the head of each screw and give it a little pinch.

•   •   •

No one tells you that crutches hurt.

Hidden in the bodily alcove of the armpit lies a large bundle of nerves, and they do not appreciate having rubber and wood jammed into them. Leaving Helen W. at my bedside had felt great in the morning, and the simple act of driving had been liberating, the first few hours of school flying by as everyone congratulated me on my return.

People also kept asking if I was okay.

Even on my best days I'm not a talkative person, and by lunch there are no words that can come out of my mouth without me having to clamp down on the shriek that wants to follow them.

Everything hurts, and no, nothing is *okay*.

My upper back is sore from leaning forward on the crutches, my left knee hurts from all the weight I'm putting on that leg, and my right knee is stiff from having to be bent constantly. My upper arms are a holy mess from having to do more work than has been asked of them in a month of Sundays, and I'm very aware that the muscles that used to be defined can now only be seen if the light is falling just right.

At some point in time, I fell out of shape.

I am never out of shape. I lift with the other sports teams during the off-season, just to keep that from happening. I run with the cross-country team even though I'm not on it.

"Eat your vegetables," Carolina says, pushing my tray back toward me.

"You eat my vegetables," I say back. She shrugs and does exactly that, eyeing me over a plastic spoonful of lima beans. Carolina knows better than to ask if I'm okay, so instead she's doing her best to acknowledge that I'm not, without saying it.

"You lifting tomorrow after school?" I ask Carolina, who carries both our trays in her one good hand, gracefully weaving through the crowd to return them. I follow in her wake, a lumbering beast.

"Leg day, yeah," she says, pausing to check her phone even though I know it didn't go off. She's giving me a chance to catch my breath, and I realize that her little moments of kindness are what's going to get me through today. That, and if Edith ever texts me back.

"Every day is leg day for now," she says, lifting the arm that still sports a brace.

"I'll be there," I say, and Carolina shoots me a side-eye.

"That smart?"

"It's not about being smart," I tell her, as I feel my phone vibrate in my hoodie pocket. "It's about being better."

CHAPTER NINE

need: *to be in want of; to lack; to require, as supply or relief*

Edith lives in a part of town where all the houses look the same: like someone with no imagination was given some boards and a box of nails and they went for it. Everything is squares and right angles, even the yards, perfectly segmented with a hedgerow or a picket fence running down the property line to ensure no one is confused about which blades of grass belong to who. I spot a tan Buick in the driveway, parked under a maple, one of its dangling, naked winter branches almost scraping the hood.

I find myself in the odd situation of not knowing whether to go to the front or the side door of my dealer's house. Edith saves me by coming out the front door and waving me in, a steaming cup of something in her hand losing its warmth into the gray sky, which has just begun to spit tiny, perfectly formed snowflakes.

I don't know how to buy drugs, don't know what I'm supposed to say to her, or if there is bargaining involved. Carolina says that Americans in Puerto Rico are easy game because they don't haggle, and she remembers her grandma telling stories about the tourists she just relieved of their chavos, parting with her goods as if it were an emotional moment, but actually garnering five or six times their worth.

I'm a tourist here.

But I don't feel like Edith is taking advantage of me when she pops two cookies in my hands, still warm and gooey from the oven, and invites me to sit down at her kitchen table.

"How you feeling, darlin'?" she asks me, patting my shoulder as I lower myself into a chair, wincing, and lean my crutches against the table.

People have been asking me all day how I'm feeling, teammates and teachers, counselors and coaches. For them, I gave the expected answer. I am strong. I am a survivor. But I'm here for a reason, and Edith knows what it is.

"I hurt."

"I know it, hon. I know it," she says, putting a glass

of milk in front of me. She tells me she'll be right back and disappears down the hallway. I break apart one of the cookies, melted chocolate forming delicious bridges between the two pieces. I haven't had an after-school snack since Mom went back to full time when I was in sixth grade. On the kitchen counter, a police scanner spews out codes and static, reporting as people get hurt, go to the hospital, die. God, why do old people love those things?

"How many you need?" Edith's voice calls from the back of the house.

I like how she says *need*, not *want*.

"Um . . ." I think about it, while chocolate drips onto my fingers.

"Right now I've only got ten 30s, five 60s, and a handful of 80s."

I try to do the math. I was prescribed two doses of 20 milligrams per day—one for the morning, one at night—and I stuck to it pretty good until physical therapy started kicking my ass.

"Hon?" Edith's voice, high-pitched and inquisitive.

"Give me all the 30s," I say real fast, before I can crunch the numbers. I don't want her to walk out of the back and find me doing math on my phone like . . . well, like a tourist. She doesn't answer me, but I hear the familiar noise of a bottle cap being popped, then the sound of pills sliding across a surface as she counts them under her breath.

I'm about to be out of pain, out of the private hell of pretending that I limped through all day. Sitting here with my bad leg propped up, in an overheated kitchen with a gooey cookie in my hand, I realize that for the first time all day I feel . . . comfortable.

That's when the side door crashes open, and a girl my age walks in. "Edie?" She calls, flipping a glossy mane of hair over her shoulder. "Edes? Jesus Christ, it's ninety degrees in here, woman. I know you have bad circulation but—"

She stops when she spots me, perfectly painted nails pulling her hair back to where it had been.

"Oh, hey," she says. "That your car in the drive?"

These are the kinds of girls I can't talk to, never have been able. We're the same sex of the same species, but I always feel like an orca flopping around on dry land while gazelles like her hover around me, unsure of the large awkwardness that has claimed space among them. It doesn't help that I just took my first bite of cookie and my jaws are stuck together. I go with nodding.

She tosses her purse—a Coach, I notice—onto Edith's table and flops onto the chair opposite me. "Josie," she says, holding out a hand. Both of mine are greasy, but one has less crumbs than the other, so I shake with that one.

"Mickey," I finally manage to say, when I unstick my

jaws, then wonder if I'm supposed to give a fake name or something, since I'm here buying drugs.

"Jos? That you?" Edith's voice interrupts us.

"Yeah," she calls back, glancing down at her phone when it buzzes.

"Mickey wiped me out of my 30s, hon, so if you want something you'll have to go with 60s or 80s for now."

So much for secrecy.

"How many 60s you got?" Josie asks, while answering a text.

There's a pause. "Four." Funny, I could swear Edith told me she had five.

"I'll take 'em," Josie says, reaching into her purse and pulling out a wad of cash.

Shit.

I was so busy trying to figure out how many pills I needed until the next appointment with Dr. Ferriman that I didn't even think about if I had enough money to buy them. I asked Edith for ten 30s, so at a dollar a milligram . . . I just bought three hundred dollars' worth of pills and I only have two hundred in my pocket.

What I have is birthday money, and it was going to go toward a tougher phone case and new workout playlists. Now, I'm recounting it in front of a stranger, as if I think the twenty-dollar bills in my pocket might have multiplied since I put them there.

"You short?" Josie asks.

I've got two choices. I can either admit to Edith that I don't have it, and try to make it through the rest of the month by cutting pills in half, or I can be honest. It's the idea of dividing pills that takes my pride down a notch.

"Yeah," I say. "By a hundred."

Josie peels five twenties off without blinking, and tosses them in front of me.

"Thanks," I say. "I'm good for it."

"So's my mom," she says, eyes back on her phone.

On the counter, the scanner crackles.

`32 to 7300 . . . Go ahead 32 . . . 7300 signal 13 at the gas station.`

"Somebody's gotta pee," Josie says.

"What?"

"The scanner," she says without looking up from her phone. "A thirteen means the officer is taking a leak."

"How do you know that?" I ask her.

"I spend a lot of time here." She shrugs. "Listen long enough, you figure it out."

Edith comes back in with two brown bags that she's written our names on in old-lady cursive, like she's packed our lunches for us. We pay her and she sends us off with more cookies and a reminder that she's restocking next Monday, to get ahold of her then. I tell her I should be good, but she just nods and pats my shoulder. Josie walks with me to my car and even opens the door for me, as I do my awkward, stilted dance that's required to get behind the wheel.

"You in?" she asks, before she closes the door.

"Yep," I say, then roll down my window. "Hey, seriously. I . . . thanks."

"No problem," she says. "It's on me. You look like you need it more than I do."

"I was in a car accident." It comes out almost apologetic, like I had to have done something wrong in order to be rendered so weak and helpless. "What about you?"

"I'm just bored." Josie shrugs. "See you next Monday, Mickey."

I want to tell her she won't, but she's already gone. I catch a glimpse of her little sports car driving away in my rearview mirror, where I also see that I've had a strand of chocolate sitting on my chin this entire time.

CHAPTER TEN

sleep: *to take rest by a suspension of the voluntary exercise of the powers of the body and mind*

I drive slow all the way home, and only partly because of the mix of snow and ice falling from the sky. A real fear gripped me at Edith's when I got behind the wheel, the confidence of the morning gone along with the sun. I'm barely doing thirty when I pull into the driveway, and my hip is starting to burn.

It's bearable, but my left crutch slips out from underneath me a little bit at the door and I put more weight on my right foot than I should. Any good feelings I had left from warm cookies and cold milk are driven out of me in a rush, leaving behind a spike of pain.

I push open the back door with my shoulder and Mom is there in a second, untangling me from my backpack and crutches, then guiding me into a seat at the kitchen table.

"First day back went that well, huh?" she asks.

I grit my teeth and nod, deciding not to tell her about my slip on the pavement.

"There's potato soup on the stove, and I thought I'd make grilled cheese," she offers, doing her best not to hover.

It sounds like the best possible end to my day, if only I didn't feel like my hip exploded.

"Cool," I say. "I'll just grab a shower."

I do, leaning heavily on the suction-cup bar that Mom put in there for me, as I test putting weight on my leg. I'm cautious, starting first with the ball of my foot, then easing back onto the heel, aware of the rubber grip on the shower floor that also showed up right after I got home from the hospital.

I feel better as my muscles unknot under the hot water, enough so that I try not to think about the pills stuffed in the pocket of my varsity jacket. If I can get through the evening after taking a jolt like I did at the garage door, then maybe I can get through to my next appointment without having to go back to Edith.

Mom's got her own approach to pain relief—hot food and a whole bunch of kitchen towels duct-taped to the armpit rests of my crutches.

"You on call?" I ask her, sitting back from the table after eating.

She shakes her head. "I know it was potato soup and not chili, but maybe we could do some Netflix?"

I look at her blankly.

"You know," she says, spinning her hand around. "Netflix and chili?"

"Oh my God, Mom," I say. "It's Netflix and *chill*, not Netflix and chili. And don't ask just anyone to do that, either. It doesn't mean what you think it means."

Her eyebrows go together. "What does it mean?"

"Google it," I tell her. "Or even better, don't." I get my crutches under me and am hobbling for the stairs before she can get her phone out.

"Is this like a sixty-nine thing?" she calls after me. "I know what that is."

"GOOD NIGHT, MOM," I yell.

Sleep is impossible.

I thought I could do it, thought after the boost I felt from driving myself, returning to school, and watching my mom get just about everything wrong over dinner, that I could grit my teeth and push through the night.

I was wrong.

I probably shouldn't have put so much weight on my leg during the day. Should have taken a couple people up on their offers to get things for me, rather than doing it myself. Should have gone for a bath instead of a shower, taken some pressure off my pulsating hip. A lot of bad decisions put me where I am right now—standing in front of my varsity jacket and digging for the baggie.

It's two in the morning. I made it that far, which should count for something. I rode out waves of pain and told myself that I'd been through worse before. And maybe I had, but before I didn't have an answer sitting just a few short steps away, a promise that I didn't have to feel this way if I didn't want to.

And maybe taking an Oxy right now isn't a bad idea, after all. Maybe everything else was a bad choice, and this is a good one. Maybe I need that relief in order to relax, all my muscles going slack and sleep giving my body a chance to rejuvenate. Sleep, that's another thing. I've got to be up in four hours, ready to convince the world that there is nothing wrong with me. And I can't do that without some solid rest.

Edith had texted me after I left her place, to tell me that if I needed relief right away I should chew up the pills, eliminating the time-release element to get the full benefit without waiting.

I do it now, because I might as well be out of pain sooner rather than later, if I'm going to take them any-way. And I take two because one is only going to take the edge off, not send me straight down into unconsciousness, where I need to be in order to be ready to do it all again tomorrow.

I get back into bed, already warmer, already better.

I'm only taking medicine that has been prescribed to me, and if I ran out early it's because Dr. Ferriman went a little light with my dosage in the first place. I know he's worried about addiction, could see it in his face when I asked about the refill. But I'm not worried about it, because I just lay here for hours with the fires of hell burning in my leg. I'm not worried about it because I didn't go for the pills as soon as I got out of the shower. I'm not worried about it because I'm not like that Josie girl, who is popping pills out of boredom.

No, I tell myself as I slide into a sweet, slippery sleep.

I'm not like *that*.

CHAPTER ELEVEN

weight: *a ponderous mass; something heavy to be lifted in athletic contest—or—a burden or pressure that is intangible*

The clank of weights echoes down the hallway, along with the low hum of male voices punctuated by the girls' higher cries. I hear Carolina's familiar noise, the one she makes at the end of a set when she's verging on collapse but determined to get one more rep out. There's a thump of bass as well, and a string of lyrics my mom wouldn't approve of fills the air, along with the funk of sweat.

It's like coming home.

When I open the door to the weight room, everyone shouts my name. I get fist bumps and back slaps, hugs from my teammates and a few awkward shoulder squeezes from the guys, my crutches pinched tight in my armpits. My mood was good before; now I'm lifted right through the roof. These are my people; this is my place.

"MickeyCatalan,"BellaRightyells."Hoo—fucking—ray!"

Words come to me easily here, always have. I can talk to anyone because we're all speaking the same language, asking if they're done with a piece of equipment, borrowing a weight, lending a towel. We all smell bad and nobody cares. We yell encouragement, push somebody to add another five to their bar, and spot each other.

The Bellas are here, working out with the basketball team. Our second baseman, Lydia, is also the point guard. She gives me a full-on hug, chest pressing against mine. She's given a few solid attempts at convincing me I'm a lesbian but hasn't had any luck. Carolina gives me a smirk from the corner where she's on the leg press, anyway.

"What?" I snap my towel at her as she sprays down the equipment.

"You could get laid by like five people in this room right now," she says. "Hail the conquering hero, and all that."

"Which five?" I ask.

"Probably your pick, just leave me mine," she says as

Aaron comes over to us.

"Mick," Aaron says, putting his fist out for a bump, which I do a little harder than necessary. Aaron's a good guy, but I still don't like it when his arm goes around Carolina's waist. She usually lifts with me, but it's obvious that they've been working out together as he switches the weight on the leg press and takes his turn.

"How are you going to lift with crutches?" Carolina asks.

"I'll only do arms today. And I'll sit," I say, avoiding her eyes as I load up the curl bar, aiming for my usual weight even though I haven't lifted since I got hurt.

"¿Eso es una buena idea?"

"Estoy bien. Te lo prometo," I tell her, and to prove it, I hoist up the curl bar and start doing reps. The truth is that, no, it's not a good idea, but I sucked down two 30s right after school. I feel great right now, and I'm going to take advantage of it.

"¿Cómo está tu brazo?" I ask after her arm, ignoring the sweat that starts running down my face when I'm only five reps in.

"Estoy bien," she says, bending her elbow where the brace has replaced her cast. "Just like you."

"Ha," I say, ignoring the poke. I'm past the point where I can speak while lifting, anyway. I'm not in pain yet—the Oxy isn't allowing it—but Edith doesn't deal in steroids and I'm not anywhere near the shape I was in before.

I get about an hour in before the assistant basketball coach turns the lights out, telling us to go home and look at our phones like normal teenagers. I'm crossing the parking lot, talking with one of the guys about the latest boxing matchup—Mom sprang for HBO when she found out how long I was going to be laid up—when Carolina yells from the gym doors.

"Hey, Mickey, can a broki get a ride?"

I wave her over and she gets in, each of us doing what it takes to make it possible. She has to keep her bad arm straight and pull her gym bag over it carefully before she tosses it in the back seat. I've got to do the shimmy-slide behind the wheel and maneuver my crutches into the back.

It's the first time Carolina and I have been in a car together since the accident, and it's awkward. Some things are different, for sure. We're both slightly crippled, there's no pizza, and it's not even the same car because the insurance company decided my old one was a lost cause. Still, there's enough to remind us both. Our words at first come out a little stilted, the conversation cramped.

But those few, horrific seconds are balanced against hours of good times sitting this same way—me driving, her giving me shit from the passenger seat. So it doesn't take long before we're good again, her music filling the car, both of us talking over it.

"Not to be all your mom on you or anything, but how is being back at school?" she asks.

"School sucks," I tell her honestly. "But being in the weight room did me good."

"It definitely did Lydia some good."

"Shut your face," I say. "I'm not into her. Straight girls can be awesome at softball."

"Uh, duh," Carolina shoots back. "You're talking to a straight girl with a free ride."

"You mean on Aaron or to college?"

"It's *all* free," she says, laughing. I'm behind her just a tick, laughing because I'm supposed to. We'd both agreed a long time ago that having sex wasn't worth the risk, having seen too many great athletes become mothers, their sports career sidelined while the father carried on uninterrupted. But those conversations were before Aaron, and before this new awkwardness, where I feel like I can't flat out ask her if they're doing it.

I drop her off and she hauls her bag out of the back, pulling it onto her good shoulder. It's below freezing, ice falling from the sky. She winces as a pellet hits her in the face.

"You use those crutches going inside back at your

place, you hear me? I see you putting more weight on that leg than you're supposed to." She gives me a stern look, and I do my best to look innocent.

"Only toe touch to the ground. I swear."

"I'm calling bullshit on that," she says.

She's right and she knows it. I've been straightening my knee, trying out a little weight on my heel when I think the Oxy will let me get away with it. If I can shave one week off my recovery time—*one week*—I can be ready for conditioning.

Carolina stays by my car despite the ice, teeth gnawing her bottom lip in indecision. "I'm not going to ask you how you're feeling because you're just going to tell me you're fine," she says. "But I saw what you were benching. Don't overdo it, okay?"

"I'm not fine," I tell her. "I'm awesome."

And right now, it's true.

CHAPTER TWELVE

understand: *to apprehend the meaning or intention of; to have knowledge of; to comprehend; to know; to have sympathy for*

"Mickey Catalan, I'll be damned."

"Hey, Big Ed," I say, holding the door of the local market open with one crutch while I swing myself through. Ed stays behind the lunch counter, not offering to help or fussing over me one bit, exactly like he knows I want. Instead, he makes my Monday morning coffee like there hasn't been a month break between this one and the last one.

It's shit coffee, which is why Ed stopped asking me to pay him for it, and it's not why I come every week, anyway. I'm here because Ed can talk sports—any sport—better than anyone I know. He puts the coffee in front of me as I settle onto a stool at the lunch counter.

"You hear about the Griffith girl?"

I sip my coffee, letting the familiarity of bad coffee and Ed's terrible story introductions settle over me.

"She's the shortstop from Left Bank, isn't she?"

"Yep," Ed confirms, then rounds his arms out in front of his belly.

"Huh, I thought she was smarter than that," I say.

"Smart tends to go out the door when sex is involved," Ed says, pulling his own stool underneath him on the other side of the counter.

"Yep," I say, reminding myself that I need to have a conversation with Carolina, whether it's awkward or not. "So what else is new?"

"Haven't seen you in a while, let me think." Ed sighs, pushing his ball cap up to scratch his balding spot. "The big kid from Baylor Springs, basketball player . . . what's his name?"

"Luther Drake," I tell him.

"Yeah, the Drake kid. He shattered the backboard over at West Union last weekend, so they've got to play in the junior-high gym till it's fixed."

"Screw them anyway," I say, having harbored a resentment ever since their point guard broke Lydia's nose in an intentional foul.

"Yep," Ed agrees. We both sip our coffee, and I hear

the squawk of a scanner from the back room.

"Why do old people like those so much?" I ask him.

"Well, I'll tell you," he says, fishing a day-old dough-nut out of the glass case and putting it in front of me. "It's our version of you kids with your phones and your head book."

"Facebook, Ed."

"I'm proud to not know that. Now eat your dough-nut, looks like you could use it."

It's the most he's going to say about my injury, about the thinness of my arms and legs, the absence of mus-cle. My varsity jacket feels big on me, my shoulders no longer filling it out. I take a bite of doughnut. It's awful.

"I don't know how much healing properties this has, Ed."

"Healing is you just being here, talking," he says.

I hear the scanner again, and I wonder if he was lis-tening the night of the accident, if he heard the details of how my leg had been separated from my body, my blood strewn across snow.

"You sign with anyone yet?"

"Not yet," I tell him. "Couple Division Three coaches have talked to me, but you know how that is."

Ed nods. "Can't give athletic scholarships."

"Nope. So I've got to keep my grades up, hope for

an academic one that comes with an invite to play D3.
So . . . we'll see."

"Carolina still headed to Ohio State?"

"You bet," I tell him, pride swelling, even if it's not
for myself. "Division One athletic scholarship. All the
way. Free ride."

"I didn't know if . . ." He trails off, letting me put
together the rest.

"If getting hurt ruined things?" I shake my head.
"She's on track, doing fine. She'll be throwing opening
day."

Ed doesn't ask about me. I don't offer, and the bubble
of happiness I felt for my friend deflates a little.

"Westwood lost a wrestler," Ed goes on.

"He pregnant too?" I ask, mouth full of doughnut.

"Nope, he's dead."

"Shit," I say, wiping my mouth. "Sorry."

"Overdosed." Ed shakes his head. "I'll tell you what
the problem is, it's that truck stop out at the interstate.
Kids can go out there, get anything they want. Get stuff
they don't have any business with."

"What was it?" I ask. "Pills?"

"Yep," Ed says. "You believe that? When I was your
age, you know what we did? We drank. These days . . ."
He shakes his head again. "I don't know, kiddo. It's not
good, understand me?

"Yep," I agree.

"And you know what else?"

"No, Ed," I say. "What else?"

"Daisy—the lady cop?"

"You know you can just say *cop*, Ed."

"Yeah, well, she told me they got a call from a mom the other day, all upset. Her kid was hanging out at the park after school and found a bunch of needles behind the dugout at the diamond."

Okay, now that actually does upset me.

"People are shooting up at the park?"

I haven't played on that field since youth summer league, but I still don't like the idea of dirty hypodermics lying where Lydia and I used to have spitting contests with sunflower seeds. The thought makes me shiver.

"Terrible," Ed says. "Why would anyone ever stick a needle in their arm?"

"I don't know, Ed," I say, glancing at the clock as I throw back the rest of my coffee. "I've got to get to school."

"All right. You be careful out there."

Ed's said this to me every Monday since I started coming in here, but today feels different. Maybe I'm being paranoid, taking it the wrong way since I'm on crutches and I don't want him thinking about me as a hurt thing. Maybe it's because there's a couple white pills in my jacket pocket that are going to be in my stomach before lunch. Or maybe it's because, as I'm leaving, I hear Ed mutter to himself, "I just don't understand."

And maybe it's because I'm starting to.

CHAPTER THIRTEEN

graduate: *to mark with degrees; to divide into regular steps, grades, or intervals—or—to admit or elevate to a certain grade or degree*

School has never been easy for me.

It's never been my goal to be the prettiest girl, or the funniest girl, and definitely not the nicest girl in the room. But right now it sure would be great to be the smartest one.

My conversation with Big Ed only served to remind me that while colleges have shown interest in me, nobody is going to give me a degree to play ball. It'll be a mix of athletic ability and good grades that get me anywhere I'm going, and I've been set pretty far back on both of those things by the accident.

As Carolina likes to remind me, it sucks to suck.

What sucks right now is that I've got to write out definitions for twenty different words I don't know the meaning of, plus finish *Lord of the Flies*, and I've got one study hall period to do it in. Time is against me, and I'm not at my sharpest thanks to the double shot of Oxy I just did in the bathroom.

I let out a long sigh and shake my head, hoping to clear it. If I'm not careful I'll slide back down into sleep and be late to English, which isn't going to get me any closer to a better GPA. I'm thinking about the fact that I can't fall asleep when my head hits my chest and I jump, knocking over my crutches and attracting the attention of everyone in the room.

A freshman named Nikki comes running over to help, propping them against my desk. I know she plays basketball and made varsity, something that Lydia and the Bellas weren't quite sure what to think of, until they saw her box out. Apparently she knocked the overbearing assistant coach on her ass, and immediately became everyone's best friend. Rumor is she plays softball, too.

"You okay?" she asks.

"Fine," I say, stifling a yawn. "Just tired and . . ." I gesture toward the pile of books in front of me.

"No time for naps?" she finishes for me.

"Nope."

She pulls a chair over and sits across from me, sifting through my pile to pull out *Lord of the Flies*.

"This isn't so bad," she says. "Worth reading."

"Maybe," I agree. "But I've got to decide between that or vocab, and the clock's ticking."

"You don't have to decide between shit," she says, surprising me. "You do your vocab. I'll read to you."

"Are you serious?" I haven't had anyone read to me since Dad put away "The Night Before Christmas" on December 24 when I was in fifth grade.

"I . . ." Nikki suddenly doesn't look quite as confident. "I mean, yeah. If you want."

I glance at the clock. "Yes," I tell her. "I want."

We're deep into chapter seven, me half listening to her while my pencil scratches out definitions, when the bell goes off. Nikki dog-ears a page and hands the book to me while I jam everything else into my backpack.

"Just FYI, Piggy dies," she tells me.

I take the battered copy, years of other people's thumbprints marking the edges. "Good tip."

Nikki and I part ways in the hall as I head to English, my head mostly turning over a different problem altogether from English class. I've got to figure out how to space the Oxy I've got left in order to get through the day and get to sleep at night. Jamming up my leg on the ice did not do me any favors, and I remember just as I get to the door of the English room—I've got physical therapy after school.

Down the hall, Carolina gives Aaron a quick peck and dashes to class before the tardy bell rings, holding the door for me.

"Ready for the quiz?" she asks, slightly breathless.

"Can you believe Piggy died?" I ask.

"Aww . . . ," Carolina says, pushing my hair out of my face and tucking it behind my ear. "My girl read a book."

I'm headed out to my car, picking my way around ice patches and analyzing every inch in front of me, when I hear Aaron yelling my name.

"Yo, Mick! Wait up."

I reach my car and rest against it, envying Aaron's easy movements as he jogs across the parking lot to me.

"Hey," he says, a touch out of breath.

"Better get in shape before baseball," I warn him. "Carolina could outrun you right now."

"You might be able to outrun me right now," he admits.

"Doubt it," I say, kicking my crutches where they rest beside me. "So what's up?"

Aaron and I are close enough to fist-bump and for him to shorten my name, but it doesn't go much beyond that. I can't think of a good reason for him to run me down after school.

"How's Carolina seem to you?" he asks

It's a weird question, and I'm immediately on the defensive, searching his face for some indication of what he's asking me.

"What do you mean?"

"Like, physically," he says. "I watched you guys lifting the other day."

"And?"

He runs his hands through his hair, knocking some snowflakes loose. "I don't know, I just think she's pushing too hard. She curled ten more pounds with you than she did with me."

Okay, I get it now.

"So you want me to babysit her? C'mon, nobody tells Carolina Galarza what to do."

"Not babysit her," he says. "Maybe just . . . don't encourage her so much."

"Don't encourage her?" I repeat. "Don't encourage my friend to recover?"

"Not . . . God—that's not what I meant," Aaron says. The words aren't coming out right, and he's frustrated. Normally I would sympathize.

Not right now.

"Just don't push her, I guess," he says.

"I'm not pushing anybody but myself," I tell him.

"That's bullshit and you know it, Catalan. She's not going to let you show her up. She'll match you in the weight room, even if she shouldn't."

"Whatever, man," I say, opening my car door and tossing my crutches inside. "Carolina's not stupid."

"I didn't say she was," Aaron argues as I get in, raising his voice to be heard over the engine as I start the car. "Carolina's not stupid, but she is in pain."

"That's not my fault," I snap at him.

"It's not?"

I stop moving, hands frozen on the steering wheel. We're not talking about lifting anymore, or adding weight that we're not prepared for. We're talking about ice on the road and wheels in the air, my blood on the ground and Carolina's voice as she calls for me. I snap the engine off.

"Are you serious?" I ask Aaron. "Do you blame me for that?"

I'm waiting for him to back off, an apologetic retrieval of words he didn't mean to say. That doesn't happen. Instead he jams his hands in his pockets, eyes not meeting mine. My throat tightens.

"Does *she*?"

"Look, I'm not . . . just take it easy on the weights. That's all I wanted to say." Aaron shuts my door, the

conversation having gone somewhere he never wanted
it to.

Somewhere I never expected.

"You are doing amazing, Mickey. That's awesome. You
look so strong." Kyleigh is a sunburst of positivity
behind me as I make my way through the parallel bars.
I *am* flying, there's no doubt. I wouldn't be surprised if
she yells at me that I'm beautiful and a genius, too.

Even Jolene doesn't have anything negative to say, I'm
doing so well. I'm at the end of the bars in a couple minutes, and pivot for the return journey without a pause.
Last month they had to both hold me up when I turned,
one of them wiping tears off my face while the other
moved my leg for me.

"You are on fire," Kyleigh yells.

At the moment, no, I'm actually not. I definitely was,
right after school. I made it out to my car with a straight
face but I was running on fumes; every molecule of air
that my hip moved through felt like a needle going
straight down into bone. I dug into the center console
of my car for an old Doritos bag, and the pills tucked in
the corner. I took two because I knew Mom was meeting
me and I didn't want to upset her by collapsing into a
pile of inability before my session even started.

This is the best rehab place in three counties, and

Mom and Dad are paying through the nose for it, insurance only covering so much. If I have to wander into the gray area of appropriate use of my medication in order to make this appointment worthwhile, then I'll do it. The look on Mom's face when my hour is up is more than worth it. She looks the way she does right after she gets home from delivering a baby, like something new just happened in the world and she was a part of it.

I'm not something new. I'm just trying to get back to my old self.

Which, Jolene informs me, I'm way closer to than anyone expected at this point.

"You're ahead of where I thought you'd be," she says, handing me a paper cup of water while I do my cooldown stretches. "At your first appointment, I wouldn't have expected you to be able to do more than a toe touch to the ground at the beginning of February. But you're bearing weight on your heel. You've been doing all your exercises at home?"

I nod, too tired for words.

"Every night," Mom says.

Jolene puts both her hands on my shoulders, crouching down in front of me. "Your recovery is a testament to what hard work can do."

"Can I graduate to putting weight on it regularly?"

She glances at her clipboard, but I don't need a

calendar to know what I'm asking. If she'll let me move on to putting half my weight on it with crutches, I'll be a full two weeks ahead of recovery schedule.

"That's a lot, Mickey," she says. "But if you can do it without too much pain some of the time, I would say it's okay."

"Awesome," I say.

"*Some* of the time," she repeats. "I know you want to be ready for your season in time, and it is feasible. But right now I'm happy that you can walk. You should be, too."

"I am," I tell her. And it's true.

But it's not enough.

Mom's still beaming as we leave therapy, her pride overflowing into a pizza stop. I convince her to let me walk into the restaurant without the crutches, and even though it's slow, I do it. Then I ease into the booth without holding on to the tabletop for balance, just to show her I can. She reaches across the table for my hands.

"Mickey, I can't even say what I thought when I first saw your X-rays. They were—"

"Bad," I finish for her. "I know."

"To see what you did today . . . honey, I'm so proud."

She's so proud that the waiter has to ask her if she's okay, while she wipes away tears, explaining that she's happy, and yes, everything is okay.

It's not, not yet. But it's going to be. I'm going to make it that way. Because I realized when I saw her face light up at therapy that this isn't just about my pain.

Every time I pop a pill I'm doing it so that Mom has a kid she can be proud of, something good to focus on with Dad's second family on the way. I'm doing it so that I can be behind the plate for Carolina when our senior season starts, showing the OSU scout she's still got what it takes. I'm doing it so that she and I can go on with our lives like that night never happened, like I wasn't behind the wheel in a car that landed upside down in a ditch. I'm doing it so that my teammates aren't exchanging worried looks when I limp past them in the hallway. Yeah, I manage to tell myself as I sink my teeth into a bread stick, I'm not taking Oxy because it makes me feel good.

I'm taking it for other people.

CHAPTER FOURTEEN

tolerance: *the power or capacity of enduring—or—the power acquired by some persons of bearing doses of medicine that in ordinary cases would prove injurious or fatal*

While I might be able to convince myself that I'm taking OxyContin for other people, it's still my money paying for it. And right now, I don't have much.

I'm back at Edith's, somewhere I told myself I wouldn't be. But with physical therapy going so well and softball conditioning starting in a month, I have to prioritize. Just thinking about running the two miles that Coach Mattix asks out of us during training makes me dig my fingers into my hip, punishing the injury that has sidelined my former confident self.

I dig, feeling the screws, but the pain isn't near what

it was last week after therapy. The Oxy is making sure of that. I've figured out that two can get me through the day, and if I chew them up before bed, two will send me right to sleep, taking care of my nights. But today the familiar echo of pain began snaking shadowy fingers out from my hip right after lunch, something I'd been able to keep at bay until at least after dinner with two 30s.

"That means you need to increase your dosage," Josie says, eyeing me from across Edith's table. She's wearing an expensive winter coat, long hair artfully hanging over one shoulder, new nails tapping away at her phone while she talks. She sounds so confident and looks so well kept that I feel like I'm getting advice from a medical professional. Josie slips her phone back into her pocket, and there's a prolonged silence.

"Where do you go to school?" I finally ask her.

"Baylor Springs," she says, then yells toward the hall-way. "Edes, what's the holdup?"

Edith answers but it's unintelligible, her words lost as the furnace kicks on. "Jesus," Josie complains, pulling off her coat. "She probably forgot the combination to the safe. We'll be here all day."

"Safe?" I ask.

"Yeah," Josie says. "You really think she's just got Oxy lying around with a bunch of junkies walking in and out?"

"I'm not a junkie," I say, too fast.

"Right," Josie says. "Tell yourself whatever, but if you want to stay happy you'll need to up your milligrams. You've built up a tolerance to the 30s."

"What do you take?" I ask her.

"Right now I'm popping two 80s twice a day."

She takes way more than I do, and she looks like all her shit is together. If I did two 80s I'd be dead to the world, floating on my bed and high as hell. But Josie drove here, and doesn't fumble with her phone or have to search for words when she speaks. Me, I'm still working on putting together complete sentences in social situations when I'm one hundred percent sober.

"What do you think I should do?" I ask her.

"I'd say go to 40s, but that's not much of a bump. Buy a bunch of 60s too. Edith tell you about chewing them?"

"Yeah."

"Cool." Josie nods, reaching into her pocket and silencing her phone when it goes off again. I'm weirdly pleased that she's interested enough in me to ignore her phone. She rests her chin on her palm, perfect nails tapping against her cheek.

"You wanna hang out?"

"Sure," I say reflexively, like I've been picked first for dodgeball. I was *always* picked first for dodgeball, but I was never invited to the popular girls' birthday parties. That's what it feels like now, like I'm being acknowledged as a girl by this much better specimen of our kind.

"Cool," Josie says again, sliding my phone out from under my hand. She dials herself from my phone, then pushes it back across the table. "That's me," she says.

I glance down at her number on my recent calls list, then add her, pausing for a second. "Um . . . what's your last name?"

"Addison," she says, going through the same action on her phone. "What's yours?"

"Catalan."

Edith comes back with our brown bags, Josie's noticeably bulgier than mine. I went so far as to open the piggy bank I forgot I had, and took all the loose change down to the coin machine at the grocery store. I dumped everything into it, every penny I'd ever found in the halls, every nickel old Mr. Henderson had given me for each weed I'd pulled in his flower bed when I was just a kid. My childhood sounded loud, going into that machine.

Half of me is waiting for Josie to notice that I'm only getting a 40 off Edith and offer to help me out, the other half is ashamed of myself for wanting that. But her phone goes off yet again, and this time she answers it, not seeing my pitifully slim payment. My own phone vibrates under my hand, and Edith looks pathetically between the two of us.

"Off so soon? I've got a pie in—"

"Sorry, Edes," Josie says, yanking on her coat and taking her pill bag. "I've got to bounce."

I glance down at my phone, where a text from Dad has come in:

Baby on the way!

It's got a string of happy faces and hearts next to it. It's also part of a group text that Mom is included in. Geez.

"Yeah, I've got to go, too," I tell Edith, who is clearly hurt that we aren't staying for snacks. "I'll be back," I reassure her.

The shit thing is, it's true.

CHAPTER FIFTEEN

addict: *one who devotes themselves habitually, especially to a substance*

Dad's second wife may not be my favorite person, but I feel sorry for anybody pushing a baby out of their vagina. Dad comes out to the waiting room every so often to give us updates on how Devra is doing. Mom practices her polite smiles in between his visits, but eight hours later she's asking pointed questions, and not in her ex-wife voice, either. She's talking to Dad like a doctor.

"Is something wrong?" I ask, once Dad has disappeared back behind the double doors that separate the waiting room from the women in labor.

"No," Mom says brightly, smile back in place. "It can take a while with the first one."

I watch her carefully, familiar with every line on her face and where they're supposed to be when everything is fine. That's not where they're currently located.

"But?" I push.

"But I'm watching the staff. They may look calm to you but it's all a front. They're all wearing *oh shit* faces." Mom blows out all her air with the admission, her bangs flowing with the updraft.

"Oh," I say, a quiver of concern in my belly. I can't say I like Devra, but I do know how excited Dad has been about his second family, and as a member of his first one, I've got a stake in this, too.

I stretch out my bad leg, bending the knee a little to get some blood flowing to my foot, which has fallen asleep.

"Honey, you should just go home," Mom says. "It could be hours yet. You've got school tomorrow, and you can't be doing yourself any good right now."

I'm definitely not doing myself any good. I realized that around *Jeopardy!* time, the waiting room TV posing unanswerable questions at me as tendrils of pain took a firm grip. The one 40 I managed to buy from Edith is down in the parking lot, ready to make it all go away if I cave and take it. But then I'd be out, and with no cash left. I decide to grin and bear it, just like Mom, sitting here for the sake of solidarity while Dad's second wife delivers his first biological child.

Mom's fading into sleep, her head nodding to one side, when her phone goes off, making us both jump and sending a hot wire of pain that runs from my hip down to my little toe.

"Shit," we both say at the same time. She turns her phone around so I can read the message from Dad.

emergency see section

"Isn't a *C-section*, like *C* as in cat?" I ask.

"Yes," Mom says. "But I don't think he's overly worried about autocorrect mistakes right now."

"Right," I say.

"Although," Mom adds, rubbing the crease on her face where she fell asleep against the couch, "you do *see* a lot."

"Oh my God, Mom," I say. "You're so bad."

She starts laughing too, holding her hand over her mouth to stifle the sound as tears leak from her eyes. "Do not tell your dad I said that," she says. "That was horribly insensitive."

"You earned it," I tell her.

The sun is up by the time we're allowed back to Devra's room, my little half brother—or adopted half brother, or I don't even know what—asleep in a plastic crib near her bed. Devra is refusing pain medication, even though she's as gray as the wall behind her, and her mouth is set in a firm line that I know too well. It's the only way to stop yourself from screaming. Mom and Dad are in the hallway, arguing. I lean my head against the wall, able to pick up the hiss of their intense whispers.

"If she says she doesn't want them, then she doesn't want them, Geoff. It's her decision, period," Mom says.

"What if it's too much?" Dad argues back. "What if she can't take care of the baby?"

"I guess you'll have to take the leap of parenting your own child," Mom says, and I bite my lip so that I don't laugh again.

"That's not . . . I can't very well breastfeed him, can I?"

"Neither can she, if she's got painkillers in her system."

I hear Dad's heavy sigh, one that filled the house often before they split up. "It's been a really long day, Annette. I just saw my wife's intestines, for Christ's sake."

"I see intestines at least once a week. Suck it up."

In bed, Devra reaches into her mouth, pulling the one pill she conceded to take under the vigilant eye of her nurse out of the pocket of her cheek.

"Don't you think you should . . . ," I begin, but she shakes her head.

Our eyes meet, and I know that look. She can't even

find words right now, all her brain is overrun by agony, every nerve she has singing a song that has no lyrics. Pain can come in a quick rush, fading off into something bearable after that initial peak. But pain that endures doesn't give you that break, the moment of air that you need before you're pulled back under. And under is all there is right now for Devra.

She reaches for me, pill in her fist.

"Get it the hell away from me," she says, each word coming out low and tight, every syllable fought for.

"Devra . . ."

"Addict," she says, cutting me off. I tighten in my seat, blood rushing to my face at the accusation. Then she touches her own chest, eyes closed tight in shame.

"Recovering," she manages.

We've never touched before, but when I slide my fingers under hers and she drops the pill, slick with her spit, into my hand, I feel like I know her better than anyone in the world.

I slip into the bathroom and take it myself.

CHAPTER SIXTEEN

steal: *to take without right or leave, and with intent to keep wrongfully*

I get a free pass from school, something I'm only too grateful for. I don't think I could handle it right now. Whatever the nurse had given Devra, it definitely wasn't Oxy. It took the sharper edges off, but the comfortable numbness I've come to depend on is nowhere in sight.

Mom and I head over to Dad's new place, to get a few things for Devra. We go through their drawers, Mom matter-of-factly folding Dad's underwear and packing a bag, instructing me to find comfortable, loose clothes for Devra. I feel weird, going through her stuff. But I'm surprised to find she's more like me than I thought, veering toward sports bras and cotton undies. I toss some things together, and am about to join Mom downstairs when I see the sharp edge of a twenty-dollar bill sticking out from under Devra's jewelry box.

I pick it up to find a nice, neat stack of fresh bills, so new they look fake. I peel two off, having to rub them against each other to separate them. I head down the stairs with Devra's bag over my shoulder, face flush with shame. And while I'm not proud of myself, there's a louder, bigger thought in there.

Forty is nowhere near enough.

Mom's waiting for me in the car, reapplying mascara. She's never been in Dad's new place, and I don't know if she needs makeup because she took a few minutes to have a good cry, or if she's just trying to freshen up as we head back to the hospital.

"You okay, Mom?" I ask.

"Yeah, honey," she says. "I'm fine."

I've said it enough to know how it sounds when it's a lie, and when it's the truth. Somehow, miraculously, Mom really is okay.

"Is it hard?"

"It's not easy," she admits. "Want some coffee?" I adamantly nod yes and she pulls into a drive-through.

"It's not easy . . ." I nudge her to continue.

"Well . . . it's . . ." Mom sighs, resting her head against the driver's window as we wait. "It's like this: When I found out your dad was having an affair, I was pissed.

But when I found out how much younger she was than him, it was almost laughable. Like he was this big joke, an old guy chasing the young girls, right?"

"Yeah, I get it," I tell her.

"But then she gets pregnant," Mom goes on. "And I've got to rethink this whole thing. She's not some little home-wrecker anymore. She's a woman building her own family. And now—"

She cuts herself off, orders our coffees, and rolls the window back up against the cold. "This is strictly between you and me," she says.

"Okay."

"Now I find out she's refusing pain meds after a terribly invasive procedure, because she's a recovering addict. She wants to be able to breastfeed her child, and be a good mother to it beyond that, into the future. Devra won't take *anything* beyond aspirin, afraid it will make her relapse."

"She told me," I say.

"Yeah, well . . ." Mom pauses, rolling down the window and getting our drinks. "Now I'm right back to being pissed off again."

"Because she was an addict?"

"No," Mom says, popping her coffee open. "Because now I respect her, dammit."

∙ ∙ ∙

The hospital is different during the day. There are more people, more crying, more hugs being passed around. There's a lot of naked emotion that I'm uncomfortable with, especially when Mom picks up Dad's new baby and her face shows pure bliss. She never held me like that, never smiled down with wonder on me. I came to her already formed, for better or for worse.

I make an excuse and leave the room, leaning a little less on the crutches than I was yesterday, pushing the edges of what Jolene said I was allowed to do. I still need sleep—and a shower, if I'm being honest—but I'm not going to tear Mom away from the baby yet. I go for an awkward, lurching walk, swinging the crutches out in front of me, my body the pendulum that keeps going forward, never back.

I may have missed school and the weight room, but if I keep moving on the crutches I can get a decent workout on my arms. So I keep going, past open doors and closed ones, down hallways I recognize from my own visits and then through some I don't. I end up in the cancer ward, slightly out of breath, heart pumping harder than it should be if I want to be ready for spring training. I find an empty pair of chairs in the hall and settle into one, resting my crutches next to me.

A woman about Mom's age comes out of a patient room, phone in one hand, her purse in another.

"No," she says into the phone. "They don't want him to have meds from home . . . I don't know. No, I . . . something about they can only give him meds from the pharmacy here. . . . Yeah, and bill the insurance three times what they cost, I'm sure," she snorts. "I didn't know what he needed so I just grabbed everything . . . there were half-full bottles just lying around . . ."

She's quiet for a second, listening to the response. "Well, you know how he is, never finishes anything.

"I don't know, honey," she says, her voice dropping lower. "He's in a lot of pain." She disappears around the corner just as my phone goes off with a text from Mom.

Where are you? Ready to go?

I tell her yes, and that I'll be right there. I get my crutches under me and am heading back the way I came when I see the lady I accidentally eavesdropped on still talking into the phone, and as she heads into a bathroom I follow, telling myself that I have to pee, or take a thirteen, as the scanner on Edith's counter would say.

I don't pee.

What I do is this. I wait for her to come out of a stall, to wash her hands, and to turn her back on her purse as she dries them. It's an old-lady purse almost as big as my gym bag, mouth gaping open to reveal a gallon Ziploc bag with four orange prescription bottles inside. I grab it and duck into a stall, lowering myself onto a toilet as I listen to her gather her things and leave.

In my hands I hold Ronald Wagner's pills, a man I don't know, but I can guess by the dosage and amount of Oxy here that he's got cancer. And I just stole from him. I wait for the shame that filled me when I took money from Devra, but it doesn't come.

Mostly what I feel, when I look at all that OxyContin, is absolute relief.

CHAPTER SEVENTEEN

strong: *having active physical power, the power of exerting great bodily force—or—having passive physical power, the ability to bear or endure*

My phone vibrates with a reminder about a checkup with Dr. Ferriman. I'm a month out from conditioning, putting half weight—and sometimes more—on my leg, but still with the assistance of crutches. I get my stuff together and check in on Mom. She's napping, the small hump of her body lonely in the king-size bed she and Dad splurged on for their anniversary.

An hour later I'm back in the teddy-bear-papered room, their cherubic faces less annoying when I'm not in pain. I feel great, actually, good enough to have left the crutches at home, thanks to one of Ronald Wagner's OxyContin, the full 80 milligrams coursing through my system.

There's the two-tap knock on the door, then Dr. Ferriman comes in.

"Mickey," he says. "How are you doing?"

"Good," I say, swinging my legs to prove it.

Ferriman rotates my leg, asks me questions about my pain levels, which I can honestly answer are quite low.

"You're doing great," he finally says, finishing up. "Putting weight on the leg?"

"Yep."

"Without too much additional pain?"

"Nope." Not after taking Ronald's Oxy, for sure. "Can I get rid of the crutches?"

Ferriman crosses his arms, eyeing me up and down. "Only if you promise me you'll go back to them if necessary."

"Promise," I say quickly, as if I'm afraid he'll take it back. "Can I start conditioning in March?"

"Can I stop you?"

Technically, he can. So I don't appreciate the joke.

"Yes," he says quickly, reading my mood. "But I strongly advise you to consider a different position. All that crouching behind the plate could create long-term problems for your injury."

I nod as if I'm listening, but I only heard the first part. I can play.

Ferriman is reaching for the door when he pauses, and I wonder if he's noticed that I'm a little slow with my responses, my eyes lingering too long on certain things that catch my attention, like the changing facial expressions of the teddy bears as the pattern in the wall-paper repeats itself.

Instead he says, "I'm so impressed with your recovery, Mickey. Really. To see you doing this well, after an injury like yours, is a testament to the healing capacity of the human body, but also to your willpower."

"I . . . thank you," I say, not really knowing what else would be appropriate.

"You're a hell of a strong person, Mickey Catalan," he says.

Somehow, this makes me feel like shit.

Dinner with the Galarzas will fix that.

Carolina and I are fixtures at each other's houses, and I can almost claim to be as comfortable around their dinner table as I am on a softball field. Almost. The accident disrupted more than our health. Being housebound, unable to drive, then buried under piles of makeup work had taken me out of the weekly cycle of dinner with them. Tonight that changes. It's one more step in my return to normalcy, I think, as I let myself in the side door without knocking. Most people would find that rude, but Mrs. Galarza—Clarita—had been more offended the one time I *did* knock.

"You knock on your own door?" she'd asked, finger in the air to punctuate her question as I shook my head. "Then don't knock on mine."

Still, it's been so long that I do feel odd walking straight into their kitchen. That is, until I'm folded into Clarita's arms, a spoon dripping asopao barely missing my face in the process.

"How is this girl?" she asks, pushing me back just as forcefully as she pulled me in, to get a better look at me. "Wait . . . where are the crutches?"

"Gone," I tell her, emotion closing my throat so that I can't get more than that out.

"You look good," Mr. Galarza—Ian—says from the table, folding his laptop shut. "I told my wife it will take more than a car accident to keep you two from playing."

I nod, unable to speak. I'm saved from breaking down into actual tears when Carolina shows up, pulling a sweatshirt over her head. She's got pillow creases on one side of her face and her hair is sticking up in spots, but she gives me a smile.

"Cinco minutos," Clarita says, glancing at her pot of soup.

I've been raised past the point of a guest in the Galarza family, which means I get to walk in without knocking, but it also means I have jobs. I help Carolina set the table, pausing only when Mr. Galarza glances up at the place settings and asks, "¿Aaron no viene?"

"Not tonight," Carolina says, and her dad can barely hide his disappointment.

"¿Por qué no?" Clarita asks, carrying the soup pot over to the table. "Donde comen dos, comen tres."

What two can eat, three can eat . . . a saying I've heard more than once in this house, although it's usually being used to invite me to stay for dinner, not Aaron.

"He is a good boy," Clarita says to me. "But his Spanish . . ." She shakes her head.

"No es bueno. He has a teacher from the Midwest and speaks Spanish with a Wisconsin accent," Ian agrees, shuddering. "But he will learn, now that he has a proper instructor," he adds, giving Carolina a nudge with his elbow.

She tells him off a little too quickly for me to decipher it, then we all clasp hands and say a table prayer in Spanish. I've done it a hundred times, at least, but I'm surprised to find my tongue falling silent once or twice, the familiar words not coming. I don't know if it's because I've been away from the Galarzas too long, or if it's the 80 I helped myself to before heading over.

"¿Qué te dijo el doctor?" Carolina asks me, as we fill our bowls.

"I'm cleared to start conditioning," I tell her, and Clarita breathes a deep sigh of relief. I don't add that

Ferriman suggested I consider a different position. Our lineup has been set in stone since seventh grade, the chemistry of our starters carefully proportioned. Me not catching would be like substituting the Virgin Mary into Ian's carvings of the three kings.

"Gracias a Dios," Clarita says. "I am happy for you, Mickey."

"And for Carolina's sake," Ian adds. "She can shine on her own, but the two of you together have a special polish."

That's the truth. The pitcher is only as good as her catcher, and Carolina and I work together, hand in glove. We use our own signals, a silent communication from mound to plate forming a thread that the ball follows, back and forth, flowing free and easy. That doesn't happen naturally; you've got to have a good pair to make it work. And while the speed Carolina can put on the ball is what gets attention, there's still got to be someone with the cojones to stop it.

What I do might not be sexy, but it's useful.

"¿Cómo está tu brazo?" I ask, watching as Carolina reaches for the soup pot again, using her uninjured arm. The other one rests on the table, and I realize she's been babying it.

"Carolina está bien," Clarita answers for her, and my friend's jaw tightens.

"The doctors, they wanted to give her stronger . . . pastillas." Mr. Galarza looks to his wife, spinning his hand in the air, unsure of the English.

"Painkillers," she says, shaking her head. "I told them no, ella no lo necesita. Poison will not make her better."

"Poison?" I ask, not catching Carolina's warning glance in time.

"Sí, es veneno," Clarita says. "My brother sits in a prison in Puerto Rico because of un dolor de cabeza."

"A headache?" I ask, unsure of my translation.

"Sí, una migraña," Ian says. "Pain that split his head in two. The doctors gave him the pastillas, and . . ." He shrugs, ending the story without finishing the sentence.

"And that was it for him," Clarita says. "A man who steals is not a man, and when he steals from familia, he is no longer mi familia."

I feel my blood warming, my tongue loosened by my own pastillas. "He must have been in a lot of pain," I say.

"It was not the pain, but the poison," Clarita says sternly. "The drugs were more important to him than everyone; now everyone has found more important things than him. His wife left him, and his son has a new father who does not share that weakness."

I glance at Carolina, who is tipping her bowl up to get the last of her soup.

"Now he wishes his only problem was una migraña," Ian says, trying to lighten the mood, but his wife will have none of it.

"This is why mi hija will not take pastillas. She is strong, and smart. Carolina does not need it."

I look down at my dinner, jaw clenched.

Because if Carolina is strong and smart, then what would the Galarzas have to say about me?

CHAPTER EIGHTEEN

choke: *to render unable to breathe by filling, pressing upon, or squeezing the windpipe; to affect with a sense of strangulation by passion or strong feeling; to fail in a critical situation*

"Hail the conquering hero!" Big Ed shouts at me when I walk into the market, a bitter end-of-February gust blowing me most of the way in. That became my official greeting right after I lost the crutches.

"Heroine, Ed," I correct him as I settle onto my stool.

"How's lifting?" he asks, pouring my coffee.

"Pretty good," I say, and it's mostly true. I've had a couple setbacks when I pushed too hard, got optimistic with the weights. But always the Oxy took the edge off. I've even started experimenting with squats. Slowly, it's true, and with no weight and the trainer keeping a steady eye on me.

But I did it.

"I heard the Gatts twins both signed with Ashland," Ed says.

"Heard that too," I say. "Baylor Springs always has D1 and D2 scouts crawling all over them. Money likes money."

"And there's more of that in the suburbs. But OSU came all the way out here to the sticks for Carolina," Ed reminds me, like I could forget.

"Yeah, but that's Carolina," I tell him. OSU wasn't the only Division One school to send scouts to take a look at our pitcher, but they usually only stayed for a few innings, and I guarantee their notes included only her name. All of us are good, some of us are great, a few might be gifted. But Carolina is exceptional.

"You'll get an offer, Mickey," Ed says. "They're just waiting to see what you can do on that leg."

"Maybe," I say.

"Yep," he says confidently. "You'll show 'em. Get you back behind the plate, Carolina on the mound, them three Bellas on the grass. You guys will make it this year; I guarantee it. State champs, I'm calling it right now."

"That's ballsy, Ed."

"Nothing to it." He shakes his head. "I'm not jinxing it to say you've got conference champs buttoned up. Sectional tournaments, no problem."

I can't really argue with that. We've won sectionals since my freshman year.

"District, the only team I see giving you any issue is Calcutta, and they lost that shortstop . . ."

"Vixon," I supply.

"Yeah, Vixon. She graduated. So I say you've got districts." He starts ticking off his fingers, raising them one at a time. "Regionals—"

"Is where we choke," I tell him, more bitterly than I intended. "Every time."

"Maybe," Ed allows. "But you got hosed on that play at third last year." He ticks the regional tournament off his fingers like it's a done deal.

"State," he says, holding up his index finger. "You're going to get there this year, and you're going to win."

"That's the plan," I say. "We'd be the first softball team to make it that far."

"Check your school history," Ed corrects me. "You'd be the first ball team, period. Baseball never made it that far."

"Nice," I say.

Ed takes a sip of his coffee while he searches for a different topic, and the police scanner disrupts the silence from the back room, though I can't quite make out the words.

"You hear about the dollar store?" he asks.

"I know they got broke into," I say, but he waves that away.

"Nah, I mean yesterday. Young mother hits the ground over in the diaper section, and Dolores—you know her, she's the one with the real short hair—she gets there and this kid, couldn't be more than two, is tugging on her mom's arm, trying to get her up, just crying and crying."

"What was wrong with her?"

"She's a goddamn idiot, that's what's wrong with her," Ed says. "OD'd, right there in the dollar store with her kid holding her hand."

"She's not dead, is she?" I ask.

"Nope." Ed shakes his head. "Squad Narcan'd her and she's fine. Fine as someone like that can get, I guess."

"Mmmmm," I say, burying my face in my coffee cup. I take a sip, letting it burn all the way down, to meet the heat gathering in my veins from the two 80s I took right before I walked in here.

"Do you know who it was?" I ask. Chances are, if she's that young, I'll at least recognize the name.

"Heather Bellinger," Ed says. "Used to be Heather Donahue; she married one of the Bellinger boys from Left Bank."

"Shit, Ed," I say. "She TA'd my gym class, freshman year."

Heather was pretty cool. Even though she was supposed to check off her clipboard to make sure all the girls showered after class, she'd ignore it if some of us just ran our hair under the sink. There were some heavier girls in that class too, and one skinny girl who was so mortified at the idea of undressing in front of everyone else that Heather made sure anyone who wanted a stall with a curtain got first pick.

"Damn," I say, sipping my coffee again even though the last swallow scalded my throat.

The scanner goes off again, and this time Ed tilts his head to catch the sound, and I glance up at the clock.

"I gotta get to school," I tell him. "Have a good week."

"You too, kiddo," he says. "Be careful out there. Keep your grades up and you'll get a scholarship, I know it."

"See you later" is all I've got to say to that.

I make my way to the car, shoulders hunched against the wind, scanning the ground for icy patches as I walk. But I can't get Heather out of my head, or the image of her unconscious on the tiles of the dollar store, a panicked toddler beside her.

I get behind the wheel and flick on the wipers, scattering the fresh coat of snow that accumulated just while I was talking to Ed. The heat comes on, and I hold my hands up to the vents, hands that were shaking a little before I took the Oxy this morning.

I think of Heather again as I pull out of the parking spot.

But I don't have a little kid.

So it's kind of different.

CHAPTER NINETEEN

justification: *a sufficient reason why a person behaves or acts as they do*

Lifting improves my spirits, especially when I get to the weight room before Aaron, and Carolina partners with me instead of him. We're both careful with our injured limbs, her arm pale and too thin, the scars on my leg a vibrant red against the whiteness of my skin, my strong leg clearly larger than the other. We look like somebody took toddler parts and stuck them on our bodies, the muscular outlines on the rest of us wildly out of proportion.

"You sure?" she asks me, standing by as I lie down on the leg press.

"Yep," I say. Carolina would only let me put sixty pounds on it. It should be like pressing a feather. Maybe two feathers and one piece of paper.

I take a deep breath and extend, keeping my hips straight so that I'm not pushing more with one leg than the other. Everything stretches. Time. Muscles. The thin covering of Oxy that my whole consciousness is bathed in these days. But as the weights lift, nothing breaks through. I feel no pain, no puncture of this bubble I've created, within which I can do anything.

"One," counts Carolina as the weight comes back down. I push again.

We agreed on a set of ten, and I do it, easily. I want to tell her to add more weight, or let me go to fifteen on my next set, but when I swing off the bench my leg spasms. It's not painful, just a reminder that the muscle there has been taken by surprise and pushing it to exhaustion isn't to my benefit.

"You good?" Carolina asks as I come to my feet.

"Yeah," I say, experimentally standing.

"Cool. Wanna see if my arm falls off when I try to curl?"

I glance at Aaron, who is over on the butterfly machine, his face red in concentration as he pushes his elbows together.

"It won't," I tell her.

And it doesn't. The weights might be lower, our reps not as quick as they used to be, but we're together, and we're working on it. I can't forget what Aaron said to me in the parking lot, but I'm not going to tell Carolina to ease up on her workout, and I'm sure as hell not backing off mine. I spot her as she does a bench press, maybe helping more than I usually do. She shakes her head at me in warning, her hair swishing against my knees.

"Do I look like a bebé to you?" she asks.

"No," I tell her.

"Then don't treat me like one."

I step back, only eyeing her as she benches, hoping that Aaron overheard, that he knows his girlfriend doesn't need him—or anyone else—taking care of her. Carolina racks the bar, then gets up from the bench, tripping over a twenty-pound plate I had set out for myself.

"Sorry," I say.

"Not your fault." She waves me off.

I hold on to those words as I set up my bar.

Not my fault.

The others had stopped watching us as we go through our workout, no longer keeping an eye out to gauge how the season is going to go, or whether they might need to dive in to help if one of us struggles. We're two girls getting ready for the upcoming season.

I can almost forget that I was broken.

When I get home there's a note from Mom saying

she's been called to the hospital, so I take over her tub with the jets. The water feels good, rolling over me, the outside world matching the inside waves that the Oxy seems to bring to my mind. I settle in, resting happily. The feeling of normality hasn't left, almost as if I could look down in the driveway and see my old car there, glass still intact, wheels on the ground like they're supposed to be, not up in the air and spinning like they were last time I saw them.

I get out of the water, suddenly too warm.

The weekend stretches out before me and I don't have a lot to fill it with. I've exhausted my Netflix options while recovering, and I swear I've looked at most of the internet, too. I shoot Carolina a text, asking if she wants to see a movie, get a pizza, or just come over. I'm getting dressed when she answers.

Can't tonight. At Aaron's. ☹

I know the frowny face means she's bummed that she can't hang out with me, not that she doesn't want to be with Aaron.

Don't get pregnant, I shoot back.

She sends me a thumbs-up, which doesn't exactly make me feel better.

I toss my phone on the bed, my body following shortly thereafter. It's not like I don't have other numbers in my phone. The Bellas. Lydia. Even Nikki. But the Bellas require a level of energy I don't have right now, and I don't want Lydia to misinterpret anything. I'm considering texting Nikki and seeing if she wants to do something other than read required novels to me when my phone goes off.

Wanna hang?

It's a text from Josie Addison.

I look at my ceiling, then check the time. It's only six. An entire night of hanging out alone in my room isn't something that used to bother me, but now it feels too much like convalescing, something I'm very done with.

I text back, **yes.**

It turns out that hanging with Josie also includes hanging with Edith. She instructs me to head over to "Ede's place," where I find the two of them watching QVC while eating dinner.

"Hey, darlin'," Edith calls after I let myself in, following the sounds of the TV to Edith's living room. "There's dinner in the oven, if you're hungry."

I feel kind of weird about it, but I get myself a plate and load up with mashed potatoes, ham loaf, and green beans. I grab a Coke from the fridge and settle in with Josie on the couch.

"Hey," Josie says, scraping the last of her dinner off her plate. "You're here just in time. They're almost out of the double-encrusted emerald pendant."

"Oh good," I say.

"Don't knock it till you've tried it," she says.

And dammit if she isn't right. I end up watching the pendant go out of stock and get weirdly excited about the next item, a set of kitchen knives that the guy throws pineapples at, the three of us making an *ooooh* noise when they split in midair.

From the kitchen, the scanner squawks.

Unit 32, respond to 1525 County Road 46 for a Code 12.

"Somebody's got no cash for their stash," Josie says. "That's the third B & E this week."

"Seriously, that's impressive," I tell her.

"I'm even better at scanner codes than I am at blow jobs," she says, sucking on her fork.

"Josie," Edith chides her.

"Not that I give those," she adds easily.

I laugh, no longer caring that Carolina is with Aaron and Mom is at the hospital. My empty house fades into the background as the knives are replaced with a line of skin-care products, and Josie pops a pill.

"It's the weekend," she says. "Have an 80 on me."

I feel fine, my legs stretched in front of me, muscles

sore—in a good way—from working out. But I take it.
I take it because it's free Oxy, and an offering of friendship from Josie. I take it because she just took one too,
and that means I don't have to feel bad about it. I take it
because I don't have to justify to anyone that I'm taking
it even though I'm not in pain.

I'm taking this Oxy because I like the way it makes
me feel.

And nobody here is going to call me out on that.

By ten o'clock Josie has raided Edith's liquor cabinet and
I've texted Mom to tell her I'm spending the night at a
friend's house. She answers quickly—**ok**. In the midst
of a delivery I doubt she has time to even question it.

Josie offers me a shot of something amber-colored,
but I hold my hand up.

"I don't drink."

"Seriously?"

"Yeah," I say. "If I get caught drinking, I'm off the
team. Not worth it."

"Um, but Oxy is fine?"

"That's different," I explain. "I've been prescribed
Oxy."

"And that pill you just took was given to you by a
doctor, right?" She throws back the shot she poured for
herself, then mine as well.

"Dr. Edith, accredited by the School of Hard Knocks," Edith shouts from her recliner, where she's taken up residency after a failed attempt at standing. "You leave Mickey alone, Josie. No fighting."

"We're not fighting, Grandma," Josie says, gathering up the bottle and reclaiming her spot next to me on the couch. "You don't drink, whatever. More for me."

"'Kay," Edith says, her eyelids drooping.

Josie mutes the TV and leans her head back on the couch, two bright spots of intoxication sprouting on her cheeks.

"Wait, Edith is your grandma?" I ask.

Josie starts to shake her head, then thinks better of it when it goes too far to one side. "No," she says. "I just call her that."

"Oh," I say. "My mom isn't actually my mom, but I call her that."

It's more than I've ever said to anyone about being adopted, even Carolina. I touch my face, as if I'm wondering how this is the same Mickey who makes friends on the field but can't seem to find things to say in the hallway. I'm never guilty of oversharing, unless I'm talking to Carolina about that underwear you can menstruate in, which might be my new religion. I'm about to ask Josie if she has a pair when I realize I must be high to even consider it.

She's moved again, anyway. Off the couch and over to the end table next to Edith's chair, where her purse sits. Josie waves her hand in front of Edith's face, and when she doesn't react, motions to me to be quiet as she reaches into Edith's purse and pulls out an orange bottle.

"So you're like her granddaughter, but the one that steals from her while she's asleep?"

"Yep," Josie says. "Go ahead and tell me you've never stolen anything."

I don't.

"Uh-huh." She tips a single pill into her palm and hands the bottle over to me. "Besides, she's like my grandma, but the one who would totally tell me she deserves to be stolen from if she's stupid enough to leave pills out of the safe when there are two junkies in the house."

"One junkie," I correct.

"Yeah, you're here for the green beans. I forgot." I don't argue with her, instead proving my point by putting the cap back on the bottle. Josie rolls her eyes.

"They're only 20s, anyway. Just topping myself off."

I check the label. She's right. It's a bottle of 20 milligrams of Oxy, prescribed to Betsy Vellon.

"Who is Betsy Vellon?"

"One of the ladies from the senior center," Josie

explains, curling up opposite me with a throw pillow.

I remember the van I saw in Dr. Ferriman's parking lot, the frail woman Edith was leading down the hallway there. "She drives for them, doesn't she?"

"Yeah, that's her *job.*" Josie puts air quotes around the last word.

"Job," I echo back at her, with my own quotes. "What do you mean?"

"The county doesn't pay Edes shit," Josie says. "So she supplements her income with the old people's meds. Betsy's got rheumatoid arthritis, Ruth has something going on with her nerves, and Helen . . . I don't remember what Helen had."

"Had?" I ask. "Helen's dead?"

"Yep," Josie says, unconcerned.

"Wait, what was Helen's last name?"

"I don't know," Josie says, stretching her legs out to rest in my lap. I tap her foot a little harder than necessary.

"Did it start with a *W*?"

"Maybe, yeah. Why?"

"I think I have her walker," I say. And Josie, who was almost asleep, bursts out laughing, kicking me a little in her convulsion. Enough to ping my hip and send a splinter of pain into the happy cocoon I formed around myself.

"To Helen," Josie says, reaching for her glass, which still has a small pool of alcohol in it. "I can honestly say I miss her. She got 80s refilled, no questions asked."

"So why again does Edith have everyone else's meds?"

"A lot of them don't actually need them, or don't like using them. They just want to get out of the house, even if it is only going to the doctor again," Josie says, settling back into the pillow fort she's built for herself. "Medicaid pays for the prescription, Edith gives them half the street value in cash, drives them to their appointments, and takes them to McDonald's after. Everybody gets drugs. Everybody makes money. Everybody eats french fries. Not a bad scam."

"Guess not," I have to agree as I get up to put the pills back in Edith's purse. It's the same one I remember from the parking lot at Dr. Ferriman's, with the three blond kids staring out from the plastic slots on the sides.

"You could almost pass as her actual granddaughter," I tell Josie when I sit back down. She moves her feet for me, then puts them back on my lap, as natural as can be. "Do you know them?"

"No," Josie says, suddenly serious. "They're dead."

"What? No way." I look back over at Edith's purse, as if the posed, stolen moments of their small faces can argue in their own defense.

"House fire," Josie says, her eyelids slipping shut. "Edith's only son. His whole family. Poof. Gone."

"Jesus," I say quietly.

"Apparently he was not there," Josie says, her voice somehow tight even as she slides into sleep. I let her go all the way under before I get up and go back to the purse, uncapping the bottle silently and going to the sink for a quick sip of water.

All my life people have told me how strong I am, like it's the best thing I've got to offer. I know they mean it in all the ways—physically, emotionally, mentally—and I am. But I'm also tired, worn out from hurting and being expected to come out on top of everything—even a car crash. I'm exhausted in all the ways I'm supposed to be strong, so I take comfort in the last 20 as it wraps me up, warm and comforting, happy to be taken care of for once.

Sometimes it's so damn nice to not have to be Mickey Catalan.

CHAPTER TWENTY

lie: *an intentional violation of truth; an untruth spoken with the intention to deceive*

I wake up with my legs tangled in Josie's, unsure where I am or why it's so damn hard to wake up. I feel sluggish and heavy, everything in me insisting that it's perfectly fine to go back to sleep. But my buzzing phone says otherwise, and I cringe when I see that I've missed two calls from my mom, and a text from Carolina that just says **?????**

"Shit," I say, sitting up too quickly. My head feels like it's moving forward even when I know it's stopped, and I stumble to my feet. I wish I had my crutches, or even Helen W., not because I'm in pain, but because my legs aren't all the way awake. Or my brain isn't. Or both.

Edith had put the blinds down last night, muttering something about nosy neighbors. I spread them with
my fingers now, reeling back from the sunlight that's so
bright it's painful.

"Shit," I say again when I check the time.

It's one in the afternoon, and I'm sure that my believable fib to Mom about spending the night at a friend's
just got stretched too far. Edith and Josie are both happily curled up with pillows and blankets, oblivious to
my exit. I call Carolina and put her on speaker the second I'm behind the wheel, her voice rising accusatorily
from my cup holder.

"Where are you even at right now?" she asks as soon
as she picks up.

"I was at a friend's," I tell her, which isn't exactly a lie.

"Your mom thought that friend was me," Carolina
says. "I covered for you, but you weren't with the Bellas or Lydia either. I checked. So either you suddenly
sprouted a social life or something's up."

"Maybe I did," I snap. "Is that so hard to believe?"

"Yeah," Carolina says flatly.

Fair enough.

"I was with a friend," I insist. "She goes to Baylor
Springs."

"Fancy."

"I met her in physical therapy." I don't think about

the fact that the only thing Josie Addison is in danger of breaking is a nail.

"'Kay," Carolina concedes. "But next time give your mom the details. I don't want to lie to her again."

"My bad," I tell her.

"She cool?"

"My mom?"

"This chick. What sport she play?"

I blank. I can't picture Josie playing anything other than beer pong. "She wrecked her bike," I say. "Screwed up her wrist."

"She sounds like fun. We should hang out." I'm pretty sure Carolina's dry sarcasm is at work, but I can't be sure after the adrenaline push my heart just gave at the thought of Josie casually inviting Carolina to pop an 80, and then Carolina informing Josie that she's weak.

"Ha," I say, hoping she doesn't push it. "I don't think you two have a lot in common."

Which is an understatement.

"All right, later," Carolina says, hanging up.

I'm about to stop her, about to ask if she thinks that the car crash was my fault, that her best friend is the reason why she has to worry about losing a free ride to a DI school if she's not up to snuff in time for the season. But she's already gone, and I don't know if it's a conversation you have over the phone, anyway. It's not a conversation I know how to have face-to-face, either.

I pull into my driveway, inspecting the story I fed Carolina for cracks, to see if it will stand up to a mom inspection. It should, technically. I never specified that I was staying with Carolina, and if she covered for me I should be in the clear this time. I'll have to introduce the idea of Josie as a fellow therapy patient to Mom, who will probably be thrilled that I'm meeting new people.

As I lock my car door, I realize that if I'm already thinking about last night as *this time*, that means I'm going to do it again. I think about laughing with Josie, how her shiny facade slipped for a moment while she talked about Edith's grandchildren. And Edith herself, filling her house with people she can care for, luring us there with cookies, and OxyContin. I think about the warm feeling that enveloped me there, like the sun beating down on the softball field, but coming from the inside, like maybe I belonged there with them, too.

I'm down with that.

Mom's at the kitchen table nursing a cup of coffee when I walk in. She glances up, dark circles under her eyes.

"Rough one?" I ask.

"Fairly," she admits. "Baby and mother both okay, though. So, in the end, a good day. How's Carolina doing?"

"Good," I tell her, pretty sure it's the right answer. "We lifted together yesterday and she did arms, I did legs."

"Was that smart?"

"We went light, Mom."

She gives me a hard look over what I know is a cold cup of coffee, and I wonder how much she's buying of what I'm selling.

"Seriously, I feel good."

"You *look* good," Mom admits, resting her chin in her hands. "You're barely limping."

"I know, right?"

"Well . . ." She gets up, begins clearing her space. "You've only got one more therapy session scheduled. If you think . . ."

"I think that'll do it," I say quickly, both because I know it's not cheap, and because I worry that my miraculous delivery from pain might raise some eyebrows.

"Coach Mattix called," Mom says from the sink, raising her voice over the water as she rinses her cup. "She asked if she could stop by next week, said she'd like to come over and talk before conditioning starts."

"Right," I say, wondering if Coach knows I'm doing leg workouts, and what she thinks of that.

"I know Ferriman cleared you for it, but Mickey . . ."

"Don't, Mom," I warn her. "I've been walking without

the crutches and I feel fine. I started lifting with Carolina, and I've got two weeks before conditioning starts. I've got time to ease into it. I can do this, Mom."

"I know you *can*, Mickey. Ferriman wouldn't have cleared you otherwise. But he's not the one that has to watch you stop a ball moving sixty-five miles an hour."

"Seventy," I correct her. "Carolina was up to seventy at the end of last season."

"A lot's happened since then," Mom says quietly.

"We're *ready*," I snap at her. "Both of us are."

I slam my door just to prove there's nothing wrong with my arms either, and fall onto my bed. My hip lets me know I shouldn't have gone up the stairs so fast, so I dig into the bag of Ronald Wagner's pills, which is stuck under my mattress. Ten minutes later I'm warm and drowsy, pain no longer a problem.

My only issue is time.

CHAPTER TWENTY-ONE

scar: *a mark in the skin made by a wound, remaining after the wound has healed*

Coach Mattix is a zero-fucks-given, all-bullshit-off-the-table type of coach.

She's made me—and everyone else on the team—cry on more than one occasion, but the school has always had her back. The fact that she also coaches the girls' basketball team and they fill the gym—and therefore the athletic association's cash box—probably has something to do with it.

Mom and Dad have never had a problem with her style, but I haven't ever given them reason to, either. I know Mattix is hard on us, but we're tough as a result. I might not like it when she's screaming at me for screwing up, but it does ensure that I don't make the same mistake twice. People who do that aren't on the team.

One of Coach's favorite sayings is that scar tissue is stronger than skin, and anybody who makes it to twenty without a mark on them isn't trying hard enough. I've tried—and it shows. She can tell the stories behind most of my scars as well as I can, and with as much pride. We're cut from the same cloth, no doubt—and I don't think she'd be impressed with my newfound shortcut through pain.

I spend extra time in the hot shower after an afternoon nap, trying to dispel the last of the fog from my head. I dig into my hip, like a warning to my screws to behave in front of Coach. I'm gaining muscle, can barely get down to them, but I think I can detect one head, pushing out farther than the others. The old bruise from all my digging is still there, deep in my tissue. I give it a nudge, letting it know I'm still here, too.

I've got a towel in my hair and am headed to my room when Mom yells up the stairs that I've got a visitor. I change fast, my hair a tangled mess that hangs down my back and leaves a wet spot on my shirt. But I don't take the time to brush it out or put it up. Coach is here, and she's waiting. I hurry downstairs as quick as I can, to find her at the sofa, accepting a steaming cup of coffee from Mom.

"You're moving well," she says, eyes already dissecting

my gait as I cross the room, checking to see if my weight is distributed evenly or if I'm favoring my bad leg.

"Therapy has been awesome," I tell her. "And I've been lifting."

"I heard," she says, and I can't tell from her tone whether she approves. I should've known that the boys' basketball coach would've told her as much. Carolina has sworn for months now that they share more than stats with each other, but nobody has the guts to ask either one of them.

"I'm just going to jump right in," Coach says, talking to me instead of Mom. "You know I want you behind the plate for the first pitch. You're the best catcher I've got and you've got a chemistry with Carolina that nobody else does."

"Yep," I say. "And I swear to you I'm—"

Coach holds up her hand to stop me. And I stop. It's like running bases.

"But," she says, and my stomach drops; the only thing preventing it from falling right down to my feet are the tips of the three screws that hold my body together. I feel the blood leave my face, and Mom puts her hand on my knee.

"But," Coach goes on. "You were in an accident, Mickey. You sustained a serious injury."

I think of a Barbie leg, snapping away from the body,

a hole in her plasticized hip where the peg goes, how she pops back together and functions just the same. Well, almost. I bet that Barbie comes apart a little more easily every time.

"My point is, no one would think less of you if you needed to sit a few games out at the start of the season."

"Sit a few games out?" I repeat it, in shock, like Coach just told me to execute a puppy.

"Mickey, I know what this means to you and—"

"I'm fine," I say, interrupting Coach. Which is something you do *not* do.

"I understand, but Nikki showed promise in the summer leagues as an eighth grader. If we put her back there for some of the weaker teams at the beginning—"

"I'm fine," I say again. "Nikki is capable. I'm better."

Coach is quiet for a second, a little muscle at the edge of her mouth jumping as she decides whether to let me have it for cutting her off not once but twice. She looks to my mom.

"You've got a say in this, too," she says. "This is your daughter's health."

"It is," Mom says, taking a deep breath. "But it's her body. Nobody knows how she feels besides Mickey. If she says she's ready, then she is."

I relax a little, realizing that I wasn't sure if Mom would back me.

"All right." Coach stands, not even feigning interest in the coffee Mom gave her. She came here to talk to me about softball, and now that conversation is over. We follow her to the door.

"You've said you're ready, and I believe you," Coach says as she leaves. "But two weeks from now, you're going to have to show me."

"I will," I tell her, chin out.

"'Kay," is all she says.

Later, I try to convince myself that she didn't notice how stiff my right leg was when I got up from the couch. That Coach didn't see the shift of my hips as I put all my weight on my left leg at the door, something that has become more of a habit than anything. One I'm going to have to break.

Just like a Barbie leg.

CHAPTER TWENTY-TWO

team: *a number of persons banded together for a common endeavor, or to compete in a contest*

When conditioning starts the only thing I allow myself to be is a softball player.

I am not someone who was in an accident. I am not a person recovering from an injury. I am not a girl who has upped her Oxy over the last two weeks in order to calm the anxious voices and quell the tide of anxiety as each day got me closer to this, my day of reckoning.

All I am today is an athlete.

I see it in the other girls' faces in the hall, a stony preparation with tiny fissures where our doubts go. The ones who don't play basketball have the most cracks in their composure, and the one-sport athletes who have let themselves be lazy in the off-season. And then there's me, the girl who had crutches in January and today claims she will be running two miles.

They usually look to me for confidence, so I convey that, giving them an up-nod in the hallway, a reassuring "see you after school," to Bella Center, who never, ever finishes a run without puking. Carolina is a little pale, too. She's not a distance runner, and even though the most we'll ever have to run during a game is 240 feet—in the case of a home run—Coach says she won't play anyone who's on the plate. Equipment won't even come out of the lockers for four weeks; this is all about running. And I have to act like that's something I can do.

Nikki is positively gray when I see her in study hall, which isn't uncommon for the freshmen.

"Does she really chase you if you lag?" Nikki asks me, her feet at the edge of our shared table, knees pulled up to her chest.

"Only toward the end of practice," I tell her. "Coach says there's more in you than you think, and if there's someone chasing you people tend to find that last energy reserve."

"What does she do if she catches you?"

"Then the whole team runs an extra mile."

"Ouch," Nikki says, going from gray to white. "That's . . . harsh."

"That's softball," I tell her. "Oh, and don't tell Coach

you're going to puke, either. She'll tell you if you can still talk, you aren't going to puke. Which is actually true. Same with passing out. If you're really going to, you don't get time to announce it."

"Okay." Nikki closes her eyes and rests her chin on her knees.

"You'll be fine," I tell her, and I mean it. It's something I can see in her, a grittiness that might not be obvious in her small build, but can be spotted in her eyes. It's what I see in my childhood pictures—pure determination.

"Really?"

"Yeah," I say. "I know it sounds stupid, but just keep putting one foot in front of the other."

To someone watching it might seem like I'm being a good team leader, calming the anxiety of a younger player. But really this is what I've been saying to myself for weeks, every time I get out of bed and want to crawl back in, each step across the parking lot to the school, then out again. It's not Nikki I'm talking to when I say these things; it's myself—keep putting one foot in front of the other.

Just today I'm going to have to do it faster.

"Ladies, two miles."

It's how my season has started every year since I hit

high school, a greeting that Coach yells to our semicircle of stretching girls before even introducing herself to the freshmen. I know I'm about to experience pain, maybe even enough to punch through the protective fuzziness of the Oxy tablet I quickly bit in half and chewed before practice. But those words still send a spike of adrenaline through my veins, warming up my blood along with the black tarmac of the track as the sun eases behind a low-hanging March cloud.

"That's eight laps," Carolina says for the younger players, as we get to our feet. I reach down to pull up Nikki, whose color hasn't improved.

"You've got this," I tell her, pulling my heel up to my rear end, feeling the stretch of my quad. "Pace with me. Longer strides eat up the distance faster."

"'Kay," she says, and joins me with Carolina at the head of the pack.

"Shorter strides feel easier," I continue as we take the first curve, the girls fanning out behind us already, weakest at the back. "But they make you take more steps than you actually need to. You're working harder—"

"Catalan!"

Coach's voice cuts from where she's standing at the fifty-yard line, eyeing our progress.

"Yeah?" I shout back.

"What the hell do you think you're doing?"

I shoot Carolina a glance, but she shakes her head, as clueless as I am.

"Running." I'm careful how I say it. Coach doesn't care for smart-asses.

"No, you're not."

Shit.

I cut into the grass, headed toward Mattix at a slow jog. "Coach, I'm—"

"Fine?" she asks.

I stop in front of her, aware of Carolina's back as she passes us, Nikki's dark ponytail flopping between her shoulder blades.

"Yes," I tell her.

"I decide if you're fine, and I'm telling you to walk these laps." She sees my face fall, though I try to hide it.

"Just for this week," Coach adds in a lighter voice, one that won't carry to the rest of the team.

I don't argue, although everything inside of me screams as I step back onto the track. I take a lane on the outside, so that others can pass me easily. Soon even the slowest girls have lapped me, and I'm overhearing snatches of Nikki and Carolina's conversation as they drift by.

Two times. Four. Six.

By the end Nikki is struggling and Carolina is talking her through it, even though her own face is red and

I can hear the strain in her voice. Others slip past me, teammates casting me curious glances. I'm sure it's odd to see Mickey Catalan walking.

And it sure as hell doesn't feel right to finish last.

When I was ten we should have won first place in the county tournament, but it didn't happen. That's because of a girl name Lana Patrick, who now plays trumpet in the marching band. Lana was a good kid, the cute kind with two little blond braids and matching ribbons on the ends, a button nose, and a sweet voice that always said, "yes, sir," or "no, sir," to our coach, even though he was just somebody's dad.

Lana had a pink batting helmet that she dusted off after every practice, a shiny bat that remained that way throughout the season because she never connected it to a ball, and a glove that apparently had a hole in the middle of it even though it was brand-new. She couldn't stop shit.

To be fair, her parents weren't the type that insisted she play infield just because she wanted to. They knew her head might get cleaned from her shoulders. Instead, Lana was perfectly happy to hang out in right field, searching for four-leaf clovers and telling the first baseman what her mom had brought for team snack.

Carolina hadn't come along yet, but the three Bellas,

Lydia, and I were enough talent to pull us through the bracket. One by one other teams fell, their names crossed off and the scores recorded on the big sheet tacked on the side of the pop shack. We'd play three games in a day, sweat pouring out, dirt crusted in the corners of our eyes, running on hot dogs, walking tacos, and Mountain Dew. By the end of Saturday, double elimination had taken its toll, and the second team we faced was done. We lined up on the baseline, everyone clapping for them as they got their trophies, Lana too.

"I don't get it," she said to me, barely there blond eyebrows coming together, the tight pink skin of her sunburn creasing.

"Get what?"

"They lost," she said. "But they get a trophy?"

"Yeah," I told her. "They're done. So they get their trophies now."

Lana clapped as the coach from the other team announced the next girl's name, the dirt on her face smudged with tears as she took hers, trying to smile as her mom snapped a pic.

"But *we* won," Lana said. "They get trophies and they get to go home. What do we get?"

"We get to play more," I told her.

And I meant it. I didn't play for trophies or ice cream or for the chance to go home. I played because I loved it, and winning meant I got to do the best thing in the world one more time this summer, one more game in this jersey, with this team.

None of that made sense to Lana, who kept clapping for the other girls, even though I saw her kick aside a cup when we went back into the dugout, not pick it up and put it in the trash can like she usually would.

I don't know for a fact that she missed the fly ball in the seventh inning on purpose, or that she struck out every time she batted in order to get eliminated faster. It's hard to say because those things probably would have happened anyway. I do know that when the team stopped for ice cream later, Lana was the happiest of any of us. She ordered extra sprinkles on her cone and got selfies with all of us, even though Lydia, the Bellas, and I looked more pissed in them than celebratory, our cones half melted, unwanted third-place trophies in our hands. When she took her picture with our coach she told him he was the best coach in the world.

"And you're the best little player in the world," he said.

I threw my cone in the trash and walked away.

I'm thinking about this now because it's something I've never been able to let go, never came close to understanding. But I've never been last before, never been the weak link, never been the one people clap for to encourage rather than congratulate.

I get it now. Lana stuck with the adults because they valued her talents—being cute and doing the right thing all the time. She couldn't stop a ball or hit one for the life of her, so she steered clear of us, some primal instinct aware that if we had a chance we'd tear her to pieces to strengthen the herd.

Today is about conditioning; it's not a race. But that doesn't mean that we aren't all keeping track of who was first, middle, and last. It doesn't mean that it hurts less when Carolina doesn't wait for me to finish my two miles, heading into the school instead with Nikki, offering her water bottle since the freshman's is empty. What it means is that the winners are going to go back to the weight room and stay awhile, a stationary victory lap.

The loser gets to go home and take an Oxy.

CHAPTER TWENTY-THREE

awkward: *wanting dexterity in the use of the hands or of instruments; clumsy; wanting ease, grace, or effectiveness in movement or social situations—or—not easily managed; embarrassing*

Ronald Wagner's pills get me through the first week of conditioning, but I'm not biting the second one in half anymore once Coach Mattix agrees to let me run with everyone else. I don't have time to go to my car after school, so I risk keeping an 80 in my pocket, once gulping down a ball of lint alongside it when Bella Center surprises me in the locker room and I just want everything out of sight.

I've reclaimed my place at the head of the pack, Carolina by my side, but it's cost me. She didn't question me when I handed her an earbud on the first day Coach said

I could run. We took off together, striding in sync, my playlist powering us both. I made all two miles, the cord between us never tightening because I didn't fall back. And if Nikki looked a little bummed that she'd lost her running partner, it sure as shit didn't hurt as bad as my hip.

The ache radiates, swelling outward from the screws like an explosion, the debris primed to reach all the way to my toes. I never let it, stopping the fallout with Ronald Wagner's assistance, may he rest in peace.

I've started checking the obituaries, a new, very morbid habit. Ronald departed this world not long after I lifted his meds, which made me feel better rather than worse since it meant he didn't need them anymore. I got curious after that, and found Helen Whitmore. She was eighty-five, passed away after a short illness, leaving behind eight children and twenty-five grandchildren.

I'm not exactly looking for Betsy Vellon's name, the last provider of Edith's OxyContin stock, but it would jump out at me if I saw it. With only her and Edith left to refill the safe, things could get sticky if Betsy bows out early. Edith's prescription for osteoarthritis isn't enough to take care of herself, let alone me, Josie, and anyone else she sells to.

There are other names in the obituaries, pictures that I don't expect to see. Parents who *died suddenly*, and a few people my own age who *passed away unexpectedly*. Some of the obits skip the euphemisms and flat out say that their loved one overdosed. My internet searches catch up with me and pretty soon I'm getting ads in my sidebar for cremation services, mattresses with remotes, and discreet adult diapers.

So I stop looking.

I tell myself that it's because I want to get back to pop-ups about the World Series, not because I'm bothered by that word.

Overdose.

Yes, I know that people die from this shit. But the obits are for washed-up dreamers who didn't hit their goals before thirty, stressed-out parents who needed a little break and ended up taking a long one, and people who just plain *look* like junkies, who have been messing around with this, that, and the other for so long that they tried too much of something new.

The obits I'm reading aren't for athletes who know exactly how much to take in order to perform. They aren't for bored prima donnas like Josie trying to fill up their spare time.

The obits are for people who are nothing like us.

"I can't remember the last time I took a shit."

It's not something I would usually share, but it slips

out. Josie almost does a spit-take with the whiskey that she's sipping, and over in her chair, Edith lets out a snort. It's Saturday night, the ache of a full week of real practice settled into my bones, sending me over here instead of to Carolina's for "Netflix and chili," as we'd started calling it, specifically for my mom's benefit.

"That's the Oxy," Josie says, wiping her chin clean of a dribble of whiskey. "Take some Metamucil, that'll clean you out."

"Prune juice," Edith argues as she flips the channel. "You don't need to be putting all that stuff in your body, darlin'."

"Says your dealer," Josie adds.

I laugh, but the truth is there's nothing funny about not being able to take a shit. "Does Metamucil work?" I ask Josie, who is crushing an Oxy with the base of one of Edith's Precious Moments figurines.

"I guess so." She shrugs. "I don't really worry about it. It's got to come out sometime, right?"

Actually, it doesn't. But Josie doesn't seem concerned, and while the Oxy has loosened my tongue, I don't think she keeps me around for constipation stories.

"What are you doing?" I ask, as Josie forms powder into a line with her nail file.

"Somebody told me if you snort it, you get high faster," Josie says.

"Somebody?"

"Yeah." She doesn't elaborate and doesn't look at me. Instead she checks her phone, then looks down at the white streak she's created, a fine wrinkle appearing between her eyebrows. "Do you know how to do this?"

I almost laugh, but catch it just in time. Josie's never asked me how to do anything, and I've always followed her lead when we're under Edith's roof. Outdoors I could run circles around her, or even pick her up and throw her a good distance. In here, she's the one who knows what's up. Except right now she doesn't, and the part of me that got left behind when Coach had Lydia show the freshmen how to slide last week is ready to show off, even if I have no idea what I'm doing.

I come over to the end table, eyeing the line. "How much is this?"

"I crushed up a forty," Josie says.

I lean over the table, unsure. "I guess you just plug one nostril and snort, right?"

"I don't know, yeah?" Josie's phone goes off and she grabs for it.

Without her attention on me, I rock back on my heels, enjoying the stretch of the long muscles of my quads. I love even more that I can do this, that I can bend without crying, move as if the accident never happened. If Coach could see me like this . . . my eyes go to the white powder, the Precious Moments next to it, cuddling her puppy.

Yeah, if Coach could see me like this.

Josie tosses her phone onto the end table, knocking the statue over the edge. I'm supple and warm, snagging it from midair with little effort. I put it back, for some reason turning her so that the little girl isn't looking at the Oxy.

"Nice save," Josie says. "Hey, Edes, the guys are coming over."

Edith's eyes open slowly. "They buying?"

"I don't know."

"The guys?" I ask, sudden, hot anxiety peaking in my gut. I'm comfortable here in Edith's house, my muscles long and relaxed, the heat of her living room matching the warmth blooming inside. I don't want more people here, ones I have never met and don't know how to talk to.

"Don't worry, they're cool," Josie says.

She doesn't seem to get that that's exactly what I'm worried about. Boys don't intimidate me in a weight room or in a gym, but put me in a social situation with them and nothing to lift, throw, or kick, and I'm deadweight. Girls like Josie know how to drop their shoulders, tilt their heads, and use their hips to make conversation. Me, I ask them their stats.

"Who is it?" Edith asks from the chair. She digs the

remote out from under her hip, awake enough now to care again what's on TV.

"Luther and Derrick."

"That's fine, hon," Edith says. "But nobody else. There's enough cars in the driveway as it is. And tell them there's no meat loaf left."

"Okay," Josie says, clicking out a response on her phone.

Edith flips through a few channels, then seems to reconsider. "I can make more though, if they want to stop and get some ground beef."

"I think they're good, Grandma," Josie says.

"Actually, tell them if they want to come they need to stop and get prune juice," Edith says.

"No, hey—" I begin.

Edith waves away my complaint. "Prune juice."

"Done," Josie says.

I find my sweatshirt in a ball at the end of the couch and pull it over my head. "I'm out," I tell them.

"Sorry, darlin'," Edith says. "You're not driving anywhere. I don't want your death on my conscience . . . or a police record."

"I'm fine." I'm digging in the hoodie pocket for my keys when Josie stops me.

"You're not fine," she says, hand on my arm. "And you'll like Luther and Derrick."

That's not the issue, and I don't know how to explain it to Josie. I'm sure I will like them well enough. But I won't have anything to say, and I'll just stand in the middle of the room, an awkward girl as big as they are. They won't quite know how to handle my silence, or worse—if I open my mouth and say something stupid. But Josie has delayed me long enough, because a few minutes later headlights sweep the front of the house, the back door opens, and Luther Drake walks in.

Athletes in small towns know each other—or at least, we know *of* each other. Even though Luther goes to Baylor Springs—a much nicer school than mine— and plays basketball—not my sport—I could still tell you his highest scoring game, just like I'm pretty sure he probably knows my batting average.

"Mickey Catalan, what the hell?" Luther says, fist raised for a bump.

"You know each other?" Josie raises an eyebrow.

"All-County athletes three years in a row," Luther says, fist still out. I bump it, both stricken and flattered. "Heard you got tore up pretty bad."

"Car accident," I say. "You ripped your ACL, right?"

"Last year. In half," Luther says, with a perverse sort of pride in his injury.

"My leg popped out of its socket," I say, aware that we're competing.

"My muscle rolled up like a window shade," he comes back.

"I've got three screws in my hip."

"I screw with my third leg."

I laugh, loud and easy, a sound that doesn't usually come out anywhere other than the dugout or at home.

"Um, who's this for?" Luther's friend, Derrick, holds up a jug of prune juice.

"Mickey," Josie says. "She can't shit."

"Nice, thanks," I tell her.

"You got the Oxy-can'ts?" Derrick asks.

"Go a few days without," Luther says to me, pulling his jacket off. "Then go for a run. You'll be fine."

"Thanks," I tell him, weirdly comforted even though we're still talking about poop, and mine specifically.

Luther is a true athlete, someone whose movements are suffused with grace at all times. Everyday things, like him taking off his jacket, or moving a pillow on the couch, become fascinating to watch, large muscles flowing in small gestures.

Josie elbows me. "You're staring."

"What's up, Edith?" Derrick asks. "That reunion happen yet?"

"Reunion?" I ask, hoping Luther didn't catch Josie giving me a hard time. "What's that about?"

"Fiftieth class reunion, down in West Virginia," she

says, turning off the TV. "I don't know what I'm going to wear."

"I'll take you shopping," Josie volunteers, but Derrick cuts her off.

"What's going on over here?" he asks, spotting the line Josie had made.

"Josie wants us to show her how to snort," Luther says. "Check your texts."

"It's easy," Derrick says, leaning over the table. "You just—"

It's gone in a second and Josie smacks him between the shoulder blades. "Asshole! That was mine."

"There's more where that came from. No fighting," Edith says. "And I've got a closet full of clothes, Josie. I don't need to go shopping."

"I'll help you pick something out then," Josie says, still sulking about her lost line, and cradling the hand she hit Derrick with. He's swaying on his feet now, and she tips him over onto the couch, where Luther slides over, effortlessly, making room as Derrick falls.

"Fashion *show*," Derrick says, clapping his hands together. "Fashion *show*. Fashion *show*."

I don't know Derrick. He must not be in any sports, or if he is he doesn't get a lot of playing time. The first impression I have of him is of a little kid, clapping his hands and bouncing on a couch, incredibly small next to Luther. I like him. I like him enough to start clapping too, and yelling for a fashion show, even though I don't think I've ever said that phrase in my life, and I really don't care at all what we do for the rest of the night.

I don't care, and that's the glory of it.

So when Josie pulls a wad of cash from her pocket and Edith goes back to her bedroom for the safe, I don't question it. I don't say anything when Derrick crushes up an Oxy for Luther, then holds Josie's hair while she snorts another. She does the same for me, her fingers cool on the back of my impossibly hot earlobes.

I'm afraid it'll hurt. Burn the inside of my nose, like the time I choked on Pepsi and lost it out of everywhere. But it's not like that at all. It's like silk reaching up into my face, sliding past my eyes to cradle my brain and rock it, slowly, gently, into a drifting peace.

I'm not worried about saying something stupid or looking dumb, even when Josie starts raiding Edith's closet and we end up wearing her clothes. In the bathroom, I allow Josie to streak a shaky slash of lipstick across my mouth, and zip up her dress for her, something that Edith wore to the prom in 1973.

She looks gorgeous, and I'm high enough to be happy for her, knowing that we'll walk out to the living room and the boys will only look at her. I don't look beautiful, exactly, but as I study myself in the mirror I can

admit that I don't look like Mickey Catalan, either. Josie
had put some shadow around my eyes that makes them
stand out, and my constricted pupils make them bluer
than usual.

"Let's go make some boys happy," Josie says, swinging the door open dramatically. But whatever effect she
was hoping for is immediately lost when she starts bray-
ing laughter, the feathery layers of her dress rippling
around her. "Oh my God."

She grabs me, pulling me out into the living room,
where we find Edith putting final primps on both Derrick and Luther, who are wearing matching powder-blue
leisure suits.

"Bob loved this suit so much he bought two," Edith
says, brushing off Luther's shoulder, which she can barely
reach. Derrick's is too big on him, loose and floppy,
but Luther looks amazing, even if his neck bulges out a
little over the light-blue collar.

"Fashion *show*! Fashion *show*!" Derrick says, spinning,
whiskey spilling out of the glass he took from Josie.

"Hey!" She lurches toward him, awkward in heels
that are too tight for her. "That's mine. Stop taking my
shit, Derrick!"

"You look nice," I'm saying to Luther, somehow
having crossed the distance between us. Usually I'm
crafting the words, weighing each one to see if it's right

or wrong, the topic at hand having changed by the time I'm ready to contribute. But right now I'm saying what I think, as I think it.

"You're not so bad yourself, Catalan," Luther says.

I hug him, suddenly and forcefully. It's rare to be around guys who are bigger than me, but Luther definitely is, and that's part of the reason why I go for it. He's warm, and my face rests nicely against his chest, the impossibly slow beat of his heart next to my ear. I feel small, safe, and feminine, tucked in next to him. I'm not turned on, or thinking about anything other than safety, warmth, and the incredible feeling of arms stronger than my own around me.

I don't care that Derrick and Josie are pointing at us, or that Edith makes us all line up to take a picture as if we were actually going to prom. I don't care that the zipper on this dress is only halfway up because my shoulders are way broader than Edith's were in the 1970s, or that my hand comes away with makeup on it when I wipe the sweat from my forehead. I can't remember the last time I wore a dress, or if I've ever had makeup on in my life. I'm doing things I usually wouldn't, saying things I normally couldn't.

Right now, I'm not me.

And I'm so damn happy.

CHAPTER TWENTY-FOUR

withdrawal: *a collection of psychological symptoms*
as well as physically painful symptoms following the
discontinued use of a drug

Being so damn happy on a Saturday when you're high
and with friends is one thing; going through withdrawal two days later while trying to perform on the
diamond is another.

"¿Estás bien?" Carolina calls from the mound.

"Fine," I yell back. My brain is slippery, and I don't
trust my tongue.

Up until now Mattix wouldn't let me get down in
a crouch. She's had me sitting on a bucket, the plastic
edges biting into my ass. It threw Carolina off, her speed
still there, but her control had slipped. One curveball
came so close to Bella Left that she had to throw herself

out of the box, kicking dirt into my face.

Now, two weeks out from our first game, Coach finally gave me the go-ahead to get down behind the plate. I know Carolina is worried about my leg, and it's not unfounded. Without the Oxy I feel an ache, but it's not the explosion I remember. It's deeper, more sinister, like a wound that healed on the surface but is hiding a rot that's going to break through sooner rather than later.

I signal Carolina for a changeup and she gives me a perfect one, slinging her arm around like she's about to take somebody's head off, then floating it in, nice and slow like we're playing in a church league. I've seen batters take a swing before the ball is even halfway to the mound, their swing timed for her amazing speed right when she takes the heat off.

Coach trusts me to spot the batters who will fall for it, and I usually know the type. The girls who make a show of hitting their cleats with the bat before they step into the box, like a little bit of dirt on their spikes might slow them down. They always dig in then, heel turning into the soft grit of the box, keeping one hand up for a time-out so that Carolina is prevented from going into her windup until they're ready.

I love making a fool of them.

So does Carolina, and we've worked out exactly who

we want to burn with the changeup this year, a carefully curated list that includes the pitcher from Peckinah who threw at me twice last season and the shortstop from Palma Falls who cleated our first baseman, and if a wild pitch were to hit the dad from Left Bank who screams at his daughter no matter how good she does . . . well, I can't be expected to stop *everything*.

"Nice," I yell at Carolina when she puts a fastball right in my glove. I swear I don't have to move it a centimeter. I know how to frame a pitch so that it looks like a strike, even if it's a little to the inside or out. But right now there's no ump behind me, and that thing hit dead center, regardless. I toss it back, still crouched, every muscle in my body flickering to keep my balance and make the throw, a thoughtless act that I've always taken for granted.

I can still do this. I can still be Mickey Catalan. And my friend is still Carolina Galarza, a taut line of energy between us that the ball travels over, back and forth, then again, an easy journey each time with zero interruptions.

"Take a break?" Carolina calls, and I'm about to tell her that I'm okay when I see that she's holding her arm oddly, at an angle. I flip my mask up, cool spring air evaporating the sweat on my face quickly.

"Yep," I say, coming to my feet.

It happens easily enough, although I know my weight is planted more firmly on my left leg than my right. At my very last physical therapy appointment both Kyleigh and Jolene had given me shit about it, told me that it might get me through the day now but eventually I'll be a crippled old lady if I don't distribute my weight evenly. They didn't understand that getting through the day is what matters to me right now. The day, the week, the season.

I walk out to the mound, tossing the ball from one hand to the other, face mask pushed on top of my head, shin guards creaking as I go. Coach has me wear all my gear when I'm catching for Carolina, game or no game. I never complain, knowing full well that if one of her fastballs were to hit me in the chest it could stop my heart.

"You're walking funny," Carolina says when I toss her the ball.

"You look funny," I tell her. She rolls her eyes but lets it go, swiping the ball from the air.

"Well?" she asks, and I don't need clarification.

"Changeup is spot on," I tell her. "Inside corner looks good. Lots of batters will swing at it."

We both know any bat that gets around on her inside pitch will go foul, and usually fly, the majority of them picked off by our third baseman. Carolina got good at this last year, and her no-hitter record owes a lot to that pitch.

"And?" she asks, thumbnail picking at a loose stitch in the ball.

"And you're slowing down after the first five or so fastballs," I tell her. "It's still got a zip, but you're not getting three up three down anytime soon."

It's harsh but it's true, and me telling Carolina we don't even need infielders would be a lie. Last year there were a few games where just me and her could've taken the field and been fine. But now . . .

"You shouldn't gun for the top of the lineup," I tell her. "They'll get hits off you."

I know she doesn't want to hear it, just like I didn't want Coach telling me to walk that first week of conditioning. Carolina's chin sticks out and her fingernail digs into the stitch she's working at, like tearing it out is the goal.

"Hey." I reach out, taking the ball back and resting my gloved hand on her shoulder. "You're fine."

"Dammit, I'm not," she says, ducking out from under my touch. "I *hurt*, Mickey."

Carolina looks me straight in the eyes for a moment and I realize how long it's been since she has. There's something different in her gaze now, the pupils still the same dark brown, yet shadowed more deeply, with a surprising glimmer of tears.

"Whoa, hey," I say, unsure of myself. I'm suddenly stupid and awkward, one hand trapped in a glove, my bulk added to by straps and plastic, metal and grips. I'm with my best friend, standing in my favorite place in the whole world. I shouldn't feel this way. Not here, not now, not with this person.

Maybe it's the fact that she's about to cry, and Carolina Galarza *does not* cry on the pitcher's mound. Maybe it's because I've got exactly what it would take to fix it out in my car in a Doritos bag, but I'm afraid if I offer it to her she'll echo her mom, tell me it's poison, and that I'm weak.

Plus it would be one less Oxy for me, and Ronald's pills won't last forever.

"I hurt, too," I tell her. And while it's not the sharp pain I knew from before, the snap of a body tearing apart at the seams, it is spreading. Not from my hip, like I'm used to, but my spine, radiating out to my skin, where sweat starts to pop even though I feel a chill.

"Yeah? You hide it good," Carolina says, pulling up the neck of her practice shirt to wipe a tear away before anyone sees.

In the outfield Coach yells, "Dammit, Becker! Where did your depth perception go?" We turn together to watch Mattix toss a ball and hit it as far as possible in the opposite direction, out toward the cow pasture, where more than a few heifers have accidentally been involved in a game or two.

"Go get it," Coach yells at Bella Center, who lopes after it good-naturedly, more than familiar with the punishment.

"I'm getting good at hiding things," I admit quietly.

"Like what?" Carolina asks.

Like pain. Like fear. Like dead people's OxyContin prescriptions.

"Dick pics from your boyfriend," I say.

"Whatever, chica," Carolina laughs, the odd sheen on her eyes evaporating. "Your screen is too small."

"So are your boobs," I tell her. "Curveball?"

"Yeah." She nods, taking the ball from me. "I can do that."

"Cool," I say, flipping my mask back down.

I get behind the plate and crouch into position, giving her the signal for the curve. I ignore the pull in my hip. I ignore the tremor that's started in my bare hand. I ignore the nausea welling in my gut. I ignore everything I don't want to see.

I pull over on the way home to puke.

I'm so close to keeping it all together that I don't realize I'm about to lose it until it's almost too late. I've got to slam on the brakes, tires screaming and gravel flying. For a moment all I've got is panic, nothing else. Then fear gets a good grip and I'm thinking I fucked everything up again and am about to take my car right off the road, ruin my leg and any chance I've got at a scholarship.

Then I'm stopped, half on, half off the road. I'm clenching my teeth shut against vomit when I throw the door open, leaning out just enough that I don't splatter on the running board. I manage it, mostly. Then the incline I stopped on works against me and the car door swings back, with me nowhere near done puking. I stick my leg out, getting a good pinch for my effort, then unhook my belt and throw myself out the door. I land on my hands and knees, lunch coming back up all over the shoulder of the road.

Somebody honks at me, a good-natured *toot-toot* like maybe I just provided the day's entertainment. I managed to get my car mostly off the road, but not all the way, something I can't acknowledge or apologize for because I'm still emptying my gut. The next driver leans on the horn, but I hear brakes on the third, followed by the familiar *tick-tock* of hazard lights blinking, then a voice I know.

"Mickey?"

It's Lydia, her words edged with a mix of disbelief and

concern, but mostly the former. I doubt she expected to turn the corner to find me on all fours, staring down at a steaming puddle. I can't do more than nod that, yes, it is in fact me. Lydia gets her hands in my armpits and hauls me to my feet, carefully sidestepping the mess I made. It's so mortifying, so against who I am and what I project to my teammates, that I don't know what to say to her.

"You're a wreck, girl," Lydia says, standing back to take me all in, the exhibit of what Mickey Catalan has become in the small stretch of time between the end of practice and now. "Stomach flu get you?"

I nod. It's believable. Our government teacher went home halfway through the day today, and I saw a line of kids in the office waiting to call their parents to come get them, green around the gills.

"Can you drive?"

I nod again, searching for the words required to get me away from the mess I've made at our feet, the scraped bare earth where my tires screeched to a halt, the embarrassingly black dirt where I went into the ditch.

"I'm fine," I assure Lydia. "Thanks for . . . stopping."

"No problem." She shrugs and gets into her own car. Her hazards go off, but she's not going anywhere until I do. I thank her again, in my head. Lydia's not going to freak out or make a big deal about it, won't make me feel helpless. But she's not leaving until she knows I'm really okay.

I'm not, and I know it. I did as Luther said, went without Oxy until I could finally take a crap. It got things moving, all right, but it's all coming up, not out. I put my car back in gear, giving Lydia a wave as I pull away, gripping the steering wheel tightly so that I don't have to see how much my hands are shaking.

It's not just in my fingers though. I can feel the small movements, tiny tremors, rippling out from the center of me, every nerve I have sparking and jerking, the energy flying out into nothingness as I quake in the driver's seat. I'm struggling to get a good grip on the doorknob once I'm home, and Mom's face when I walk into the kitchen is enough to tell me that I look the same as I feel.

"Mickey!" Her shock is pervasive, sending pings of alarm across my brain. I can't let her know. *Cannot* let her guess what is actually going on here. She's got a hand on my arm but I'm slick with cold sweat and it slides right off.

"Sit down, honey," she says. "You look terrible. What happened?"

Mom leads me to the kitchen table, where I can smell dinner cooking. It sends another wave of nausea through me and I have to put my head down, my own rancid breath reflected back in my face off the smooth surface of the table.

"Mickey?" Her hand is on the middle of my back, the touch painful even though it is light. Every piece of me hurts, every inch of skin feels as if it has been sliced, every bone insisting to my brain that it has been broken.

"Flu. And I can't shit." I'd been meaning to tell her about the constipation, after Edith's miracle cure of prune juice did nothing other than make my pee smell funny.

"If you've really got the flu, that should take care of it," she says, trying to keep her tone light, but her face changes again when I lift my head. "Are you sure it's the flu? Honey, you look . . ."

I swear if she says *like you're going through withdrawal* I will run out the front door as far as my shaky legs will carry me.

"When is the last time you had a bowel movement?" Mom asks, suddenly brisk, no longer a parent, now a doctor. "If you're becoming toxic or have a renal tear we need to get you to the hospital."

"It's a stomach bug. Going around," I tell her, finding the strength to hold my head still. "Bunch of kids went home today."

"Okay." Her hand is still on my back, tremulous, unsure. "But you can get really sick if you don't use the bathroom. I can give you an enema if you need me to, and if that doesn't work I can manually evacuate—"

I'm saved from having to react to that when my phone

goes off. It's Dad, and I answer fast, putting him on speaker.

"Hey," he says. "What's going on?"

"Mom just offered to stick her finger up my butt," I tell him.

"You too?"

"*Geoff!*" Mom grabs the phone, her face a sudden, blazing red.

"Oh my God," I groan, half in reaction to whatever just happened, half because I think my constipation is about to be solved in a very abrupt manner. Mom misses my dash for the stairs as she makes her own embarrassed exit, my phone to her ear.

I make it to the bathroom in time, but only just.

Shivering, I collapse onto my bed a few minutes later, burrowing under the covers like an injured animal. That's what I feel like, a lost feral thing that got clipped by a car, dragging my hurt leg behind me while I make for my hole in the ground.

I keep my Oxy next to the bed, hidden in plain sight. The prescription bottle might have my name on it, but those are Ronald Wagner's pills inside. I resupply my bottle out of the baggie stuffed under my mattress, tossing his empty bottles in a recycling bin outside the gas station. Even if Mom doesn't buy my stomach flu story, the pill bottle next to my bed has pills in it, long after my prescription has run out. There's nothing here to suggest that anything is wrong.

Except the girl on the bed going through withdrawal.

I curl into a ball, but the fetal position brings no comfort. My spine feels like it's spiked, each curve threatening to tear through skin. I can pinpoint each screw in my hip, where they enter bone and where they end, gripping. I roll over, stifling an involuntary sound that escapes as I do. It's like the flu, only heightened, so that even the touch of the pillow against my face is unbearable.

But the stomach flu that's going around only lasts a day, and I have no idea how long withdrawal can hold on. Right now I can't conceive of even getting up to turn off my light, and the idea of going to school in ten hours is laughable. After that comes practice, and there's no way I'm letting Nikki catch for Carolina with our first game on the horizon. Besides, if I don't show up at school after spending most of today's practice crouched down, Coach might think I'm nursing an injury. If she suspects that at all, I'm benched.

"Shit," I whisper to myself, the word rattling out between my teeth.

Downstairs I hear Mom laughing. I wonder if she's still on my phone, talking to Dad, and what Devra would think of that. It's that normal sound that does it:

Mom's laughter. I could ruin it, walk downstairs right now and tell her that I think I've got a problem, reduce whatever life she's managed to rebuild for herself into rubble.

Mom would blame herself for not seeing it. Dad would feel guilty for not being here to notice. The Galarzas would no longer tell me that what two can eat, three can eat. Coach would be done with me, since our school has a zero-tolerance drug policy. I imagine the harsh cutoff of Mom's laughter when I tell her, the collapse of each face as they flood with disappointment.

Or I can reach for the bottle, knowing that one pill can fix it, restore my balance and put my skin back in the right place and realign my bones, my feet planted firmly on the ground in the morning. Those are my choices. I can derail the lives of everyone I care about, or I can take one white pill and make it all better.

When you think about it that way, it's easy.

CHAPTER TWENTY-FIVE

friction: *the resistance with which a body meets from the surface on which it moves—or—a clashing between two persons in opinion*

I think of it as a maintenance drug, taking two 80s every day the same way Bella Right takes her birth control pills or Mom does for her Cymbalta. Even though upping my dosage means Ronald's pills are almost gone, I tell myself I don't need to be ashamed of it. My goal has always been to drop the pills as soon as possible, and right now, it's not possible. If withdrawal is going to leave me with liquid guts that come out both ends and hands that can't make the throw to second, there's no question of putting myself—and my team—through that right now. When the season is over, when my leg is healed. That's when I'll do it.

For sure.

At school, the Bellas got the okay to set off confetti cannons in front of the locker room after school for the first game of the season. They get the JV team to make a tunnel and two girls at the end set off the cannons, streamers flying out in school colors, the band lining the hall and blaring the fight song. Carolina and I lead the charge, running under the outstretched arms of the JV players, the Bellas, Lydia, and the rest of the starters behind us. We run through the halls, slapping hands, chest-bumping some of the guys who lift with us.

Aaron sweeps Carolina up in his arms when she finds him, spinning her, and I pause, waiting for them to end whatever this is so that we can finish the circuit and get back to the locker room. Finally, he sets her down, gives me a fist bump that's hard enough to send a jolt up to my shoulder. We take off again, yelling and slapping hands down the hall, our adrenaline spiking to exactly the right spot—slippery anticipation that makes it difficult for the butterflies in my stomach to land. By the time we're back at the locker room I'm exactly where I belong—a hot, feverish pitch of emotion where I'm perfectly capable of slaughtering an opposing team member or dying to protect one of my own.

Lydia hooks up a speaker to her phone and the locker room is ours, school clothes stripped off, carefully folded uniforms emerging from gym bags. Some of the JV girls pull brand-new cleats from unopened boxes, a mistake. Their feet will be pinched and sore by the second inning, the pristine leather of the shoes ruined the second they hit the dirt. My shoes slide on easy, the same pair I had last year, nicely broken in and appropriately filthy.

There's a wealth of skin apparent, some girls walking around without a stitch on, others strutting in sports bras and underwear. Calls for necessary things—forgotten tampons, a hair tie, deodorant—fly back and forth—as does whatever we requested. Some girls change in the showers, a few taking their turns in the one toilet stall we've got in here. But mostly those are the JV girls, the freshmen and sophomores, plus one or two unlucky juniors who don't have quite what it takes to make varsity.

But those of us who have been together forever don't care—me, Carolina, the Bellas, and Lydia, plus the rest of the infield. We were wearing diapers when we started playing, and have no secrets between us. Everyone has seen the long magenta scar that curves around my hip, hugging the edge of my underwear. We all know that Bella Right has horrible back acne and that the first baseman has a wine-colored birthmark between her shoulder blades.

The Bellas have formed a braiding line and are wrist-deep in each other's hair when Nikki comes in. She glances around the locker room, taking in the long muscles of our naked legs, the tight forearms of the girls who are stretching out sports bras. Nikki doesn't hesitate, simply plops her gym bag onto a bench and starts to strip down. I'm the one who tosses her deodorant when she realizes she forgot hers, and Carolina puts her hair up in a tight ponytail when her nervous hands can't quite get the job done without bumps.

"Well, hoo—fucking—ray for you!" Bella Right says suddenly, and I look up to see her slapping Nikki on the shoulder.

Nikki's putting on a black jersey—our home color. The JV is traveling today, wearing red, and while I knew that Nikki was good enough to earn a spot on the varsity bench, I didn't expect her to prefer that over actually getting playing time in JV. I don't say anything until I'm cutting across the grass of the outfield with Carolina, equipment bag slung over my shoulder.

"Why's Nikki dressing varsity?"

"'Cause she earned it," Carolina says.

"Yeah, totally," I agree. "But who's catching JV?"

Carolina shrugs. "Some other freshman, I guess."

My best friend isn't exactly inviting conversation right now, so I don't think it's a good time to dig into my words, find a way to express what I'm feeling. Which is that if Nikki is here, Coach doesn't think I can make it a whole seven innings on my bum leg. And it's entirely possible that Mattix asked Carolina her opinion before deciding whether Nikki got on a bus or stayed with us.

I don't say anything else.

We warm up together, like always. The whole team pairs off wordlessly, me with Carolina, Bella Left with Center, Right with Lydia, shortstop and first rotating with third on who's going to pair off with a bench rider each game. The other girls find someone, and I feel a tug at my heart when I see them searching faces, looking for that person they know will accept them when they say, "Wanna catch?"

I would be one of them, if it wasn't for Carolina. Before she moved in I was always close with my team, but I never had that one person I always threw with, the person who just assumed they'd be across from me as we lined up, midafternoon sun flashing off our sunglasses.

"Can I throw with you guys?"

It's unexpected, and I balk, bobbling the ball even as my weight shifts to release it. Nikki is standing on the edge of our two lines of girls, her words directed at Carolina. She was slow getting out to the field, and has no one to pair with. She wants to make a triangle, like we're all back in third grade or something. I'm about to tell her to throw with Coach, which is the usual punishment for being the last one out of the locker room, but Carolina waves for her to join us.

She actually misses the first ball I throw at her, and Carolina raises an eyebrow at me as the freshman runs after it, well aware that I side-armed it with a spin, just to be a bitch.

"What?" I ask, expecting a rebuke in Spanish, something that most of our teammates won't be able to follow. But Carolina only sighs, welcoming Nikki back into the triangle with a smile and a pop-up that a kitten could catch.

She's been doing that a lot lately, letting some remark of mine go without responding, or only rolling her eyes. Carolina has always given me shit, it's part of how we operate, but I'm starting to wonder if some of it is meant to stick, and if what Aaron said to me in the parking lot about the accident being my fault has anything to do with it.

I can't ask her now, not with Nikki in our space and a game about to start. The last thing we need in between our clean line of the pitching rubber and home plate is friction. So I let it go, though some of my excitement leaves with it, the fire in my center at the commencement of our last season suddenly snuffed out, leaving only empty space behind.

CHAPTER TWENTY-SIX

forget: *to lose the remembrance of; to let go from the memory; to cease to have in mind; not to think of*

"Nice win."

"Thanks," I say to Luther, but it's all I've got. Whatever confidence I carried with me last week is gone, and the ability to find that perfect space under his arm that—somehow—a very large girl fills perfectly seems only to exist after I've taken a shot of Oxy straight to the brain. So I do that, quick, wanting to recapture the feeling.

"Were you there?" I ask him, once I've wiped my upper lip to be sure it's clean, and have turned the Precious Moments girl away so I don't have to look at her.

"Third baseline," he says. "Me and Derrick came in halfway through the fourth inning."

"Sorry," I say. "I didn't see you."

"There were a ton of people," Luther says, shrugging it off. "You guys need, like, a stadium or something."

"We might draw a Baylor Springs crowd, but we don't have your money," I tell him. Instead we end up with people in long lines of lawn chairs that extend to the outfield, the tail curving inward so that late arrivals can see the batter's box.

"You get a decent seat?" I ask him.

"Guys like me stand," he says, and I laugh, the sound catching Derrick's attention from where he sits on the floor, trying desperately to figure out if Josie actually wants the bedspread set they're selling on QVC or is just yanking his chain.

"Math error," Josie yells at the screen, making us all jump.

"What the fuck, dude?" Derrick says, rubbing his elbow from where he bumped it on the coffee table.

"They're claiming that it's sixty percent off, but it's not," Josie says. "Sixty percent off 199.99 would be 80, not 79.99."

"I think they're rounding down for clarity, hon," Edith says.

"But they're *wrong*," Josie says, color rising in her cheeks.

Derrick pulls out his phone and double-checks, then

glances at Josie. "Seriously, how do you even do that?"

Edith's streaming service is crap and the picture keeps pixelating. There are no definite lines between anyone or anything, which is how I feel when Luther puts his arm around me, and I slide into the warm cocoon of space beside his body.

"I thought you were gay," Derrick says.

"Straight girls can be good at softball," I say, turning to Luther. "I swear I need a T-shirt."

"Or maybe not," he says, eyeing me up and down.

In the kitchen, the scanner goes off.

```
7300 to 45. Go ahead 7300 . . . 45
report to a 20 at 1568 Lincoln Way.
```

"What's that one?" Derrick asks Josie.

"Domestic dispute," she says. "Probably nothing serious. You'll know it's bad if they call for a sixteen-f."

"Yeah, what's that?" Derrick asks.

"Coroner," she says, eyes closed in relaxation as Edith starts to comb out her hair.

Derrick's attention comes back to me and Luther, since he can't get Josie's.

"If you two had a baby it would be, like, an Olympian."

"I'm not getting pregnant," I inform him. "Softball is more important than sex."

Josie practically doubles over laughing, the long mane of her hair stretched taut between her skull and Edith's brush.

"Softball is more important than sex," Derrick repeats, unbelieving.

"I hear you," Luther says, his voice reverberating by my ear. "On a day when I'm sinking threes I'd rather have my hands on a basketball than a girl. Every time. It's a different kind of good, but damn good."

"Damn straight," I agree.

"You kids know what's better than sex *or* sports?" Edith asks, snapping a hair tie around Josie's slick ponytail.

"What's that, Grandma?" Josie dutifully asks.

"Retirement."

Josie's laugh flares again, loud and brilliant, cut short when Edith gives her a warning tap on the crown of her head with the hairbrush. "Neighbors," she chides.

It's two in the morning, and Edith doesn't exactly live in the part of town where anyone would be up to hear us, but like Mom always says, better safe than sorry. I feel a stab in my gut at the thought of Mom, a mix of guilt and fear. She'd been at my game, of course, casting worried glances at my hip every time I crouched down, assessing my gait when I got back up. But her phone had gone off when she'd met me in the parking lot with a

hug, her cheek coming away wet from my freshly showered hair.

"I've got to go in," she said. "The Hughes girl is in
labor."

"Go," I said, waving her away as I spotted Aaron
sweeping Carolina up in another swinging embrace.
God, can't he just hug her like a normal person?

"See you when I get home?" Mom asked, already edging toward her car.

"Um . . . I might go over to Jo—Jodie's." It's the
worst cover ever, changing Josie's name to Jodie. But at
least I should be able to remember it.

"The girl from therapy?"

I nodded. When you only lie with your neck it's easier.

Mom told me to have a good time and sped off,
and when I turned to tell Carolina good game she was
already gone. The only person left in the lot was Nikki,
walking dejectedly to her car, her spikes still shiny and
new since she didn't get any playing time. I considered
calling out to her but settled for a wave, thinking that
next time maybe she'd play it smart and get on the bus
with the JV.

Then I went home and swiped Mom's wedding ring
from her jewelry drawer, hawked it at a pawn shop,
and drove here to Edith's, ready to get high and forget
everything. Forget the curveball from Carolina that I

almost dropped because I'd been adjusting my stance to take some weight off my hip. Forget how she didn't even glance my way when we left the field. Forget how Nikki's face had gone from hopeful to shattered as the innings wore on and I didn't wear down. Forget the quarter-carat wedding ring that once meant so much to two people, and now means so little that it was jammed under cheap Mardi Gras beads.

Forget that I stole from my mom.

Forget that I don't have the cash to keep this going.

Forget to be awkward when I nestle against Luther.

Forget.

CHAPTER TWENTY-SEVEN

habit: *a fixed or established custom; the involuntary tendency to perform certain actions*

I wake to midafternoon light filtered through cracked blinds, the sound of the toilet flushing, and Josie complaining about her own morning breath. Edith wanders out of the bathroom, her clothes rumpled from sleeping in the chair, her face betraying her age. I know she loves having us here, but right now she looks like all she wants to do is go back to bed, but she's too good of a hostess to do it.

"C'mon." I give Luther a nudge and his eyes come open with effort. Derrick's on the floor, refusing to do much more than huddle into a tighter ball and insist that everything hurts and he's dying the more we try to wake him.

"Derrick, I'll let you drive my car if you get up," Josie says, and that does the trick. He's up in a second, revitalized—whether at the thought of driving her car or getting some alone time with Josie is hard to say. Either way, he's got a second wind and the two of them are out the door before I get a chance in the bathroom.

Luther emerges, water still running down his face from where he splashed himself. With Josie gone, Edith's mood drops visibly and I move quickly in the bathroom, as eager to get out of her house as she is to have us gone. I eye the lone toothbrush, but it's definitely old and certainly Edith's, the bristles so worn they're splayed, a small white explosion that looks too soft to do any good.

I squeeze some toothpaste onto my finger and do the best I can, scrubbing my face with some horrific old-lady soap and drying my hands on a towel with a monogram on it. ELH and BEH are the matching pairs, and I'm thinking what it must feel like for Edith to look at her dead husband's initials every time she's in here, and why she didn't just put them away.

"Yo, Catalan. Get a move on," Luther calls from the living room, and I finish up, touched that he's waiting on me.

"See you kids later," Edith says, shepherding us to the door. "Drive safe. Tell Josie to call me."

We promise to do both and duck out the back. Winter

hasn't quite let go in Ohio yet, and a stiff breeze hits us in the face when we come around the corner of the house, Luther wrapping one arm around me as I turn into him, both of us shielding the other from the chill. It's nice.

"I s'pose you all are her grandkids too?" A voice asks, and we both jump, a little guiltily. Edith's neighbor is on the other side of the fence, gathering up dead limbs that have been knocked from trees by the wind.

"Yep," Luther says, recovering first, not taking his arm from around me. "Big genes run in our family."

I choke on a laugh and the guy gives us a glare before going about his business, muttering something under his breath that I'm sure isn't complimentary. But I'm too sluggish to take offense, too comfortable with Luther, too relieved at the thought of an entire day to myself to really care.

I say goodbye to Luther and head home, a playlist that Josie made for me filling the car. It's light and silly, pop music that Carolina would unplug a speaker from if anyone dared to play it in the locker room. I would too, usually. But today it feels right, with the sun breaking through clouds and a belated text from Josie warning me about the nosy neighbor. I'm not worried about anything or thinking too hard.

We won our first game. I've got friends outside of

softball. My leg doesn't hurt too bad. I'm happy.

Who says drugs are bad?

Mom's napping hard when I get home, both of us having had a long night. I pull her bedroom door shut with
a click so that the noise of my shower won't wake her. I
take my time under the hot water, finding all the knots
in my muscles and working them out slowly, concentrat-
ing on my quads especially. The ropy muscles of my
hips have grown since I got back to working out, and
I can't get past them to the screws anymore, no matter
how hard I dig. I give up once I've raised a bruise, aware
that I'll probably have to explain it next time we're strip-
ping down in the locker room.

I've already slept most of the daylight away, and the
shower boiled away any residual sleepiness. It's a wet
spring day, the kind where you curl up in your bed with
earbuds and a laptop, find something to sling on Netflix
and commit to being lazy. That's what normal teenagers would do, anyway. I end up cruising the obituaries
again, but this time I'm in the archives.

I know Edith's last name from her mailbox—
Holmbach—and that her husband was named Bob. I find
him on the second try—forgetting that Bob is short for
Robert—and learn that he died at the age of forty-five,
from an aneurysm.

"Oh, Edith," I say quietly, scrolling past the list of surviving family members, her son and grandchildren still alive at the time. Edith had chosen to publish their wedding picture alongside the obit.

She looks young, confident, happy. Her face is unlined and her hair magnificently large, everything about her broadcasting that she's on her way up. She doesn't suspect that all she's going to do in life is cross the river, trade West Virginia for Ohio, and sell prescription pills to teenagers to supplement her income and—I think—her family.

Bob, too, seems to think things are going to turn out okay. He looks proud, both in the woman he's married and who he himself is. I recognize the suit he's wearing, having been pressed up against it when it was Luther inside those powder-blue sleeves. I minimize the screen quickly, a bubble in my throat that refuses to either rise or pop, all my happiness of the morning evaporated.

I've used that man's towels. Shit, I've used his toilet. Neither of the people in this picture have any business knowing me, and I've got no claim on their lives, or any reason to read about his death. I pull the browser back up, ready to erase my history and hopefully this morbid curiosity along with it, but accidentally refresh the page instead, and recognize a name in the new obits.

Betsy Vellon.

I know for a fact that one of the lines that went up my nose last night was courtesy of Betsy, and that whatever Edith's legal prescription is, it's more than likely all in her bloodstream a few days after she gets it filled. There's no way she can keep up with her own habit and supply the rest of us.

Jesus, *habit.* I just said that word like it fits one of us, or all of us.

I want to close the browser window, close my eyes, not look at anything else, but there are more names today. The recently dead stare me down, and I can't not see them, or the words printed next to their pictures, in stark black and white. Some of the obituaries stick to the euphemisms—*suddenly, unexpectedly, tragically*—but more are using stark language, not open to interpretation. *Addiction. Opioids. Heroin.*

I snap the laptop shut, fear spiking adrenaline in my veins. I call Josie, who answers on the first ring.

"Hey, baby doll, nobody calls anymore. Text me if—"

"Betsy Vellon's dead," I interrupt her.

There's a pause, followed by what I think is the sound of her shifting around in bed, where she probably went as soon as she got home. "Wait—who?"

"Betsy Vellon," I say, more slowly, realizing that her speech is slow and she might have kept last night's party going into today.

"Do we, like, know her or something?"

"*Betsy Vellon*," I say again, though the words apparently don't carry the same weight with her as they do with me. "Edith's friend? One of the people she gets the . . ." I drop my voice, aware that my volume has risen with every repetition of Betsy's name. I crack my door and peek into the hallway, but Mom's door is still closed.

"The Oxy?" Josie supplies. "Shit."

"Yeah," I say.

"You know what this means, right?"

The truth is, I don't—other than the fact that me, Edith, Josie, Luther, and Derrick have all been cut off.

"It means Edes is going to drag me to another fucking funeral."

I count out what I've got left from Ronald Wagner. It's not much. Five 80s, which will only get me through a couple days, and that's only if I decrease my dosage. I slide the pills back into the bottle, my body crashing after the rush from seeing Betsy's name. I'm tired, and overwhelmed, my emotions going someplace that not even the memory of Josie's laugh or Luther's arm can follow. I've almost drifted off into something I'd forgotten existed—a natural sleep—when Mom knocks on the door.

"Late night?" she asks. She's perky and smiling, thrilled that I have friends.

"Yeah," I say.

"Don't forget you've got dinner with your dad and Devra and your baby brother tonight."

Baby brother. I'm suddenly angry at the phrase, all my anxiety and fear coupling together to lash out at the idea of him.

"He's not actually my brother," I snap. "I mean, I don't even know what to call him. My half adopted brother? And what's Dad if he's not married to you and we're not actually related? What's Devra? My adopted dad's second wife?"

Mom's face is going hard, the way it does right before she's either going to start crying or start yelling. I have no idea which one to expect, but I keep going, all my frustration finding a target in my family, or the closest version of that I have.

"Why do you have to pretend to be so happy for him?"

"Enough." She puts out one hand, palm facing me. Her tone is sharp and concise, the two syllables tearing the air between us. She only puts her hand down once she sees I'm done, and when she speaks again her tone is softer, different, and I can't help but wonder if this is how she speaks to the little ones right after they're born.

"Mickey," she says, coming to sit next to me on the bed. "I am not pretending to be happy for your father."

"He's not—" The hand goes up again.

"Whatever you want to call him is your choice, but that man raised you. I raised you. We did it together and it was a beautiful thing, and now he's doing that with someone else. Does it hurt? Yes. But how I feel about it doesn't factor into your relationship with him. I promised myself I wouldn't let it."

She's switched from angry to sad, the tears rising, though she doesn't let them fall. "Do you think of me as anything other than your mother?"

"No," I say automatically, and it's true. When the divorce came there was never any question for me of who I was going to live with. I love my dad—if that's what I'm going to continue calling him—but it was Mom who took care of me.

"You're my mom," I say, my voice cracking on the last word.

Her tears finally fall, and she wipes them away. "Good," she says, reaching for my hand. "Because you're my daughter."

I half choke, half sob, and fall into her, everything I'm feeling rushing out in a hot swell of tears, reminding me of the vomit I left behind on the road two weeks ago. She wraps her arms around me and rocks me for a little while, back and forth, the ancient calming movement so natural to mothers doing its job. I pull back finally, wiping my own face.

"You totally still have to go to your dad's," she says, and I laugh, a harsh sound that can't quite find its way up my swollen throat.

"Yeah, I'll go," I say. "It's not that I didn't want to. I just . . ."

But I don't know what I just.

"It's okay," Mom says quickly, one arm going back around me. "You were in an accident. You went through *trauma*, hon. But you kept your grades up, and you were still behind the plate for your first game. If you lose your temper over a little family drama, I can live with that."

I go back into the hug, eager for her warmth.

"I don't expect you to be perfect," she says into my ear.

My eyes stray to the pill bottle.

"Good," I say.

CHAPTER TWENTY-EIGHT

broken: *separated into pieces by force*

Mom had lingered in my room after our talk, enjoying our closeness, so I had no time to slip a pill before I left for Dad's. I was nowhere near nauseous, or in any pain, but my anxiety flew through the roof the second Devra opened the door.

"Hey, Mickey," she says. "Come on in."

The baby—Chad—is attached to her left breast, and she's making no attempt whatsoever to hide that fact. I don't care, exactly. I just didn't expect to get a boob in my face first thing. I don't know where to look, my eyes tracing down the length of Chad's tiny, perfect leg, rolling to the side of Devra's elbow. My face is flaming red, so hot I can feel it, which only makes it worse.

"Where's Dad?" I say quickly, searching for the one familiar thing in their house.

Devra's face tightens, and I realize I didn't even say hi to her. She's got deep bags under her eyes, and while her cheeks still hold a trace of the fullness of pregnancy, it looks like the skin is just hanging from her bones. She's lost the baby weight in the past two months, for sure, but I can't say she looks good, either.

"He's in the kitchen," she says, turning her back on me to close the front door.

I feel off, thrown the second I walk in. As usual I said the wrong thing or looked the wrong way. Their front hall is small and I bump into a table, my ridiculously large body not made to pass through here. A small bowl flies off, shatters on the floor, spilling keys and spare change. Startled, Chad jumps in Devra's arms. His feeding interrupted, he starts to scream.

"Sorry," I say, dropping to the floor to pick up what I've broken.

"It's okay—" Devra wants to say more, but she's prevented by the small, angry fists pummeling her face.

"Dev? Everything okay?" Dad's voice calls, and I follow it to find him, carrying shards of broken glass in my hands.

"Sorry. I broke . . ." I look down at them, unsure how to describe what I destroyed. "Something."

"No worries," Dad says, pulling out the trash can with one foot, both hands full as he stands at the stove. "Nothing in this place is priceless except the people."

"Really, Dad? Lame," I tell him, but I appreciate his effort.

"Where's Dev?" he asks, stirring one pot while lowering the flame under another.

"There was a thing, with the baby," I say. "I think I scared him."

Saying it puts me right back where I was two seconds ago, large and ungainly, a girl who isn't related to anyone in this house and who ruins things when she tries to be a part of it.

"Mick," Dad says, following my thoughts. "You're good. It's a cheap plate, probably something Devra picked up at a garage sale. Throw it away. Stop thinking about it."

I do as he says, all but the last part. It's not exactly something I can control. With no Oxy in my system and no dirt under my shoes, Dad's house has me wanting to break for the exit.

"Sit," Dad says, pulling a trivet from the wall and taking the last steaming pot to the table. "It's my night to cook, so . . ."

"Spaghetti," I say, a smile tugging on the corners of my mouth. Dad has no problem with being asked to cook; you just have to be cool with eating spaghetti. Often.

Dad hands me a plate and I scoop some noodles onto it, then sauce, then meatballs. I haven't eaten since . . . weird. I actually don't know. The first bite sends an almost painful jolt into my mouth, my taste buds waking up after being fed only Oxy for a while. Dad's three forkfuls in before he even tries to make conversation. It doesn't get far when I notice a drop of spaghetti sauce on his chin and point to my own, making a swiping gesture. He keeps missing it on purpose, dabbing his forehead or his cheek instead, then asking, "Did I get it?"

"You're an idiot," I say.

"I'm sorry I missed your first game," Dad says, and the way he drops his eyes tells me he's way more bothered by it than I was.

"It's fine." I shrug. "You've got . . ." I wave my hands around his new house, taking in the baby monitors and still unpacked boxes stacked in a corner. "Stuff."

"I do have stuff," he agrees. "But I told myself I could manage two families and I've already failed."

My eyebrows come together, and I try not to rake my fork through the cooling mass of noodles on my plate. "You don't have two families."

Dad nods his head like he's trying to think of a

better way to phrase it, but I've already beaten him to it, thinking of Mom's face drawn in a tight mask of forced pleasantry when she sees him with Devra.

"You left her, Dad. You left Mom. You can't just think of her and me still waiting at home, like you can bounce back and forth between us all."

"That's not . . ." He's got his hand out to stop my words. Just like Mom. Just like Coach Mattix. "Mickey, that's not what I meant."

I can't answer. I don't know how else to feel about what he said.

"Yes," he says carefully. "I left your mother, okay? But I didn't leave you."

Another person might be able to come up with a quick rebuttal, a comeback to end the conversation. Me, I just sit, painfully aware of the rising tension in the room and the fact that he still has that stupid drip of spaghetti sauce on his chin.

"I have to go to the bathroom," I say, and push out from the table, my chair knocking to the floor behind me. I head for the hallway, where Devra is popping out of a side room, her finger raised to her lips in a warning as she pulls the door shut behind her.

"Bathroom," I say, and she waves me down the hall. I find it, and am about to pull the door shut on everything and everyone when I hear Devra complaining to

Dad about us not waiting for her to start eating.

Fuck. This. Place.

I should've stuffed an Oxy in my pocket, or just said to Mom that I was in some pain and taken one right in front her, making it natural. No, instead I tried to keep her happy by not popping a pill, and keep Dad happy by showing up here, somewhere I don't belong. I am so tired of keeping other people happy. Of making sure I say just the right thing to Carolina about Aaron. Of not letting Coach know how shitty it feels that she's got Nikki on the bench waiting for me to fail.

I don't feel this way at Edith's, and no one there expects anything out of me. I don't have to make anybody happy because we *are* happy.

I'm going through drawers before I can question myself, shoving aside Devra's makeup and nail files, hoping an ex-junkie keeps a little something back for the hard nights. I don't find anything, but I turn on the water to cover the noise as I try another drawer, and another. I run my hands through the folds of the towels to see if she's tucked something there, empty the tooth-brush holder and turn it upside down, but nothing falls out. I turn off the water, thinking hard. I can hear an argument starting in the dining room, in low tones the way adults do, but an argument nonetheless.

Right now Devra *looks* like more of a junkie than I

do. Or Josie. Or Luther. Or Derrick. There's got to be
something here. I cross the hall, catching the phrase
"least have the decency to—" and duck into the mas-
ter bedroom. There's a bathroom here too, and I start
in her tampon supply—somewhere Dad would never
venture. I'm cross-legged on the floor, tampons strewn
around me, peering up into an empty box when Devra
walks in.

"Oh, Mickey—" She's startled, not expecting to find
me here. She swipes tears from her face, like just having
them gone means she wasn't crying.

"Do you . . ." Devra looks at the mess I've made. "Do
you need something?"

"Yeah," I say fast, jumping at the convenient excuse
she just made for me. It doesn't explain why I threw
everything on the floor first, but whatever, I'll take it.
I grab one tampon and throw the rest in the box, shoving it back in the drawer awkwardly, the corner bending
when I try to jam it shut.

"It's okay, just leave it," Devra says, flipping the seat
of the toilet down so she can sit, head in her hands,
ready to be rid of me.

"I . . ." I struggle, wanting to say something to make
it all better, to erase the horrible awkwardness of this
night. A disappearing father. A frightened baby. A broken dish. A woman trying too hard.

"Are you okay?" I settle on a stupid question to ask someone who is crying on the toilet. Devra turns, one bright, red-rimmed eye staring at me through her fingers.

"Are you?" she asks.

I don't answer her. I leave. I go home. I take an Oxy. I feel better.

CHAPTER TWENTY-NINE

accusation: *the act of charging with an offense*

I could almost be okay the next night.

Carolina comes over for dinner, and she even silences her phone before she puts it in her hoodie pocket. Mom gets takeout, and we're falling back into a familiar pattern—dissecting the game just past, analyzing who did and did not do certain things, and talking about the next team we'll face on Thursday. It's almost the same, but not quite.

Dad isn't here to listen intently to Carolina like he was last season, chin resting in his hand while she explains the best way to hit another pitcher's curveball. And even though she did put it on vibrate, I can still hear texts coming in on her phone—probably from Aaron—as we talk. Carolina ignores it, which I appreciate, but every time I hear a buzz coming from her direction it sets my teeth a little more on edge.

We've almost put away the entire order of wonton soup, the egg rolls are gone, and Carolina is diving back into the General Tso's chicken when Mom's phone goes off. She's on call again, so silencing is not an option. Mom pops a fortune cookie into her mouth and puts it on speaker when she sees that it's Dad.

"Hey, what's up?"

"Um . . . there's no good way to say this," Dad says, his voice uncharacteristically cautious. "So I'm just going to spit it out. Devra thinks Mickey is on something."

Mom's hand slaps down onto the phone, taking it off speaker before he can say any more. I stop chewing, the last bits of Chinese food that I've managed to force down turning tasteless in my mouth. Carolina drops her eyes, suddenly interested in arranging her chicken a certain way on her plate.

"What the hell, Geoff?" Mom is up and leaving the table in an effort to make this a private conversation, but there's too much emotion in her voice to bring the volume level down. I clear my throat, looking for words to use, anything to say that can drown out Mom.

"You get enough to eat?" I ask Carolina.

It's a stupid thing to say, something a mom or a grandma would ask. Not a best friend. Or any friend.

But it's all I can come up with, a question that doesn't require a vocal answer, so Carolina only nods her head as more of Mom's responses drift to the table.

"Because she needed a *tampon*? Geoff, do I really have to explain menstruation to you again?"

"The soup was good," I say.

"Right, right . . . of course," Mom goes on, voice rising again. "Of *course* everything is falling apart here, without you. That's right. The second you leave your daughter becomes an addict. I couldn't possibly be a good doctor *and* a good mother—"

"Mickey . . . ," Carolina says, turning her spoon upside down so that rice cascades off it.

"Oh, fuck you, Geoff. FUCK. YOU."

"I think I should probably go," Carolina says, pulling her phone out so she doesn't have to look at me. I glance at it too, seeing texts from Aaron, as expected. But there's also a group text with Lydia and the Bellas, one I'm not in on.

What are they talking about?

"Carolina, wait," I say, getting up to follow her to the door.

"Thanks for dinner," she says, pulling her jacket on. "It was nice to . . . hang out."

It was nice, but it wasn't like it used to be. And I can tell by the tone of her voice that she can't quite figure out why either, and doesn't know how to fix it.

"See you later," she says, leaving without waiting for me to respond. I close the door behind her just as Mom finds me, white-knuckling her phone.

"Mickey, you never, *ever* have to go over there again if you don't want to, okay?" She swipes angry tears from her face, flicking them away so that they splatter on a framed picture of us from last Christmas, Dad included.

"If you can't even get a tampon without being accused of something . . ."

Except, I didn't just get a tampon. I also rifled all the drawers in both bathrooms, and bolted from the dinner table.

". . . just because he started a new, happy family, it doesn't mean that this one is falling apart!"

"Yeah," I agree, too shaken to even find the energy to be angry alongside her.

Because Mom just went somewhere I hadn't expected. She got mad, sure, but she wasn't just pissed that Devra thinks I'm an addict. She's pissed that Dad thinks it happened on her watch, that she can't hold down the fort here without him. She's barreling down the hallway now, toward my room, and I hurry to catch up with her.

"You've still got pills," Mom is yelling when I get into my room, holding up my prescription bottle and shaking what's left inside. "If you were an addict, would you still have pills from a prescription filled that long ago?"

It's not a question I'm supposed to answer. These are all the things she wanted to say to Dad, the words bubbling up now, after she's hung up. I know how this feels so I let her go, let her talk about all the things that illustrate how I'm not an addict, most of them carefully orchestrated by me so that she wouldn't know.

This tells me two things:

Mom can never, ever find out the truth.

And I'm getting really good at lying.

CHAPTER THIRTY

heroine: *a woman of heroic spirit; the principal female person who figures in a remarkable action*

Game day.

Those two words mean so much to me, the equivalent of *I love you* for so many other people. I wear my jersey with jeans, and Nikki braids my hair in study hall. Varsity is away today and she's coming with us, something that would have bothered me if I hadn't made it through the entire game last week. But I did, so when Nikki asks if I want her to do my hair so someone else doesn't have to on the bus—resulting in bumps galore—I say okay.

Not that it matters. The first time my catching gear goes over my head it'll tear out the perfection that Nikki is concocting, a web of fishtail braids that is somewhat painful as she does it, but has other girls coming in close to comment over. I'm not used to being complimented on my hair, and it feels good. That, mixed with the warmth in my bloodstream as I grind an Oxy between my molars on the way to the bus, has me feeling like a million dollars when my feet hit the ground in Palma Falls.

I'm even able to ignore the awkwardness between me and Carolina, stiff at first, as we make our way out to the grass to warm up, then fading as we follow the routine, reestablished now that the first and third basemen have adopted Nikki into their throwing triangle. We know each other. We know these movements. We might not talk as the ball goes back and forth between us, but it's a conversation nonetheless. She slaps my ass as we jog to the dugout and I stick it out farther, like I'm asking for another.

"Whatever, Catalan. Lydia says you're just a tease," Carolina says, tipping back her water bottle.

"Not that I've given up," Lydia calls from the corner, where she's tightening her spikes.

Coach leans against the edge of the cinder-block building, eyeing her lineup. "Catalan, you good for cleanup?"

"Yep," I say, trying not to let pride sneak into the single syllable.

Last week she didn't let me bat fourth, too worried that the strain on my hip from catching might make it difficult for me to rotate all the way around in the box. Behind the plate is my place, but I've got no problem standing next to it, either. I can place a shot where I spot a hole, and drop a fly in front of outfielders who expected me to power it over their heads.

"You got this," Carolina agrees, holding out a fist for me to bump.

The bleachers are starting to fill, our side with faces that I know. Lydia's parents—and grandparents, both sets—show up with their air horns, something Coach Mattix has asked them not to use. Last time she tried to make her case, Lydia's grandpa kept setting it off every time she spoke. We just sat in the dugout, faces buried in our hands, red with suppressed laughter that we knew *could not* get out.

The three Bellas' moms come together, carting a cooler that I know has postgame snacks even though we outgrew those forever ago. Guy Who Always Brings His Wiener Dog shows, yappy friend following on his heels. Woman with Victoria's Secret Umbrella makes an appearance, carrying it along to shade her face from the sun. Even the Elderly Couple in Matching Scooters comes rolling in a few minutes before game time, which says a lot about fan loyalty. Palma Falls is a half-hour drive, and I'm sure it takes most of their combined energy to get out here, and back home.

The Galarzas show up in matching sweatshirts that say *Pitchin' Mom & Dad*, and Big Ed rolls in right when the umpires do. I spot Mom as we're gearing up, the top three in the lineup—Carolina, Lydia, and Bella Center—pulling on batting helmets, while I wait in the wings. Mom waves, but I spot a tightness in her smile that makes it not quite honest. As vehement as she was following Devra's accusation, I'm sure whispers of doubt have started to surface, ones that contradict all her yelling.

Dad doesn't show. I try not to care.

Carolina drops a sweet bunt and runs out the throw easily, bringing up Lydia, who scores an easy single. Bella Center gets a full count before fouling out when the third baseman snags her line drive that's just on the wrong side of the baseline. That brings me to the plate, and everyone cheers.

My blood swells, pushing the Oxy through me faster and heating my veins. The sun bakes into my jersey so that I can feel every thread, am aware of each voice saying my name.

I don't fuck around in the box, never have. Coach likes us to take at least one strike to put the pressure on the pitcher to make her throw, but if I think I can get the bat on it, I swing. Coach has given me an earful once or twice, but since this is the one thing I don't defer to her on, she's let it go. My batting average is solid, so she's got no leg to stand on.

I do the same thing now. The pitcher is already rattled; with two on and staring down Mickey Catalan, she's aware things are not going her way. Beside me, the catcher shifts, throwing a signal that I don't need to see to know what it is. They're going to try to get a fastball past me.

So stupid, when you're pitching to someone who catches for Carolina Galarza.

I can judge a fastball better than anyone, and there's the perfect moment when I'm dissecting the trajectory, the speed, the shift of my hips, the angle of my bat, the dip of my shoulder. My muscles take over and a million calculations are made in a nanosecond, right before I loosen my grip on the bat ever so slightly, then clutch down harder than before and fucking smash it.

The first thing my grandpa taught me was not to watch your shot. You put your head down and run, looking to the base coach for signals, and that's it. It doesn't matter if the ball's in the dirt or on the grass, because if you're doing it right you won't even know. You just run. That's your job, and you do it or you get your ass reamed.

I run. Stretching out my legs so that they eat distance, clipping the corner of first base with my spikes when I get the signal to keep going and focus on rounding second to see Coach pinwheeling her arms, telling me to go.

So I go.

I go all the way home, crashing into Carolina and Lydia, who are waiting for me, the other team's catcher standing three feet out in front of it with her helmet in the dirt beside her and her glove at her side, useless. That ball isn't coming back in anytime soon.

"You're my hero, Mickey Catalan," Lydia says into my ear, over the roar of the crowd.

"Heroine," I correct her.

"Hoo—fucking—ray!" Bella Right screams at me when I get into the dugout.

Everyone is yelling my name.

Right now, everyone loves me.

Right now, I even love myself.

CHAPTER THIRTY-ONE

intravenous: *entering by way of a vein*

"How many RBIs, Catalan?" Luther asks me on Friday.

"Five," I say, peeling the wrapper back from the warm cupcake Edith offered me when I got in the door.

"Dang. Your stats should be looking pretty sweet."

"Yep," I agree.

"Sports. Hooray, go team. Can we talk about something else?" Josie asks, from where she sits cross-legged on the floor, running her fingernail under a piece of enamel that is splintering from Edith's coffee table.

"I thought Betsy's service was nice," Edith says, from her recliner.

"Yeah, really not what I was going for, Grandma," Josie says. Edith frowns and changes the channel, switching it from QVC, which makes Josie's mouth go into a flat line. Without the boost of Betsy's prescription, we're all a little on edge.

Josie had texted me earlier to say that even though she had a wad of cash, Edith wasn't selling.

Fucking selfish, Josie texted, and I answered with an agreement, highly aware that Ronald Wagner's last 80 was dissipating in my bloodstream even though I'd stretched them as long as I could.

Josie had hoped that the arrival of Luther, Derrick, and me would make Edith crack, but instead she made us cupcakes. The only pills she had on hand were her own, and they weren't for sale. Apparently her deep love for her granddaughter-of-her-heart didn't dip past her Oxy supply, and this revelation had put Josie in a foul mood.

"Hey." She slaps Derrick's knee, and he glances up from his phone. "You know anybody?"

"Uh . . ." He shares a glance with Luther, who shakes his head, almost imperceptibly.

"What? *What!*" Josie hits Derrick's knee again, harder this time.

"Okay, so . . . I do know where we could probably get it, but he's not exactly the kind of guy I want to buy from, know what I mean?"

"Yeah, I do know what you mean," Josie says. "You're a pussy."

Derrick's face falls and I want to call her out on it, tell her to stop being rude to him and to Edith. But I don't, because there isn't enough Oxy in my bloodstream to make the words come up. Luther has no problem with it, though.

"Back off," he says. "Derrick's right. If we go around buying from him it's not like it is here at Edith's. We get spotted, people know what's up. I'm not losing my spot on a college team next year because of a felony. You hear me?"

"Yeah, I hear you." Josie rolls her eyes. "Blah, blah, blah. Sports."

"Whatever," Luther shoots back, then nudges Derrick. "Wanna bounce?"

"Yep," Derrick says, putting his phone away and not looking at Josie.

"What? Hey . . . guys!" Josie is up in a second. "You don't have to . . ." Her voice fades as she follows them through the house. Edith sighs deeply, changing the channel again.

"Goddammit!" I hear Josie yell as the back door swings. "Fuck them," she says, coming back into the room. "Just fuck those guys."

"Language," Edith says, sounding bored.

"And f—" Josie barely catches herself from telling Edith to fuck off as well. Her hands tremor as she brushes her hair off her shoulder, the tears standing in her eyes. I know where she's at. I didn't like being there, and I don't want to be around someone else going through it either. My phone goes off with a text from Luther.

Come outside

I glance between Josie and Edith, both pouting. It's not a hard call.

Luther is leaning against his car when I go out, Derrick in the passenger seat scrolling through his phone.

"What's up?" I ask.

"Wanna come with us?" Luther asks.

"Where?"

"Party with some Baylor kids. Just drinking, nothing else," he adds, like he's afraid I'll get my hopes up.

"I don't drink," I tell him.

"Still better than hanging around here," he says, and while that might be true, there's no way I'm wandering into a party where I don't know anyone, everybody has more money than me, and there's no Oxy in my blood to boost my confidence.

"Maybe next time," I tell him, heading back toward the house.

"Hey," he calls after me, and I turn. "There's a basketball game tomorrow night, college tournament. I got tickets, if you wanted to . . ."

Basketball is not my sport, but I can stand watching it. What I don't know is if I can hang with Luther without Oxy and be as cool as he seems to think I am. Maybe one evening with regular Mickey Catalan—or worse, a withdrawing one—will be a huge turnoff. In any case, I've been debating it too long, and my lack of an answer makes his smile falter.

"I mean, whatever," he says. "If you're not into it, it's cool."

I take a step forward, involuntarily. "No, yeah, let's," I say, before I think about it.

"Yeah?" Luther asks, the smile back.

"Yeah," I say, my heart stuttering a little bit.

"Hey, do you . . ." Luther fumbles in his pocket, pulling out two pills that rest on his hand, small and white in that huge space. My heart takes a full leap, way out-distancing the reaction to Luther's smile.

"Do you want these?" Luther asks, holding his palm out to me. I cover the distance between us in a moment.

"Yeah. You don't?"

"Meh." Luther shrugs. "It's okay, I guess, but if it'll get Josie off your ass for tonight, I'd rather you have them."

I hug him. It's spontaneous and a little awkward, since I'm grabbing for the Oxy at the same time. But it works out.

"Thanks, man," I tell him as I pull away.

"I'll text you tomorrow. About the game," he adds, when I look confused.

"Yep, sounds good," I call over my shoulder.

Josie is on me the second I walk through the door, and I don't have time to pop the pills Luther gave me at the kitchen sink, like I was planning on.

"Hey," she cries when she spots me. "You holding out on me?"

"It's for both of us," I lie, slipping one pill into my other hand so that I've got something to get me through tomorrow. "I got us covered."

"You've got shit covered, Mickey," Josie says, leading me into the living room. "That's one pill, between the both of us. Even if we snort it, all it will do is—"

"Help," I say. "It'll help."

"Not much," Josie mutters, shooting Edith a dark look even as she starts to grind the pill down with the edge of a coaster. Her phone goes off and her grip slips, sending the coaster rolling, a fine edge of white powder trailing it.

"FUCK," Josie says.

Edith turns up the volume on *60 Minutes*.

I grab the coaster, setting it aside in favor of the Precious Moments girl, while Josie answers her phone.

"What?" she says, as I feel the hard edge of the Oxy

give way under pressure, the resistance melting to nothing as I grind.

"Yeah, I'm at Edith's. No, you can't take my—*hey!* I said no." She's quiet for a second, eyebrows furrowed together as she watches me make short work of the pill.

"Yeah, and Mom will be thrilled to hear that, won't she?" Josie spits back at whoever she's talking to.

I take a subscription card out of one of Edith's magazines—*Prevention*—and start making two lines out of the powder. They're short and thin, not nearly enough to lift Josie out of her funk or keep me in a good place.

"Yeah, well . . . ," Josie goes on, back to picking at the piece of enamel on the table. "Not my problem."

There's a knock on the door. Edith jumps in her chair and I come to my feet.

"Seriously?!" Josie shouts into her phone. "That had better not fucking be you, Jadine, or I swear . . ."

"Hellllooooooo . . . ," a high-pitched voice sings from the kitchen, wobbly and more than a little grating. "Anybody home?"

"Oh, shit." It's Edith's turn to swear, as she flips off the TV. Lost, I look at her.

"Jadine," Edith repeats the name, as if it should explain itself. "Josie's older sister."

If I had seen her before I heard her, I wouldn't have had to ask. The girl who saunters into Edith's living room somewhat unsteadily is like a glance into Josie's future, a place where all her baby fat is gone, as is any hint of innocence. Jadine is thin, but with curves in the right places. I can see her hip bones where they jut out above her jeans, the edge of her shirt barely grazing the denim. It'd be a trashy look if the clothes weren't so obviously expensive.

The hollows in her cheeks could be from hunger or because she's learned how to suck them in, holding her face perfectly. And something tells me Jadine has studied her reflection in the mirror enough to know exactly how far to drop her shoulder, how high to cock a hip. There's a calculation to each of her movements as she leans in the doorway, even with only us as her audience.

"Awww . . . cute," Jadine says, looking at the table. "You're snorting." I flip the copy of *Prevention* over on top of the lines reflexively, but she only laughs.

"I'm not giving you my keys," Josie says indignantly, arms crossed.

"Yeah, you are. And I need the car that goes with those keys," Jadine says.

"You're so full of shit," Josie shoots back, but I can see how the tears that had started to subside when the guys left are welling again.

"No, but I'm going to *be* in deep shit if anybody sees my car after I took out that mailbox. We stuck it in

Brad's garage and he said he can bang out the dents, but I've got to get back to campus and he wasn't exactly hot on me driving that far."

"You shouldn't be driving at all, sweetheart," Edith says from her chair, the endearment falling somewhere short of kind. "Mailbox won't be the last thing you hit tonight if you keep going."

"So call the cops on me, *Edes*," Jadine says, drawing out her little sister's nickname for Edith. "Just make sure you clean up those lines on the coffee table first."

Edith makes a noise in the back of her throat, but turns away from the conversation.

"C'mon, let's go," Jadine says to Josie, impatient. "It'll take me two hours to get back and Kappa Sig is doing a toga party tonight."

"It's my car. Mom bought it for me," Josie insists.

"She bought me one too, and I fucked it up. So now I need yours," Jadine says, stepping closer to Josie. Close enough to see the sweat beading along her hairline. Close enough to spot the quiver in her breath.

I wish I'd done that line before Josie's phone rang. That silk thread running up my nose and into my brain would have helped me find words to say to Jadine, to this girl who looks the way a girl should, the way I don't. But the line is on the table, not in my brain, so as usual I don't know what to say or do, how to act or even how to stand. Jadine has sucked all the air out of the room, but I'm not the only one gasping for breath.

I've never seen Josie this way, and I don't just mean going through withdrawal. She's smaller than usual, shrunken in the presence of her sister. The first time I saw Josie I thought she was bright and shiny, the best example of femininity I'd ever seen. But next to Jadine I notice that she's begun to bite her nails, and that her hair has split ends.

I wonder if this is how Josie sees herself when she's around Jadine, too.

I wonder if Jadine knows it.

I think she does, just by the way she moves around her little sister, a cat messing with a mouse. But a cat will eventually pounce, instinct taking over in the end. Jadine is more interested in playing.

"It's my car," Josie says again.

"Annnddd . . . these are my pills," Jadine says, pulling a bottle from her purse. "Wanna trade?"

Josie perks up. Edith turns in her chair.

"I don't have a whole lot left, but I can show you how to make it count," Jadine says, shaking the bottle like that makes it more attractive, as if Josie is a baby and she has a rattle.

"Done," Josie says, handing over her keys and swiping the bottle from Jadine's hand before she can change her mind. "You can take me home tomorrow, right, Mickey?"

"Yep. Yes," I say, suddenly with more words than I need.

"'Kay," Jadine says, curling her fingers around the keys. "Grab a bottle of water from the fridge and I'll show you how adults do drugs."

I go, to save Josie what little bit of pride she might have left. I reach past part of a meat loaf wrapped in foil and what looks like leftovers from the potatoes Edith made us almost a month ago, butter and grease heavily congealed on top

"Got it," I say, going back to the living room. "Now wh—"

I stop cold. Jadine is pulling needles out of her purse. They're on a roll like lottery tickets, and sealed in paper like a Band-Aid. It looks sterile and proper, like we're playing doctor or something. But this isn't a hospital, and Jadine is no nurse. Josie has gone white, but she does what her sister says, mixing the Oxy I already crushed with water, then filling a syringe.

"Okay, so," Jadine says, as she flicks the syringe. "This is actually really simple. Look at my arm."

She holds it out, thin and white, her veins easy to spot when she makes a fist. She tells us how to find a good vein, how to make sure it won't roll, how to tell if you're in it or not.

"Who's first?" she asks, needle in hand.

Josie and I look at each other, and Jadine laughs.

"Look, kids, all the needle does is take out the middleman. The Oxy goes straight into your bloodstream; you don't have to wait for it to get absorbed."

It's pure logic, not taking into account the wicked edge of the needle, the slant of the tip and the drop of Oxy-infused water glimmering there. Jadine doesn't mention the tearing of our skin when it goes in, or the hole left behind from where we crossed that line.

Jadine glances at her phone. "I got to go, guys. Either I help you out or you fumble around poking each other after I leave."

That does it for me, as I imagine Josie's shaky hands or Edith's soft, unfamiliar ones having a go at the inside of my elbow. At least Jadine knows what she's doing. I roll up my sleeve and do as she says, making a fist, then watching as she finds a vein. She shows us how to pull back on the syringe so we see the blood flowing into the water, proof that we've hit a vein.

I'm used to waiting for my Oxy, and I almost enjoy those ten minutes or so of anticipation, knowing that relief is on the way and all I have to do is relax and enjoy it. But then Jadine pushes the plunger and I get everything, all at once, pure bliss in a rush that almost lifts me right up off the ground.

Fuck waiting.

One glance at my face and Josie is rolling up her own sleeve, though she doesn't watch as her sister finds a vein and does the same for her, using a new needle. She makes a small noise, something in between either pleasure or pain, and I don't know if it's because of the poke or what comes after.

"Better?" Jadine asks, rubbing the inside of her sister's arm almost tenderly.

"Better," Josie agrees automatically, her voice soft and dreamy.

"How 'bout it, Edes?" Jadine asks, but at some point our host has dropped off to sleep in her chair. Jadine gets to her feet, tearing off a few more needles from the roll in her purse.

"I'll leave you a few, sis," she says. "Thanks for the car, and let me know when you're ready to graduate."

"Graduate?" Josie looks up from the string of needles tossed across the table.

"To heroin," Jadine calls over her shoulder.

CHAPTER THIRTY-TWO

manipulate: *to manage artfully or fraudulently, especially in regard to other persons*

Josie is quiet in the morning on the ride to her place, breaking her silence only to give me directions, or to sniffle. Letting Jadine inject us had felt amazing, but what was in the needle had been weak and wore off quick. Neither one of us had the guts to try the needle without Jadine's help. Instead a fair amount had gone up our noses before Josie thought to check the strength of the bottle she'd traded her car for. They were way weak—only 20s—so we blew through most of it, leaving us with red nostrils and a constant need to clear our throats.

It lingers into the morning, dripping out of my sinuses and down into my stomach. Not a good feeling, or a good taste. All I want to do is get home and stand in the hot shower.

"So what's up with you and Luther?" Josie asks.

"What? Nothing," I say, sounding as guilty as I looked last night standing over the sink with the Oxy Josie didn't know I had.

"Left here," Josie says, her voice thick and wet. "Okay, whatever on the Luther thing, but if you need to talk about boy stuff I can . . . I mean, like, maybe you don't know a lot about . . . that."

Josie is blushing as I make the turn, rolling into a neighborhood I've never visited and have no reason to go. Baylor Springs has always been the kind of place most people can't afford to shop in, but I doubt I could even browse at Josie's yard sales—if they do those in this town.

"I know enough about *that*," I tell her. "What about you and Derrick?"

"Ha," Josie says, confirming what I already knew.

"He doesn't have a chance, does he?"

"Nobody does," Josie says. "Guys have always been after what I've got, and that used to feel good. Now . . . I've got Oxy."

"And?"

She shrugs. "And it makes me feel better than they ever did. You'll see. Right now, Luther is a bright, shiny new thing. Everything he says is funny, or charming. But eventually you'll fight—probably about something stupid like whether to watch basketball or baseball tonight—and then he'll start to irritate you."

I think of the way he looked at me last night by his car. I don't think it's something I could ever get tired of.

"Trust me," Josie says, following my thoughts. "He will. And as far as *that* . . . all I can say is most of the guys I've been with had no idea what they're doing. Oxy delivers every time."

"Right," I say, my own blush starting.

"Three houses down, the brick," she says, but that's not terribly helpful because I think everything here is brick. Or stone. I haven't seen any siding in a mile and a half. I stop in front of the house she points at, putting the car in park.

"What does your mom do?" I ask her.

"Divorce," she mutters, as she gathers her things.

"She's a lawyer?"

"No, like she gets married and then gets divorced and then gets married again. Alimony is a full-time job."

"Oh," I say, unsure of what else fits.

Josie cracks the door, one foot on the sidewalk, then hesitates. "Do you wanna come in?"

"Huh?" The invitation is so unexpected, the idiotic syllable escapes before I can stop it.

"Hang out," Josie says, flipping down the visor and grimacing when she sees how red her nose is. "Netflix. Maybe some pizza? Mom's out of town. Jadine's gone. I've got nothing to—"

"I can't," I say quickly. The idea of going into Josie's house has me frozen. I could break something when I turn too quickly or tread too hard. In a house like that I doubt it would be as easily replaceable as the plate I shattered at Dad's.

"Oh," Josie says, her face shifting from the placid, detached look she had worn to something more guarded, a look I've seen on plenty of girls as they assess one another. "Fine."

She tries to get out fast now that she's been rejected, pulling all her things into her lap and standing up at the same time. The shoulder strap of her purse gets snagged on the gear shift and there's an awkward moment where I'm trying to unwrap it and she's stubbornly pulling, like she means to rip the whole stick out of the car along with her purse if that's what it takes to get out of here.

"Thanks for the ride," Josie calls over her shoulder as she makes her escape, not making eye contact.

The door slams and I close my eyes, pissed at myself. There's no reason I couldn't hang out at Josie's, other than my own stupid self. The truth is that I'm worried the easy closeness between us will be gone without Oxy to bind us, that just like the Bellas or Lydia, when I'm not on the field I won't quite know what to say.

I don't want to find out, but there is one thing I need to know. I roll down the window and call to her before she makes the front door.

"Hey," I yell, and she spins on the stone walkway, hair fanning around her.

"Yeah?"

"What are we going to do?"

Elaboration isn't necessary. She knows what I'm asking. With Betsy gone, Edith hoarding her own stash, and Jadine's 20s almost blasted through in one night, our options are more than limited.

They don't exist.

Josie glances up and down the street before answering. "Text me later," she says. "I'll see what I can come up with."

I shoot Josie a text as soon as I get home, but she doesn't answer right away. I'm lying in bed, studying the empty pill bottle on my dresser, and thinking about the Oxy from Luther in my jeans pocket, when my door slams open hard enough for the knob to crack into the wall and bounce away. The sound of pulverized drywall trailing to the floor fills the room as I stare at Mom.

"What the hell?" I ask.

"Where is my wedding ring, Mickey Catalan?" she shouts at the same time.

"I . . . *Mom!*" I yell, as she swipes the orange bottle off my bed stand. Instinctively, I lunge for it, but she's on her feet and quicker than me, pulling it out of my reach as my legs get tangled in the sheets and I roll to the floor. There's a solid smack when I hit, and my teeth click together, but she doesn't move to help me, or ask if I'm okay.

"My wedding ring," she repeats, holding the bottle above her head.

"How would I know?" I say, running a finger along the inside of my lip where it connected with the floor, soft tissue already swelling.

"Did you take it?" she asks.

"Why would I do that?" I ask, hauling myself back up onto the bed, crouched under her glare. I'm answering questions with questions, hoping that love will outdo logic as I lead her down the path that makes me look good, the one she wants to follow.

"For money," she cries, her voice breaking on the second word. "You drained your bank account, Mickey. I checked."

The anger is seeping out now, having already crested with her entrance. I've overheard enough fights between Mom and Dad, seen the explosion of rage and fallout of quiet tears. She's going to fold now. Her words will stick to her convictions, but her tone will be begging me to give her a believable alternative. I've got the template for this conversation down, have heard Dad talk her out of her suspicions more than once.

And she let him.

"Mom . . ." I start quiet, like he always would. "I don't know what's going on."

"I do, though, Mickey," she says, eyes narrowed. "When your dad called I was so angry I couldn't think, but then Devra texted me. She wondered if you'd been asking me for money lately, or if anything had come up missing around the house."

Mom sinks onto the bed, her fingernail working the edge of the label. "I told her she could stick it where Chad came from, but then I looked at your bank account."

I swallow once, thinking.

"And then I went through my jewelry box," she says, a hitching sigh escaping with the words. Her jewelry box, which held almost nothing. The practicalities of her profession have always kept her from wearing much, but what she did keep had emotional value. I'd taken the only piece worth anything.

"So are you going to tell me what's up, or are you going to make me keep talking?"

"Mom," I say carefully. "I'm okay."

I say this, because it's not quite a lie. I say this, because it's almost true. I *could* be okay. If I can get her calmed down and find out what Josie's idea is to keep us from withdrawal and get through this ball season, everything will be all right. I take another deep breath, then let it out with a shudder.

"Carolina needed . . ." My mind is racing, looking in all the dark corners, any thing, any reason, any person I can throw to Mom for punishment.

Just as long as it's not me.

Just as long as she doesn't know.

"Carolina needed . . . money."

"What for?"

"I . . . I really don't want to tell you." And it's true. I really don't want to say the words that are going to come out of me next.

"Mickey," Mom insists, voice going thin and hard. "What for?"

"A . . . procedure," I say, quick and fast, spitting the words before I can talk myself out of them. Mom sits up straighter, but her face clouds, the doctor in her always on duty, the mother in her ready to offer comfort.

"She could have come to me," Mom says. "I could have talked to her about her options. Did you tell her that?"

I shake my head, my throat still full of the taste of

Oxy. "She didn't want to talk. She just needed it done. She'll lose her scholarship if she can't play, and she can't play if she's . . ."

I don't say the word *pregnant*, because it would make this a real lie, not an insinuation. And maybe it's not even that much of a lie, really. For all I know Carolina *could* be pregnant.

"She couldn't go to her parents about it," I go on more confidently, because that part is certainly true. "You know how they are."

"Yes," Mom says, rolling the pill bottle in her hand. "I do."

"So . . ." I let the word drift, hoping more will come. Amazingly, they do, welling up from the depths, fed by the last dripping remnants from my head. "So she asked me for the money."

"The boy involved helped as well, I would hope?"

"I don't know, Mom. I didn't ask questions. She asked for help and I gave it. She's my best friend."

Fuck. Listen to me. How can I sound righteous while lying through my teeth?

"Right." She squeezes the bottle, wanting to believe me. My name on the label smears under her sweaty palms. "What about my wedding ring?"

"I don't know," I say again, shrugging. "When's the last time you saw it?"

"January twenty-fourth," she answers quietly, and I close my eyes against the clench of my stomach, guilt crimping the lining into a tight ball.

"Mom, I . . ."

"It's . . . okay, Mickey," she says, closing her eyes tight. "It's okay. I'm okay."

Mom's okay, and I'm okay, and we sit there crying on my bed, the space between us measured only in inches.

But neither of us crosses it.

CHAPTER THIRTY-THREE

sidekick: *someone associated with another, but not as an equal*

Luther picks me up a few hours later, coming into the house and doing the whole meet-your-mom thing. I'm flustered as I introduce him, but Mom isn't listening too intently, anyway. I think she's mentally measuring Luther's shoulders and wondering about his delivery.

I've got to adjust the passenger seat when I get in his car; my knees are touching the dashboard.

"Who was the last person in here?" I ask, panic gripping me at the thought that it was some tiny cheerleader.

"My little sister," Luther says, and my relief tells me just how much the answer mattered.

We've got a couple hours' drive ahead of us to the stadium, and the same nagging voice that warned me I wouldn't have anything to say to Josie without the assistance of Oxy is whispering in my ear again. I throw back the one pill I've got left—courtesy of Luther—when he stops at a gas station to fill up.

We're not too far out of town and Luther attracts people the second he's out of the car. I overhear most of his conversation with a guy at the pump about Baylor's ill-fated tournament run—triple overtime in their division title game when a kid from the opposing team threw up a Hail Mary three-pointer that went in. There was heated debate about whether he'd released before or after the buzzer, but the refs had already made a run for the locker room. Big Ed told me they had to be escorted out by security to ensure their safety.

That story gets replayed by the pump while I'm scrolling through my phone, attracting another guy, who glances into the car and sees me. There's a flash of recognition on both our parts when I realize it's Bella Left's dad. We give each other waves and I know it's going to be all over the county that Luther Drake and Mickey Catalan were hanging out.

Luther knocks on the window, asks me if I want anything. I ask him to grab me a water and he goes inside to pay. Judging by the arm movements of the cashier, another basketball story is being told. By the time Luther makes it back out to the car I'm feeling pretty good, my blood warm and my limbs loose.

"Sorry," he says, handing me the water. "You know how it is."

I do know how it is, and being with someone else who gets that too is awesome.

"Thanks for the water," I tell him. "Looked like a pretty interesting conversation in there."

"Ha," Luther says, pulling back out onto the highway. "Everybody likes to talk about me breaking the backboard over at West Union."

"I heard about that," I tell him. "You even impressed Big Ed."

"Big Ed?" he asks, and I think it's possible I detect a hint of the unease I felt before, when I wondered who had been in his passenger seat.

"Yeah, Big Ed. He owns the market in town."

"I've been in there," Luther says. "He's not that big."

"I'm sure no one seems big to you," I tell him, and he shakes his head.

"No, not really. It's gotta be the same for you, though, right? I mean, who seems big to you?"

"You," I tell him honestly.

And he smiles.

We're far enough away from home that nobody looks at us twice as we find our seats in the stadium, beyond the curious glances that Luther's height attracts. We settle in, and I'm content to be watching a sport—even if it is basketball and I don't know anyone on the court. Luther is friends with a few of the guys playing because he did a summer camp at their college. He points them out and I nod, only partly interested.

The one Oxy I had left is doing its job, but I can't count on such a low dose for the heavy lifting required to actually make me happy. I'm comfortable for now, but the warmth is fading and I'm very aware that I'm going home to an empty pill bottle, and a mom who is going to be making sure no cash walks out of the house in my hand from now on. I'm wondering if I should text Josie again to see if she figured out anything when my phone goes off with a text from Carolina.

Luther Drake? Are you shitting me?

That didn't take long.

How did I not know about this?

Her second text takes the smile off my face. She doesn't know about Luther because I don't think another story about meeting someone at physical therapy will fly with her, and the truth will go over like a lead brick. I settle for taking a selfie with him and sending it back to her in response.

She answers with a shot of her and Aaron, making faces of extreme shock.

You guys are assholes, I tell them in a group text, to which Aaron sends me a pic of an actual asshole.

That's not his, Carolina assures me. **Witness.**

Gross, I shoot back, adding, **don't get pregnant.**

People don't get pregnant from assholes, Aaron replies. **Do we need to talk?**

YOU don't get pregnant! Carolina says.

One of the guys Luther knows hits a three and Luther jumps up with the rest of the crowd, both arms in the air. I check once more, but Josie hasn't answered me yet. I put away my phone as Luther sits back down.

"When's the last time you talked to Josie?" I ask him.

"When she called Derrick a pussy because he didn't want to go to a crack house for her," Luther says. "I'm not in a big hurry to see her again."

I think of Josie, the loss in her eyes when they left, the shaking of her hands as she positioned Jadine's needle.

"She didn't mean it," I say. "She was just—"

"Strung out. Yeah, I know," Luther says. "Josie hits it too hard."

I don't say anything, checking to make sure my sweatshirt is pulled down to cover the tiny hole in my arm.

"Did what I give you keep her off your back last night?" Luther asks.

"Yeah," I say, but don't offer anything more.

A silence falls between us, the first one of the evening.

"So, uh . . . do you know where you're going to college yet?"

It's an awkward question, one that anyone could ask, not a guy who likes a girl. But it's a topic, so I go with it.

"I'm looking at Vencella," I tell him.

"What are you majoring in?"

"Physical education," I tell him, and he laughs.

"What?" I ask.

"No one *wants* to be a gym teacher," he tells me. "It's just somewhere they end up."

"I do," I insist, hitting him on the shoulder a little harder than necessary. "No, seriously," I go on, telling him about how I discovered this during our summer softball camps, bringing in the kids and showing them the basics. I have no patience for people my age who can't step and throw with opposite sides of their bodies, but somebody's got to teach a kid how to do it.

And it turns out I like being that person.

There was something about seeing it click in their little faces, some with sweat-streaked braids and grime around their mouths. Seeing tanned, skinny arms dotted with freckles and tiny noses scrunched up in concentration when a pitch came in really did it for me.

"Okay, cool," Luther says, hands up in surrender. "I just don't want to see you . . ." He pauses, trying to find the right words.

"What?"

"I think you sell yourself short a lot, Mickey," he says. "I'm not trying to be a downer, I'm just saying. When I came to see you play, I couldn't wrap my head around the fact you were the same girl I met at Edith's, you looked so confident."

"Yeah, well, you know what it's like when you're in your own place."

"Yep." Luther nods in agreement. "But there's more to it than that. Your pitcher gets a lot of attention, and I think you've convinced yourself you're just her sidekick."

"She's the pitcher," I remind him. "What I do, it's not sexy."

He gives me another look up and down.

"The hell it's not," he says.

CHAPTER THIRTY-FOUR

economical: *managing with frugality; guarding against waste or unnecessary expense*

Monday brings an ache in my bones as soon as I wake up, the focal point buried deep in my hip, radiating. I can pinpoint the healed cracks in every bone I've ever broken, identify every fracture as the waves of pain touch them. Everything I've got hurts, but I'm not sweating yet, and my guts aren't liquid.

I skip my Monday coffee with Big Ed, instead stopping at the dollar store on the way to school, where I grab some Imodium. I wash down four pills when I'm back in the car. I don't care if I don't shit for a week, as long as it's not running down my leg. I chase them with a few Advil so that I don't feel like my skeleton is pulling apart at the joints. I eye the bottle of water as

I feel the last capsule stick in my throat, but resist the urge to drink. I can only sweat so much if I'm dehydrated.

My phone goes off as I pull into the school parking lot with a text from Josie.

Sorry—long weekend

I answer immediately—**It's okay.** When she didn't text me back I assumed she was pissed at me for ditching her Saturday morning, and while I didn't like how that felt, I disliked even more that I might never hear her idea for keeping us in supply.

Figured something out, she texts. **Come over after school?**

The question mark hurts my heart. If Josie is really my friend it shouldn't be there, her concern that I'll say no again finding an outlet in those few pixels.

Got a game, I shoot back.

The bubble with an ellipsis inside shows up, then disappears. Shows itself again, then vanishes without a message coming through. I imagine Josie with her expensive clothes, perfect hair, and—I'm sure— re-buffed nails trying to find the right response. It's weird to think of a girl as perfectly put together as her struggling to find words. God, I know how that feels.

Like shit.

It's a home game today, so I'll have almost half an

hour to kill before we start hauling equipment out to the field.

I can come over before, I text. **But only real quick.**

The ellipsis shows again, but this time she sends her response.

Real quick is all I need. Later!

My tongue is sticking to the roof of my mouth by third period. I roll it around, trying to kick up some saliva, but it's large and heavy, awkward in my mouth. I can feel my lips stretching over my teeth as I do, tender skin ready to start peeling away if I don't drink something soon. I shift in my seat, ignoring the teacher as my guts take a spin.

At lunch I take a bite of my chicken sandwich, chewing everything into tiny bits so they can slide down my dry throat without choking me. Carolina puts the back of her hand to my forehead.

"You're not looking so hot," she says. "But you feel it."

Lydia exchanges a glance with Bella Center, while Left and Right stare down at their own sandwiches like they might escape if they aren't paying close attention.

"Just a bug, I think," I say, making a conscious effort to stop my hand as it reaches for the carton of milk on my tray. Carolina spots the move, but misreads it. She digs into the backpack at her side, plopping a bottle of water in front of me.

"Milk's not a good call if you've got a fever," she says.

"Thanks," I say, and crack it open. I take a small sip and swish it around my mouth, waiting until the last second to swallow.

"Drink up," Carolina insists, when I go to cap the bottle. "I can't have you passing out behind the plate."

"Nikki wouldn't mind though," Bella Right says.

"I'm—"

"Fine," Lydia, Carolina, and the Bellas all finish for me, in unison.

"Yeah, we know," Lydia says, pushing her tray away. "Just like you were fine when I found you puking your guts out on the road."

"Hey," I protest, reddening. But the other girls don't look surprised. I guess it was too much to hope that Lydia would keep her mouth shut about that. "Can't a girl get sick around here?"

"How often?" Carolina asks quietly, and everyone else nods.

"Mickey . . . ," Lydia begins, "if you need to talk about anything—"

I stand up, snatching my tray so forcefully that a few peas roll off the side. "What I need is for other people to *stop* talking about me when I'm not around to defend myself."

I'm thinking of that group message I saw on Carolina's phone the other night, right after my dad called to tell Mom his new wife thinks I've got a problem. I wonder if that text conversation got longer afterward, and what my supposed best friend shared with almost the entire starting lineup.

"Why would you need to defend yourself?" Bella Left asks, eyeing me. "We're not accusing you of anything."

I don't answer, because I sure as hell feel like that's exactly what just happened. As I dump most of my lunch in the trash along with the nearly full water bottle, Nikki comes up behind me, clapping a hand on my back. It's not hard, but it's enough to rattle my shoulder blades, my skin so sensitive it feels like her fingers just went straight through to my spine.

"Don't touch me," I say, louder than I intended to, gaining the attention of everyone nearby.

"Whoa, hey . . . ," Nikki says, stepping back when I spin around. Her eyes roam my face for a moment. I must look about the same as I feel, judging by her reaction. "Mickey . . . are you okay?"

"Yeah, of course she is," Bella Left says sarcastically as she appears at my side, scraping her own tray into the trash. "She's Mickey Catalan."

• • •

I speed out of the parking lot after school, anxious to get to Josie's and back. If I'm late for warm-up, Coach will rip me a new one, and the way my body aches, it might feel literal. I throw a few more Advil back, along with another Imodium. My guts are under control, but I've hardly got enough spit for everything to make the journey to my stomach. Spots swim in my vision when I get out of the car at Josie's, a wave of dizziness washing over me.

I've been dehydrated before, and doing it to myself on purpose is straight up idiotic. I'm walking a fine line between passing out because I'm not drinking, or being drenched in sweat because I'm going through withdrawal. Either way, it's not going to look good to the half of the team that already suspects something, and might make the other half start to wonder. Not to mention Mom.

Shit.

Josie answers the door immediately, talking as soon as she opens it. I follow her through the house when she motions to me, sucking on a Diet Coke as we head up to her room. My mouth waters at the sight of it, or would, if I had enough spit.

"So," she says, "remember what my sister said about graduating?"

"To heroin, yeah. No way," I tell her.

"I know, I know." Josie rolls her eyes. "You've got this whole, 'but I'm not a druggie' thing going on."

"Yeah," I tell her flatly. "Because I'm not."

"Right, and heroin is bad. I get it," Josie says, leading me into her room, where she flops onto a king-size bed and kicks off her designer shoes. "But you're already doing heroin, you know that, right?"

"What?" I settle at the foot of the bed. Even as tall as I am, I have to boost myself up onto it.

"Oxy is basically heroin, babe," Josie says. "I looked into it."

"Like you read a Wikipedia article?"

"Uh, excuse me, no," she snipes at me, producing a notebook. She flips it open so that I can see what looks like chemistry notes.

"This is the molecular structure of heroin," Josie says, pointing to a hand-drawn diagram, layers of notes in her bubbly handwriting alongside it. "And this . . ."

She turns the page.

". . . is the molecular structure of Oxy." Josie flips back to the first one. "See any difference?"

"I . . . no?"

"That a question or a statement?"

I glance at my phone. "Look, I've got to be dressed and on the field in—"

"Fine, instead of leading you to knowledge I'll spoon-feed you. Look, Oxy is basically synthetic heroin, just in a pill form. The only difference between them is the delivery system."

"Also one is illegal and one is not," I contradict her.

"Uh, you really think the way we've been using Oxy is okay? We're not taking our own pills; we're buying other people's. And that *is* illegal."

"My doctor wrote me a prescription—"

"For Oxy," Josie interrupts, "which is heroin. Then your prescription ran out and you found someone who would fill it. You're basically already doing heroin, Mick. You're even using a needle."

"Once," I correct her. "I *have used* a needle."

"Fine," Josie admits. "But chemically, it's the same drug. The way you're getting it is illegal. You've got experience with the needle. The only difference is, it's cheap."

"Cheap?" My ears perk up. With Mom already on the lookout for anything valuable coming up missing, I'm headed for a hard-core withdrawal in a day, at least.

"Yeah, cheap," Josie says, flipping another page to a column of numbers. "I talked to Jadine. Her guy said he can hook us up with someone here and we can get a balloon for maybe ten bucks or so."

"A balloon?"

"Yeah, it's like, an actual balloon, I guess. Except it's full of heroin, not helium."

"Ha," I say, when she's clearly waiting for me to acknowledge the joke.

"Anyway"—she waves away my lack of appreciation—"a balloon will have about a tenth of an ounce. Taking into account that pure heroin is about four times the strength of Oxy . . ."

She flips to another page where she's apparently made a flowchart. Her handwriting is beautiful, with swooping curls. It looks funny arranged in a tight table, numbers precisely aligned and calculated. I have no idea what I'm looking at.

"So you're, like . . . really smart."

"Uh, yeah," Josie says. "Thanks for noticing."

"No, I mean . . ." What's in her notebook goes beyond memorizing scanner codes and doing mental math while watching QVC. There are notes in the margins, scribbled questions to herself with arrows pointing to the answers she arrived at later, and a coffee spill marring one page.

Josie sat over this, her mind mulling and working a problem until she found an answer, the same way I took an entire summer to figure out how to hit an inside pitch without popping up.

"You're going to college, right?"

"Yep, pharmacy school. Mom's all excited about me bringing home pens. That *would* be the part she focuses on. I guess a few years ago Viagra made some pens that look like a dick, and if you know the right people—"

I look back at my phone.

"Jos, I've got to go."

"Fine," she says, snapping her notebook shut with frustration. "Short version: Jadine can hook us up with someone she knows who sells safe, potent stuff that will keep noobs like us really high for a long time way cheaper than Oxy."

"Huh," I say.

"Yeah." Josie throws her arms up in the air. "*Huh!* Geez, Mickey. I spent all weekend running numbers and drawing chemical bonds and all you're giving me is *Huh?*"

"I don't feel so hot," I tell her.

"Yeah, you look like shit," she agrees. "How you gonna play a game?"

"First step is being there," I say, getting up off the bed and heading for the hall. The staircase is steep and winding. I have to actually use the handrail to get down, leaning on it as my head swims again. I'm at the front door when Josie yells down from the landing.

"So you want me to call this guy or what?"

As if on cue, my stomach flips, unhappy with its load

of Imodium and Advil, plus the few bites of chicken sandwich. Sweat has started to bead on my lip as I open the door, welcoming the air that hits me.

"Yes," I yell back. "Do it."

CHAPTER THIRTY-FIVE

collapse: *a falling together suddenly, as of the sides of a hollow vessel—or—a sudden and complete failure; a breakdown*

I can't take it.

I stop at the gas station and guzzle down a bottle of water before I even pay, catching a mean side-eye from the clerk. I toss her a few dollars—trying hard not to think about the fact it's the last bit of cash I have—and bust it back to the school. Sweat has already soaked through my bra by the time I hit the locker room, met not by my teammates but by their half-open gym bags, a busted ponytail holder on the floor, and the lingering smell of deodorant. I duck into the shower for as long as I think I can spare—about ninety seconds—to make it look like I'm wet, not sweating, and throw my uniform on.

I'm tucking my jersey into the front of my pants as I jog out to the field to see that Carolina has paired off with Nikki to warm up. The Bellas pointedly ignore me when they come into the dugout while I'm unpacking my gear. I stick my bat into the holder, tuck my helmet under my usual spot on the bench, and am retying my spikes when Coach glances up from the book.

"How's the leg, Catalan?"

"Good," I say, tossing a shock of wet hair out of my face.

"Good," she replies, either not realizing that I didn't warm up, or letting it slide. I'm guessing the first one.

The bus from Peckinah pulls into the lot, girls spilling out to eye us as they take their dugout. This game will be no contest and we all know it. Peckinah hasn't beat us since perms were in style, but that doesn't mean they can stop trying, since we're in the same county league. I wonder what their coach says to them in the locker room . . . *Let's just get this over with? Try not to get killed?*

The bleachers are filling up and Mom spots me, her eyebrows coming together in a question when she sees my wet hair. I wave, but ignore it when she beckons me to come over, instead bending down to strap on my shin guards. Black dots swirl in my vision when I straighten up, and I stagger a bit. Lydia immediately reaches out to steady me, but she doesn't make eye contact or ask if I'm okay.

I get through two innings without much problem. I'm sweating like a pig, but it's the first hot day of the year and I'm wearing ten pounds of gear, so no surprise there. I allow myself a little bit more water, wincing as it hits my nearly empty stomach. Dehydration isn't my only problem. Getting pissed off and throwing away my lunch was stupid for a lot of reasons, but right now the most important one is that my body is burning energy with no fuel in my gut.

We're up 5–0 by the beginning of the third and I feel a little wobbly in the knees when I crouch to take Carolina's first pitch. We still haven't talked using words, just pitch calls and the occasional irritation from her when she shakes off a signal of mine she doesn't like. Pretty soon I realize her face isn't crunched together because she's pissed at me, and she's not refusing to throw the fastball just out of spite.

Carolina's hurting.

The first batter gets a double off her, and she walks the second—something almost unheard of. I call time and go to the mound, carrying the ball with me instead of throwing it. The infielders move to come in, but I wave them off. This is best kept between the two of us.

"How bad?" I ask.

"Not good" is all she gives me.

I roll the ball in my palm, thinking. "Top of the order coming up," I say.

"I know."

"Want me to tell Coach to warm up the relief pitcher?"

Carolina snags the ball out of my hand. "Want me to tell Coach to put Nikki in the catching gear?"

It's as straight of an answer as I'm going to get—*if you're fine, I'm fine.*

"Fair enough," I say, flipping my mask back down and reclaiming my spot behind the plate.

I don't know the name of their leadoff batter because Peckinah doesn't have the kind of players whose stats you pay attention to, but I do know she struck out the first time she was up, and judging by the explosion of breath that came with that last swing and a miss, she's pretty pissed about it.

She still looks it as she settles into the box, kicking dirt back on me and holding her palm out to Carolina to keep her in check. It's the kind of batter I hate, so I signal to Carolina to throw one inside to back her up a bit, and there's a bit of a smile on my friend's face when she nods in agreement.

Carolina goes into her motion, a fluid move that somehow turns a softball into a missile. I've seen it so many times it's almost my own, so I can spot it when

something isn't right. Timing off by a fraction, releas-
ing just a little too soon, the ball sails into me with
no spin, hardly any speed, and right in the middle. It's
an easy kill and the batter knows it, snapping her bat
around fast and sending the ball right back where it
came from.

Right back at Carolina.

She's not ready, not fully there in the moment. Pain
does that to a person, superseding anything except its
own feedback, and Carolina's brain has too many signals
coming at her right now to process what she's got to do.
I'm already on my feet and ready to run to the mound,
fully expecting my friend to catch it in the teeth. Somehow, she gets her glove up, deflecting the shot but not
catching it, the ball clipping the end of the webbing to
hit her right in the elbow.

The crowd makes a noise, a collective intake of breath
from both sides, an acknowledgment of how damn much
that had to hurt. Lydia dashes to where the ball is lying,
dead, and tries to make the throw to first, but too late.
Carolina is on her knees, face white, teeth gouging into
her bottom lip.

"Time," I call, throwing off my mask and shouting
back over my shoulder to the ump as I run to my friend,
Coach closing in from the sidelines. We reach her at the
same moment, but Carolina waves off help, coming to

her feet just as I waver a little on mine, the sprint not
doing me any favors.

"Carolina, are—Jesus, Mickey, what the hell happened to you?"

"I'm f—" I try to talk but suddenly there's too much
strength required to force words out from between my
teeth. I sit down hard, shin guards buckling and chest
protector pushed up into my chin.

"Mickey?"

Carolina has followed me down to the ground, her
arm cupped protectively in her glove. There are dots in
my vision, and if they were white like snow instead of
black this could almost be the night of the crash. Me
crumpled, Carolina standing over me, both of us hurt.
I clear my throat and spit, wiping a fresh wave of sweat
from my brow.

"You okay?" I ask her, strength returning now that I
don't have to stand.

"Yeah, yeah, I'm okay," she says. "Just some ice, I'll
be fine."

Lydia and the third baseman get underneath each of
my arms and get me to my feet, something the crowd
applauds even though they have no idea why I went down
in the first place. I make eye contact with Mom and give
her a little wave as they escort me into the dugout, where
I collapse on the bench, happy for once to see it. I'm

surprised when Carolina plops next to me, close enough that our legs touch.

"You're both done, rest of the game," Coach says, the brim of her hat almost touching our upturned faces. "I'm not crippling my starting lineup playing Peckinah. Nikki, get this gear on. Brit, you're pitching."

Her face lights up, but Nikki is nice enough to apologize as she strips me of my gear, undoing the left leg as I work on the right.

"I got it. You rest," she says, with an even mix of concern and excitement in her voice.

I let Nikki take my gear, leaning forward so she can pull the chest protector over my head. The helmet is still in the dirt halfway between home and the mound, where I left it. She runs onto the field, the relief pitcher by her side, both of them damn near giddy.

"Shit," Carolina says, her head sagging to rest on my shoulder, all the friction between us erased by shared misery and embarrassment.

"Yeah," I agree, closing my eyes. "Shit."

CHAPTER THIRTY-SIX

pretend: *to represent falsely; to put forward or offer as true or real something that is untrue or unreal*

I won't hear the end of it if I go home looking anything less than better.

I did a good job of bullshitting Mom in the dugout, telling her I didn't have enough to eat and hadn't been feeling so great to begin with—something Carolina actually backed me up on. Our team won the game, but Carolina and I still felt like we'd lost something as we trudged into the locker room together, me clenching everything I've got shut, Carolina trying hard to hold her arm naturally, which is almost impossible to do when you're thinking about it.

I don't know if my friend believed what she said in the dugout when she told Mom that I had a touch of stomach flu, but I can't exactly stick around to ask her about it, either. What's wrong with me needs fixed—now—and there's only one person who can help me out.

Josie was desperate enough to hand over her car to Jadine in order to score at Edith's the other night, but seemed fine when I saw her before the game. The only way she had steady enough hands to redo her nails was if she's got a stash at home. I won't make it through the night without screaming, and I can't count on Mom's faith in me to stand up against that. I head over to Josie's place, aware of the screws gouging into bone every time I shift gears.

I don't bother texting first, hoping that somehow the surprise of me showing up unannounced will jolt her into handing over some of her stash, enough to get me through to the weekend, at least. I've got no cash, nothing to give her except well-polished words . . . and those aren't my strong suit. But need is stronger than pride, and I'm knocking on her door before I've put together anything close to a convincing argument.

"Hey," Josie says when she opens the door, looking me up and down in my uniform, the knees permanently dirtied. "What's up?"

"I need some of whatever you've got," I tell her, squeezing the words off my dry tongue. "Please, Josie, my mom thinks something's up and if I—"

Josie motions for me to be quiet and steps out onto the porch, closing the front door behind her. "Yeah, well, I don't need my mom on the same page as yours," she snaps. "What the hell are you thinking, showing up here?"

Stung, I step back. "You *invited* me!"

"Not *now* I didn't," she says, through clenched teeth. "How's it going to look if someone she's never met before just drops in for a second to get something from me and then leaves?"

"I don't care," I say, squeezing my eyes shut, terrified that I'm about to cry.

"I do," Josie insists, digging into her pockets. "You might have blown it at your house but I've got my ass covered here."

"Josie—"

"Try Edith again," she says, shoving some bills into my hands. "Her electric bill is due next week and she's strapped."

"She won't sell her own stash," I argue, but Josie shakes her head.

"She might love her kickers, but she likes having the heat on even more."

I look down at the money in my hands. "And after that?"

Josie is about to say something, but shakes her head

when I hear a woman calling for her from inside. "Get going," Josie says, "or I'll have to introduce you and make you stay longer than either of us wants you to be here."

"I'm going to puke in like five minutes," I tell her.

"I see that," she agrees, forcefully grabbing my shoulders and spinning me around to face my car. "Later."

I make it to Edith's without getting sick all over myself, but she's about as happy to see me as Josie was.

"Neighbors," she hisses when I come to the back door, but her mood improves when she sees the wad of cash in my hands.

"I don't have much," Edith warns me, motioning for me to sit at the kitchen table as she heads back to the bedroom. Apparently I'm only granted access to the living room when Josie is with me. I feel so bad I don't care, and I rest my forehead against her table while I wait, shudders passing through my body. I never bothered to count Josie's money, and when Edith puts a brown bag in front of me I push the whole wad to her without even checking to see what's inside.

I need to get it in my system fast, but Josie has all the needles, so I chew up two 40s and wash them down at Edith's sink, hoping I'm somewhere near respectable when I get home, which needs to happen fast so Mom doesn't wonder where I've been.

I can hear Mom's shower running when I get in the

door, so I take the opportunity to head upstairs and start my own. What dirt I have on me from the game slides off with the sweat, and a little bit of balance returns as I stand under the hot water. I've still got nothing in my stomach but pills, so I yank on a pair of sweatpants and a hoodie to raid the fridge, wet hair hanging down my back.

Mom's waiting for me at the counter, a glass of wine in front of her along with a catalog for mail-order chocolates that I'm pretty sure she dug out of the recycling—which means that she's trying really hard to look casual. I cross to the fridge, taking my time gathering up the stuff to make a sandwich, putting on my own show.

"How you feeling?" she asks.

"Better," I tell her. "Think I caught a little something."

"C'mere," Mom says, holding out her palm. I walk into it, wishing that I felt like this was purely out of caring, and not a test of some sort. "You're a little warm," she admits, pulling away and wiping her hand dry on her robe. I bite into my sandwich so that I don't have to reply.

Mom turns a page of the catalog to a section that's all sugar-free candy. I chew. Neither one of us speaks. She's moved on to organic stuff and I'm halfway through my ham and cheese before she tries again.

"You really scared me today, Mickey," she says, softly.

"I know," I tell her. "I'm sorry."

And I am. I'm sorry that I collapsed on the field and I'm sorry that I yelled at my friends today and I'm sorry that I put Josie in a bad spot and I'm sorry that Edith has to balance being in pain with paying her bills. I'm sorry about all those things. But mostly I feel sorry for myself, and I'm sorry for *being* me at the same time, which gets my already fuzzy head mixed up even more.

I finish eating and rinse off my plate, heading for the stairs to save us both from this awkward semi-conversation. I'm halfway up the steps when I glance down to see that Mom isn't looking at the catalog anymore, she's just staring at where I was standing, her face unreadable.

"I love you, Mom," I say.

She glances up. "I love you too, Mickey," she says, and I get a smile. It's a real one that cracks the blank mask from a second ago, and seems to wash away that little pucker of concern that was forming between her eyebrows.

I really, really need to make sure I don't fuck this up.

I've got a text from Carolina, asking if I know what the English assignment is. I shoot her back the answer, followed by, **How's the arm?**

She answers right away. **Better. How's whatever's wrong with you?**

Better, I tell her, knowing that if I try to defend myself like I did today at lunch anything I say could end up screen-capped and part of a conversation that I'm not in on.

It's a shitty way to feel, but it's a shitty thing to do, too.

You know you can talk to me, Carolina texts.

And that's the thing, yeah, I probably could. But Carolina is a straight shooter, and I don't just mean she throws strikes right up the pipe. I can't say for sure what she'd do if I came clean to her, but I doubt it ends with her skipping practices to come to rehab meetings with me, and after that conversation at the Galarza dinner table I'm pretty sure there'd be no asopao in my future, either.

I type out my go-to response—**I'm fine**—then erase it. Maybe not answering her at all would make my point better than anything. I'm looking for the right words, weighing options and even scrolling through emojis to see if there's one for convincing people you're not an addict when a text comes through from Josie.

Got us covered. See you Friday?

There it is again, that question mark, like maybe I'll let her down.

Damn straight, I answer.

Cool, she types immediately. **Ready for this.**

There's not a question mark after that one, and as I settle into bed I can hear Mom pacing downstairs, something she usually only does when she's got a feeling there's something wrong with a patient, but can't put her finger on exactly what.

After that, it's not a question for me, either.

CHAPTER THIRTY-SEVEN

lead: *to guide or conduct, as going before, showing, influencing, or directing with authority*

Fridays used to mean getting pizza with Carolina and bingeing something on Netflix, but the last pizza we got together ended up in a field next to my upside-down car and I'm pretty sure Aaron is the only person she watches Netflix with these days, if that's what they're actually doing.

Now my Fridays mean telling Mom I'm hanging out with Jodie from physical therapy and driving to Edith's with a curious mix of guilt and anticipation in my gut. I don't know how long the fictional Jodie will hold up against her new suspicions, but using Carolina or any of the other girls could blow up in my face on both sides, and I doubt Mom would believe I'm spending the night at Dad's after what happened last time I went over there.

"Jodie, really?" Josie asks.

"Nice cover," Derrick agrees, laughing.

"Hey, if the truth is the easiest thing to remember, then the next best thing is a lie that's almost true, right?" Luther says, in my defense.

"Whatever," Josie says, checking her phone again.

"So . . . what's the deal here?" I ask.

"The deal is that I've got more balls than these two," Josie says, arching a brow at the boys. "They don't want to risk being seen buying Oxy? Fine. I'm leveling up and taking you all with me."

I can't help but notice a little bit of Jadine in her tone, like talking to her sister over the weekend might have rubbed off.

"Leveling up?" Luther asks, glancing uneasily at me. "What are you talking about?"

"Heroin," Josie says lightly, and now I definitely recognize her older sister's nonchalance in the way she says it.

"Whoa, hold up," Derrick says. "You know I'd follow you just about anywhere—"

"Mostly just to look at your ass," Luther adds.

"But I'm not hitting up some corner just to impress you," Derrick finishes.

"You don't have to." Josie shrugs. "This guy delivers."

"Delivers?" Edith sits up in her chair, suddenly invested in the conversation.

"Wait, like a pizza?" Luther asks.

"Yes, like a pizza," Josie says patiently. "And yes, Edes, he's on the way."

"I don't need another car in the driveway," Edith says. "Yesterday when I was getting the mail Mr. Baylor said it seems like my family is getting bigger all the time."

"Yeah, he's a dick," Luther says.

"He is," Edith agrees. "But I don't need him being a *suspicious* dick."

"Don't worry, I think this guy is pretty good at being discreet," Josie says, tapping a text into her phone. "He'll be here in two minutes, and I'm not telling him to turn around, like a pussy."

Luther and Derrick share a glance.

"Okay, but . . . ," Derrick says, suddenly sheepish. "I don't even know how to—"

"We do," Josie says, waving a hand between the two of us. "Mickey and I shot up last week." While that's not exactly true—we did use a needle, but we weren't doing heroin—the looks on the boys' faces leave me without words, my usual resting place.

Derrick is impressed. Luther is disappointed.

I want to explain to him—somehow—but a pair of headlights sweeps across the living room before I can

come up with anything. Edith mutters something under
her breath, but stays in the chair when Josie goes to
answer the back door. I follow her, Derrick and Luther
trailing me. There's a quick, polite tap on the screen
door and Josie opens it to let him in.

"Um . . . Patrick?" she asks, glancing down at her
phone.

"Yep," he confirms. "Josie?"

"Yeah, hi," she says, blushing a little bit.

"All right, so . . ." Patrick's eyes sweep over the four
of us, making an assessment. "You guys have no idea
what you're doing, do you?"

"No," I say, and it's Josie's turn to smack someone.

"What?" I complain, rubbing my arm. "We don't.
Might as well be straight with him."

"It's cool," Patrick says. "Somewhere we can sit?"

Josie starts clearing the table of place mats and the
salt and pepper shakers, like we're all going to sit down
and do math homework together or something. I take a
minute to look at Patrick, trying to place him. There's
something in the line of his jaw, lightly covered in stubble two shades darker than his blond hair, that has me
convinced I know him, but I'm not sure from where.

Casually, he reaches into his cheek and pulls out a
balloon.

"Ewww," Derrick says. "That's gross, man."

"Be glad that's where I store 'em," Patrick shoots back, and Derrick shuts up.

"Why, though?" Luther asks, curiosity piqued.

"If I get grabbed, I can swallow what I've got on me," Patrick explains. "I make good money doing this. I get busted, I'm out. Bosses don't need a dealer with a face the cops know."

"You got a boss?" Derrick asks.

"You think I make this shit in my basement, bro? It's not a one-man operation, and this ain't exactly weed."

"Right, I know," Derrick says, nodding.

"Now pay attention, 'cause you only get the walkthrough once," Patrick says, his eyes coming back to mine.

And really it kind of is like homework, but not math, more like science. It feels like we're doing a chemistry lab with our checklist—spoon, water, lighter—and the catalyst, a lump of something that looks like coal when Patrick bites the knot off the balloon. He shows us what to do, each step specific and somehow sacred under his hands, the concentration on his face reminding me of Carolina's when she goes into the windup. Soon, four of Josie's remaining needles rest on the table, syringes filled with what Patrick calls "a beginner's dose."

"You know how to shoot?" he asks.

"Yeah," Josie says, eyes still on the needles. "What do I owe you?"

"First one's on the house," Patrick says.

"Dude, free heroin," Derrick says. "You're my new best friend."

"Exactly," Patrick says. "You want more, you call me. If it's three in the morning, you call me. That's what friends are for. Got a pen?"

"One sec," Josie says, going to the hutch by Edith's front door and rummaging around for one. "Um, hold on."

She disappears into the living room, leaving the three of us with nothing to say and nowhere to put our eyes. Mine keep shifting between Patrick and the needles on the table, the only things that are capable of holding my attention at the moment.

Patrick suddenly snaps his fingers. "Mickey Catalan," he says. "That's who you are."

"Shit," I say. "You know me?"

"Yeah, my sister played for Hebron Hills a couple years ago. You faced off with them at sectionals. Hell of a game."

"Oh yeah," I say, remembering. "Five–two. We won, bottom of the seventh when your shortstop choked, error on a grounder that should've never made it to the grass."

"That was bullshit, man," Patrick says, shaking his head. "She had no business being on the field. Her parents paid for new uniforms for the whole team, and suddenly she's first-string."

"Dude, that sucks," Luther says, and I swear he waits for a beat to see if Patrick recognizes him, too. It doesn't happen, and I can't tell if he's relieved or disappointed.

"You were, what, a sophomore?" Patrick asks, and I nod. "This girl's got a hell of an arm on her," he tells Luther and Derrick. "She picked off two at second in one inning that game."

Patrick's gaze is back on me, even though my eyes are still on the needles because right now I'm like a kid at a birthday party, eyeing the cake to pick my piece. That's one reason I don't look up, the other being that I don't want to see the question in my dealer's eyes, the one I've been asking myself lately.

What happened?

But there's another question, more urgent and easier to answer, a primitive call versus the philosophical tangle. There aren't even words for it, just a deep, open space inside of me that's asking for something to fill it.

Josie comes back with a pen and Patrick jots down his number—one time for each of us—pushing away Luther's phone when he asks to add him.

"Number changes next week anyway," Patrick says. "All I've got are burners."

"Hey," I say as he's getting up to leave. "Do you sell to everybody around here?"

"Yeah, pretty much."

"Can you tell whoever shoots up in the park to pick up their shit? I heard there are needles lying around behind the dugout. That's not cool."

"Not cool at all." Patrick nods like he gets it.

He tells us to stay safe and says goodbye to each of us in turn, resting his hand on my shoulder for a second longer than anyone else's. There's something deeply personal and almost caring about his actions, from the eye contact right down to the way he tells Josie to say hi to Jadine for him, and asks if their mom has been feeling better after spraining her ankle.

I don't feel like I'm doing something illegal. I feel like a nice guy just brought me something I need, a friend of a friend who only wants to help me out. It's a feeling that's shared among the four of us as we choose our needles, Josie's face puckering a little with trepidation as she watches the angled tip, her eyes finding mine.

That's the thing about being a natural leader: people look to you even in situations you don't know shit about, like just because I have absolute command of a diamond means I should make the call on who is going to shoot heroin first.

And if it is my decision, it's an easy choice.

I am.

CHAPTER THIRTY-EIGHT

heroin: *an illegal addictive narcotic that produces*
euphoric effects

I make a fist.

I find a blue line.

I break my skin.

I puncture a vein.

I pull blood up into the syringe, watch it dissipate for a moment, a part of my body outside of myself, diluted in heroin, drowning.

Then I plunge.

I am suspended in warmth, elongated like my blood in the barrel, dissipating. I am wholly without pain or caring, even when I vomit. The act itself is almost graceful, robbed of its unnaturalness as everything in my stomach makes its way to my mouth as if that were only to be expected, and I turn my head in agreement, casually leaving it all on the floor next to Edith's couch.

It doesn't matter and I don't care.

My friends move around me, asking me questions. Luther pulls the needle from my arm. Josie pushes my hair back from my face. Derrick lifts my legs onto the couch. Edith cleans up my mess and covers me with a blanket, happy to have someone to care for. I have nothing but love in me, for them and for this place where not only do I not feel pain, but I cannot even remember what pain is.

There is no hurt, there is no fear, there is no stupidity or awkwardness. I am beautiful to these people and I want to share this warmth with them, press their hands to my skin and let them feel what I feel, absolute acceptance and love.

Then they do. One by one, I watch them go.

Luther hesitates after tying off, the hand that holds the needle shaky. Josie takes it from him, shows him how to hold the needle straight, not at an angle. He's about to tell her no, his mouth ready to release the word when she shoots. There is no regret on his face.

Derrick is easier, happy to have Josie's hands on him, eager to show her that he will do as she says. But even she is replaced as the object of his affection once his veins are full. Then there is only Josie, tearful, left behind and scared to stick herself. Edith does it for her.

She stops crying.

There are no tears here, no room for anything other than the feeling that everything is all right, and always will be, and always has been. I turn my head, drawn in by the pattern of Edith's couch, my eyes tracing the outline of blue roses, long frayed by years of use. I'm lost, eyes rolling, then closing, leaning into the warmth like arms enveloping me, heavy and comforting. Endlessly wrapping me inside and out, rocking, cooing, lulling.

It's as if I've found my mother.

CHAPTER THIRTY-NINE

hyperfocus: *intense concentration on a single subject*

The hate comes later, when I see the little round injection hole in my arm.

There are two, one higher up from where Jadine expertly found a vein when she dosed me with Oxy. Then there's the one I gave myself, right in the crook of my elbow where it was easiest. Bruises circle both, the one from Jadine a fading yellow that doesn't quite reach the dark blue surrounding my fresh puncture.

In the shower the newer bruise turns a livid red, the coagulating blood warmed by the water. I press on it, digging into the broken vein like I have with the screws on my hip, treating the wound with pain as punishment. There's an ache that blossoms, pulling an exhalation from my teeth as I press until I feel my pulse, hot and insistent against my fingertips.

There's still heroin in there, somewhere.

Josie told me it takes seventy-two hours to clear my system, even if I can't feel the effects. It's in there, chasing the multivitamin I take every day.

I hold my arm up to the flow of the water, studying the tiny scab that's already formed, the outline my fingers left behind. Mom is downstairs, making breakfast. I heard bacon frying when I crossed the hall to the bathroom, the smell of coffee drifting up the stairs. She's following the pattern that has kept us together since Dad left, a variation on a theme, two plates instead of three.

Mom's down there right now, thinking about the women she will see today, the babies she will deliver. I've watched her often enough to know that her hands can perform one task while her brain ponders something else. She can mother me and many others at the same time, feeding me food while giving them her thoughts. Her life is in balance, calibrated.

She is thinking of what others need.

Her daughter is upstairs, fully focused on the crook of her left elbow.

I am thinking about heroin.

And that's all.

CHAPTER FORTY

boundary: *that which indicates or creates a limit or extent; a separating line; a real or imaginary limit*

I am not a changed person.

I go to school on Monday and no one knows that I have crossed a line. I have not become someone else. There is no sign on my chest. I am not accused of anything. Ironically, Lydia pulls me aside to apologize for what went down at the lunch table last week. I tell her not to worry about it.

But I do not tell her they were wrong.

I admit to myself that I am a heroin user, while also updating in my mind what that actually means. I am not a wasted person. I am not prowling the streets. I am not an addict. I am a girl spinning her locker combination. I am a girl who got a B on her math test. I am a girl who has two holes on the inside of her arm, but they do not tell the whole story of me.

When Bella Right lost her virginity she told us all about it at Lydia's house, detailing it to a degree that left nothing to the imagination and answered most of the lingering questions any of us had, except for one.

"How did you feel the next day?" Carolina asked. "That's always my thing, you know? Like, how can I just get up and use the bathroom and brush my teeth and drive to school and talk to Mom without thinking the whole time, *I'm not a virgin anymore?*"

Bella Right only shrugged. "You just don't. It's supposed to be this big life-changing thing, right? But it's not. You've still gotta pee, and eat and go to school and do all the same shit the next day just like you did the one before. Only difference is a guy's dick has been in you. And you know what? By third period it's like it wasn't even a thing. I had sex, but oh well. I couldn't spend all day thinking about it, right? So I go to fourth period, and then someone asks me what's for lunch, and pretty soon it's just another day. Nothing's different. Not even me."

It's true for me too, although the only thing that's been in me was a needle. There is clarity to my day that I've never felt before, a distinct line between what things are and what they are not, as if my mind has found new, more accurate definitions for everything. I know who my friends are, and which ones belong in what parts of my life. I can sit at lunch and give Carolina hell for missing that line drive, and not wince when she hits my arm for it. The bruises there can't hurt when she touches them, because her hand cannot cross the boundary between the two worlds. How can I feel pain from bruises she does not know I have, and that I refuse to acknowledge when I am with her?

There is a feeling of superiority as well, something I have never carried with me off the field. I eat my sandwich, each bite heavy in my mouth, more food than I need. I listen to my friends talk, their words fluid and easy between them. For once I do not feel the need to participate, to make my own words and fit them with theirs, putting pieces of a conversation together.

I keep quiet, holding things close to me. I know things they don't know. I don't need food. I don't need words. I don't need anything.

Right now, honestly, I really am okay.

And it's not a lie.

We're eight games into the season, undefeated. It's nothing more than was expected of us, and Coach tells us in the locker room not to get cocky. We haven't seen any real competition yet. That's coming on Thursday.

Normally Coach doesn't let up during the season, pushing us at practices in between games just as hard as preseason. But it's raining now, the field nearly underwater. She tells us to do two miles in the hallways, then put in our reps in the weight room.

Bella Right rolls her eyes, mutters, "Hoo—fucking—ray."

We trade spikes for sneakers, trying not to groan. Running indoors is absolute shit. The tiled floor has no give and if you don't know how to land on your feet just right you'll wake up the next day with shin splints. Normally I can feel the impact right up to my teeth, and I'm not looking forward to putting in my time after Carolina and I are finished stretching. But once we've shot down the science hallway, circled the auditorium, and passed the vocational tech rooms, I realize I feel nothing.

It's the heroin, what's left of it, rushing through my bloodstream, feeding my brain, liberating my heart. I take a deep breath, my lungs incredibly open.

"What are you smiling about?" Carolina asks, her own breathing a little shaky, her arm held a little too close to her side, protectively.

"I feel good," I tell her as we jog through the cafeteria, a group of boys glancing up as we pass.

"You look good," she admits after a second, her eyes

trailing over me. I know she hasn't missed the fact that I'm wearing long sleeves, pushed up just below the elbow.

Behind us, the boys catcall the Bellas and Lydia, followed by yells as Bella Right wings a softball at them. She carries two with her when we run indoors, specifically for that reason. Carolina and I both laugh, the sounds mixing together as they always have, hers high and feminine, mine a lower note. I smile even wider, lengthening my stride on the last half mile, pushing Carolina to keep up with me.

"It's like that, huh?" Carolina asks, sucking wind but answering my challenge.

I pass the locker room door a split second ahead of her, momentum taking me past the drinking fountains and a few lockers before I can slow down.

"Perdedora," I say to her.

"Pendeja," she shoots back, sweat streaming down her face.

I don't remember the last time I spoke Spanish with her. It feels good, even if we are just trading insults. We set up our weights, counting reps and spotting each other, laughing at Bella Center when her squat produces a fart that can be heard over the music.

"Jesus," Lydia says, pinching her nose. "Somebody put a bucket under her."

The baseball game was rained out and their coach gave

them the day off, so we've got the room to ourselves, our muscles tearing and lengthening, our tongues loose as we tease each other. The door to the outside is open, letting in a cool breeze and a whiff of rain, washing away the smell of our sweat. No one questions my long sleeves, and I break my deadlift record.

I feel good.

I feel like I can have both things.

CHAPTER FORTY-ONE

betray: *to violate trust, prove treacherous to, or abandon another*

Luther is waiting for me by my car after Wednesday's game. I don't see him until I'm fumbling for my keys. My head is down, mind rolling over the fact that I missed a pop-up in the third inning. We won anyway, and it's the kind of catch that would have been nothing short of a full-on run-and-dive miracle move for anyone else. But for me, it should have been routine, and I couldn't do it.

I didn't react quickly enough, and when the third baseman saw that I wasn't springing up she went after it too, even though I called it. We came close to a collision and Coach gave her a hard talking-to about the fact that I called it, so it was mine, then told me I damn well better not call it unless I know I can get it.

I'm turning that over in my head, trying to decide exactly what went wrong, when Luther says, "Hey, Mickey."

"Shit." I jump, dropping my keys. We bend to get them at the same time and he doesn't miss the twitch of my mouth as I do.

"Your hip all right?"

"Yeah, just sore."

"So, uh . . . how've you been?"

I give him a funny look while I throw my gear in the car. "I just saw you on Friday, dude."

"Right, yeah," he says. "But that was . . ."

I know what that was. It was Edith and Josie, Derrick and Patrick, needles and crossing a line. It wasn't him and me at a basketball game, taking selfies. It wasn't him awkwardly holding my hand as we walked back to the car, our knuckles tight against each other.

It wasn't *us.*

"Wanna grab something to eat?" he asks. "You've got to be starving."

Actually, I'm not. But I don't want him to think I'm avoiding him, so I hop in his car when he opens the door, once more adjusting the seat all the way back.

"So what did you think of that, at Edith's?"

I don't say *heroin.*

"Meh, it was okay," he says as he pulls out of the parking lot.

"*Okay?*" I ask, unable to hide my surprise at such a lukewarm response to something that sent me straight to heaven.

"Yeah, I mean . . ." He spins his hand in the air like Mr. Galarza when he's searching for the right word in English. "I don't know. I felt good for a little bit, I guess, but then I kind of felt like puking. And I hate puking."

"I don't think anyone likes puking," I tell him.

"No." He smiles a little. "But it just didn't feel worth it. I guess I don't like it as much as you guys do."

"Huh," I say, mystified.

"I mean . . ." He trails off, his eyes cutting to me while he drives. "You do what you want to do, Mickey. I'm not judging you. Just be careful, okay?"

I think of Big Ed, always telling me to be careful out there.

"I am," I say.

"If we're all together and using it to let go a little bit on the weekend, then okay, whatever. But I'm pretty sure Josie was popping pills all through the week, and Derrick will do whatever she does, even if it gets him nowhere."

"Right," I say, my mouth suddenly tight.

"You're not doing that, are you?" Luther asks,

scanning the lot at the diner for an open spot. "You only use at Edith's, right?"

"Right," I say again, the word coming more easily after forcing the first one through my teeth. He takes my hand as we walk in, our fingers loosely linked.

I wish it felt as good as being high.

I've got a text from Josie on my phone.

Call me.

I put her on speaker as I drive. "What's up?" I ask when she answers.

"So . . ." She takes a deep breath, followed by a long exhale. I know her well enough by now to read it. Drama is what's up.

"Edith took Patrick's number."

"Why does she need it?" I ask. "She didn't even shoot."

"No. Listen," Josie says sharply, her patience thin. "She took, like, *all* Patrick's numbers. Those slips of paper he wrote on for us? I think she gathered them up while we were high."

"She doesn't want us using?"

"Nice thought, but no. She doesn't want us using *without her.*"

"Oooohhhh," I say. It makes sense. Oxy is how she gathered us to her, an adopted family. If we move on to a different drug she can't supply, the bond is broken.

"Yeah," Josie says, her tone flat. "I am so pissed right now."

"Just call Jadine and get his number from her."

"Yeah, I totally can call Jadine, but that is not the point," Josie says, irritated that I'm not getting it.

I do get it, though.

"You feel betrayed," I say, thinking of the messages on Carolina's phone that I'm not a part of.

"Yeah." Josie's voice is small now, hurt. "So I went over to talk to Edith and she was upset, said we're going to be all about Patrick now and forget about her."

"Did you tell her Patrick doesn't make us meat loaf?"

"Ha, good one," Josie says. "Didn't think of that."

I pull into the garage and turn off the car. "Look, I get that you're upset, but what's the big deal? Nothing's really changed. Call Jadine and get Patrick's number. End of problem."

"It's not the end, Mickey," she insists. "Remember that class reunion Edes went to? She reconnected with some guy that was in Vietnam and got into heroin over there and never gave it up."

"And?"

"And he's got a hookup," Josie practically wails. "And now Edes says if we want to use at her place, we'll have to buy from him. She told me he'll deliver and everything, just like Patrick. But it's not the same thing."

"Uh-huh," I say, finally understanding what the real problem is. Buying heroin from a hunky twentysomething and buying heroin from a scuzzy old dude are two different things. While I'm sure that Josie has her own reasons for wanting to put herself in front of Patrick again, I've got my own.

If I'm getting my stuff from somebody who jumped in fifty years ago and hasn't climbed back out, as opposed to a guy who looks like he can do a cologne ad, I might have to do some serious thinking.

The garage door opens behind me as Mom comes home from work.

I don't have time for serious thinking.

I take Josie off speaker and put the phone up to my ear as I wave to Mom and go inside.

"Call Jadine and get Patrick's number," I repeat to Josie, dropping my voice when I hear Mom come in downstairs. "We don't know what's in this other guy's stuff. Patrick set us up, and nobody got sick."

"You did," Josie says, and I swear she's suppressing a giggle.

"Nobody *died*," I clarify.

"Yeah, right," she agrees, all humor gone.

"Totally the biggest benefit," I add. "I don't care how hot Patrick is."

"Omigod, but he's so hot," Josie says.

"All the more reason to get his number," I say again, closing the door to my bedroom. "And Josie?"

"Yeah?"

"Sooner rather than later," I say, as I feel the familiar ache of after-workout slip into something deeper, more nagging.

"No shit to that," she says, and I hear her own breath catching.

I don't know if she hurts, or if it's the boredom she blamed the first time we met driving her to greater heights in order to relieve it.

All I know is that there's an important game coming up, and we need to win.

And that means I need some heroin.

CHAPTER FORTY-TWO

euphoria: *an intense, overwhelming state of happiness*

We win on Thursday.

And the next Monday.

And the Wednesday after that.

Carolina's face carries a little more worry than usual, a wince following every release, but she pitches the entire Thursday game, and gets us such a significant lead in the first few innings of the next two that Coach sits her. She says it's because the relief pitcher needs the experience, and tells me the same when she strips the catching gear off me on Wednesday.

"Damn, Catalan," Coach says, pulling the chest protector away from me. "We're going to have to tighten this. Where'd your tits go?"

"That's what I've been saying," Lydia says in mock

indignation, throwing her arms up in the air. "Eat some cheeseburgers, Catalan."

I laugh it off, but make a note that maybe I should actually go do that after the game. It's hard to remember to eat when you're not hungry.

"You're fine," Carolina says to me when I sit beside her, swishing water in my mouth to get the grit out from between my teeth. "Lose a little weight and suddenly everyone thinks you've got an eating disorder."

Or that you're doing drugs, I think. Carolina and I have been okay lately, and I'm not going to be the one to mess that up. I'm not happy about riding the bench, but if Carolina isn't pitching there's no challenge in it. I'd rather be next to her than out there, which is one hell of a compliment. She rests her head on my shoulder.

"Over halfway through our senior season, Mickey. What the hell?"

"I know it," I say.

Maybe even better than she does, due to the growing importance of math in my life. It's taken some experimenting, and more than one close call at home, but once Josie scored some balloons off Patrick and handed a few off to me, I've found a good method of operation.

If I shoot up two days before a game, I can get away with telling Mom I'm hitting the sack and laying low until my pupils aren't noticeably pinpointed. I can sleep off most of the high and get through the days to the end of the game without feeling a twinge in my hip or a tremor in my hand. And if I reward myself with a little bit more of a push the night after . . . well, we did win.

I keep my stuff in the box for my cleats, which still carries the scent of leather and has that little package of silica gel clearly labeled *Do Not Eat* inside. It rests next to my spoon and lighter, along with a roll of clean needles, a syringe, and a little bag of cotton balls.

And of course, the balloons.

This time I have one red and one yellow one. Last week Josie gave me a blue one at Edith's, along with a wink. Edith hasn't mentioned her buddy with the hookup again, apparently happy to let us shoot up anybody's heroin as long as we do it at her house. The fact that Josie must be buying when she's not with us makes me wonder if she's using without us, too, but I can't say much since I'm sporting three holes in my calf no one knows about but me.

On the weekend I've got a real reason to celebrate. After Monday's game, two different D3 scouts approached me, and I had solid offers from both schools by Friday. Those colleges can't give me money in exchange for playing a sport, but they can ask me to play, and give me enough academic scholarships to make tuition manageable. Luckily, I've been able to keep my GPA in a place where they can do that without raising too many eyebrows.

But it wasn't easy. None of it has been. So tonight, I reward myself.

I clean a spot on my bicep and give myself a bump more than usual. Mom's not home. I can get high, chase that feeling I remember all the way back from the hospital after the accident.

When we were little in gym class I always loved rope days, when we'd file in to find that Mrs. Mancetti had unhooked the big ropes from the side of the wall and put mats underneath them. She always gave us a choice: we could climb to the top, or sit on the big knot at the bottom and she would swing us. Three pushes were all we got, but I reveled in every second, hair flying back from my face, classmates looking up as I flew past them, then back again.

Then Mrs. Mancetti would grab the tail of the rope and my momentum would be gone, the rush of wind taken from me, my hair flat against my head, my feet back on the ground, returned to the same plane as the other kids, relegated to normality.

Right now there's no one to grab the rope, no one to take the rush away from me. So I load a little extra in the syringe, and I go far, far higher than everyone else.

CHAPTER FORTY-THREE

interference: *the act of coming into collision, being in opposition, or clashing*

"Mickey and Luther sitting in a tree," Big Ed sings at me as soon as I walk through the doors on Monday.

"Seriously?" I say, and hold up a finger in warning before he can start the next verse.

"Sorry, had to do it," he says, in a tone that tells me he has no regrets. "Haven't seen you in a while. Thought maybe you were . . . *busy.*"

"I have been, but not with Luther. We're not even at the K-I-S-S-I-N-G part, so don't go debating what sport our kids will be better at just yet."

"Fair enough," Ed says, sliding coffee—he adds a doughnut—to me. "Heard you signed with Vencella."

"I did," I tell him, the happiness of it followed quickly

by fear, the smallest of dips in my stomach. It first happened when the coach called me to let me know how thrilled she was I'd chosen their school, then passed along information about summer camps, and freshman move-in day.

I put them in my phone, with exclamation points. I have to be clean by then.

It's my new plan, a hard cutoff date for when the heroin stops being a fallback. The season is blowing past me, and if I can just see this through, I'll have the entire summer to dial back my usage and get my shit together.

"Well, congratulations, kiddo," Ed says. "Playing D3 is no small potatoes, and Vencella's a good school."

"Yep," I say, in agreement, but my mind is elsewhere. Right now getting my shit together consists of trying to not get any in my pants. "Use your bathroom, Ed?"

"You know the way."

I do, but something entirely new greets me when I open the door. Ed's bathroom is flooded in a strange light, and when I look up at the bare bulb in the ceiling, I see that it's blue. I do my thing, wash up, and inspect my reflection in this new environment.

"What's up with the bathroom, Ed?" I ask.

"That's for the junkies," he says, flipping a towel over his shoulder. "They started doing it up at the truck stop when a guy OD'd in their bathroom last week. I don't need anybody dying in my place."

"I don't get it," I say. "How's it stop them?"

"Can't see their veins under blue lights," Ed says, confident in what he's been told.

"Huh," I say, and try to pay him for the doughnut. He doesn't let me, but that's not why I'm smiling when I walk out.

Any user worth a damn can find their veins by feel.

I might have front-loaded a little too much.

Thursday morning I'm still high when my alarm goes off. I make an assessment in the mirror. It's hard to tell if my pupils are still a little pinned because of the light in the bathroom or if I actually look as fucked up as I feel. I try flicking the lights on and off, but my pupils don't change size.

I'm considering not going to school when I get a text from Coach. **Game with Baldwin Union moved to TODAY 4:30 @ HOME**

It's quickly followed by a message from Carolina, sent to the Bellas, me, and Lydia. **Uniform NOT CLEAN. Sorry if you're downwind.**

Then one from Lydia: **It's Center's shorts I'm more worried about.**

Dammit, that squat was last month, Lydia. Let it go.

You're the one that let it go.

They go on like that, back and forth. I mute my phone and do a quick Google search, learning that if I take some Benadryl it should dilate my pupils. The downside is I'm going to be lagging through school, but hopefully my eyes will be normal by the time the Benadryl wears off and I'll be awake enough to play a ball game.

I have no idea on dosage so I take three Benadryl and put on sunglasses before heading out the door. It's bright enough outside to justify it, so I keep them on all the way to my locker, not sliding them off until I have to, and then sharing a casual glance with the girl next to me to see if she reacts.

She doesn't. I must look okay.

The Benadryl hits me in second period. It's like a wall, but one built entirely out of feathers. My head dips into my chest and I jerk awake when the bell rings. I duck into the bathroom before study hall. I don't look high, but I don't exactly look right either. I don't know if a doctor could say what is going on at a glance, but you definitely don't need a degree to tell that *something* is. I walk into study hall and Nikki immediately moves her books and tells me to put my head down.

"Take a nap," she says, as if she's prescribing me something. I obey, nodding off immediately and not waking up until she shakes me forty-five minutes later.

Nikki follows me out into the hallway, staying tight to my left side.

"You want a Red Bull?" she asks.

I make a face. Lydia sometimes downs a can before a game if she's not feeling any energy. I've never been a fan. But I've never tried to play high either.

"Sure," I say, following Nikki to her locker.

There's still enough heroin in me that I feel it, an effervescent warmth radiating from my center. It's an intense calm, one that won't let me worry too much about the game, or even if people notice that I'm off. Every time I check up on myself in the bathroom it's more of an assessment than anything, data for my arsenal of cover-my-ass moves as I determine whether the Benadryl did its job.

It did. My pupils look fine, but everything is in slow motion, and I misjudge the distance from my hand to my water bottle at lunch.

"Shit, Catalan," Bella Right says, jumping up as the spill cascades over the edge of the table, just missing her lap.

"Sorry," I say as Lydia runs to get paper towels.

"What's with that?" Carolina asks when I'm on the floor, cleaning up my mess.

"People spill things," I snap.

"No, that," she says, tilting her head toward the Red

Bull waiting for me next to my lunch tray.

"Took some cold medicine. Need something to get me moving," I tell her.

"'Kay," she says. "But that stuff can eff you up. Don't wait until right before the game to slam it."

She's not kidding.

I down it after sixth period, and ten minutes later I'm a twitchy mess. My right eyelid won't stop and I feel like my skin is going to shake right off my body. I'm tapping my pen so much in English that Mr. Duncaphel takes it away from me, so I start moving my legs instead, hitting one knee with the other and then bringing it back again. But the energy doesn't go to my core. There, I'm still a little slow, very meditative. The caffeine is all surface, waking up my body but not my mind.

I change in the bathroom stall in the locker room, checking my arm before I decide whether to wear long sleeves under my jersey. My injection sites are mostly healed and the bruises are pretty much gone, but the one on my bicep extends just a touch below the edge of my sleeve. I leave it, taking the risk in order to parade the inside of my arm and hope that alleviates any lingering doubts my teammates might have.

The Red Bull has worn off slightly by the time the Baldwin Union bus shows up, and our bleachers are filling. Nikki still has to help me hook the line of clasps on my shin guards because my hands are shaky.

"You've got this, Catalan," she says, slapping the top of my catcher's helmet. The sound reverberates inside my head, and I can still hear it as I make my way to the plate. I'm moving slow, which happens when you're wearing gear, but Carolina spots the difference in my gait. There's a tiny frown on her face as I warm her up, the ball moving fast again, her arm in a better place.

"On fire," I call to her when I toss the ball back, but she doesn't answer, only wings another one at me like she's trying to send a message. Maybe she is. Maybe she knows the threat of being hit in the face by one of Carolina Galarza's fastballs is more of an incentive to perk the fuck up than Red Bull.

The caffeine did its job, but I'm crashing by the third inning and I keep zoning out on weird things. An oddly colored stone amid all the white gravel surrounding the dugout. The little pile of chalk resting beside third base where Coach dumped too much when she was lining the field. A little kid on the other team's side, stacking his blocks as high as he can until they fall.

I still had enough jolt in me to get a double my first time at bat, but when the lineup comes back around I'm a mess. I strike out, my swing so far behind the pitch that Mattix raises her hands in the air from where she's coaching third, like *what the hell?*

"You're all right, Mickey," a familiar voice calls from the stands and my stomach bottoms out.

Dad is here, seriously?

I don't look back as I head into the dugout, tearing off my batting helmet and ignoring the commiserating slaps on the back from my teammates. People strike out, it happens. Even great hitters go down against a good pitcher, and Baldwin Union's isn't exactly throwing cookies.

I put my shin guards on and have pulled the chest protector over my head when I notice that the kid from Baldwin Union has the biggest tower yet going, nearly as tall as he is. He's balancing on tiptoes, reaching up to cap it all off with a red wooden triangle when Bella Left shoves me in the back. "You taking the field or what?"

"Shit," I mutter, seeing that somehow we ended an inning and started the next one without me noticing.

"Get it together, Catalan," Coach says under her breath as I jog past, face guard dangling from my fingers.

Carolina and I get through the first two batters easily. One goes down looking, the next grounding out. I've settled into my crouch, the embarrassment of Coach reprimanding me fading, like it doesn't really matter. Usually Coach looks at me sideways and I mull over it for three days, wondering what I did wrong. Right now,

I know exactly what I'm doing wrong, but I can't dig up the energy to care.

I'm thinking about that when Carolina throws her next pitch, the curveball I signaled her for. It spins, red stitches still bright against the white leather because not many people have put a bat on it today. It's a beautiful thing, capturing my attention and drawing me in. I reach for it, conscious once again of the power it has over me, the never-ending draw of this sport.

There's a crunch and a thud, an exclamation from the crowd.

My glove is lying on the plate, ball nestled neatly inside. I don't know why it's not on my hand, or why I'm facedown in the dirt either. The ump is waving his arms above me, calling timeout, and the batter from Baldwin Union is on the ground with me, apologizing.

I have no idea what just happened.

Mattix comes running, as does the Baldwin Union coach, who gathers up her batter and walks her down to first base, telling her it wasn't her fault.

"That's interference, Coach," the ump says to Mattix, and she nods, her mouth a tight line. I'm sitting up now and Carolina has joined the growing crowd at the plate. She yanks the helmet off my head, straight up instead of back, catching my earlobes and pulling hair as it goes.

"What the hell, Mickey?" she asks, voice low and face down in mine.

I meet her eyes, unsure. "What happened?"

"What happened?" she repeats. "You reached for the damn ball, stuck your arm out like you're a first baseman or something. Batter took a crack at it, got you instead."

"Oh," I say.

Coach gets me to my feet, and there's scattered, confused applause from the bleachers. This is the second time they've seen me on the ground this year for no good reason.

"Oh?" Carolina echoes, any concern for me now overridden with irritation. She's about to say more, but Coach sends her back to the mound.

"Let's go, Catalan," she says, keeping an arm around my waist. Coach gets me into the dugout and strips the gear off me wordlessly, handing it over to Nikki. Mattix waits until the inning starts again and no one is paying attention to us and then checks my hand.

It's swelling, but I don't think anything is broken. A dark bruise is already starting across the fine bones on the back, but I can move all my fingers and manage not to yelp when Coach gives it a squeeze. She crouches in front of me, somehow intimidating even when she's the one looking up.

"Mickey," she says. "I don't know what's going on with you."

I open my mouth to explain about Benadryl and Red Bull, how beautiful a softball can be when you haven't really looked at one in a while. She doesn't give me a chance to speak.

"But figure it the fuck out," she says.

Coach walks away from me. I don't play the rest of the game. Nikki does well catching for Carolina and the two of them are laughing by the fifth inning, all concern for me evaporated. It's a close game, and I'm forgotten, everyone else lining the fence and yelling, their voices echoing in the dugout, bouncing off the cinder-block walls.

I don't join them, instead icing my hand and watching the melt accumulate in a puddle around my feet. Dad comes to talk to me, a definite violation of Coach's rules about family in the dugout. He's digging me into deeper shit than I'm already in so I say very little to him, and he walks away looking more worried than he did when he came over.

I don't let it bother me. Try not to care about the backs of my teammates, their jersey numbers lined up in front of me, missing my own. I don't think about Nikki doing a more than okay job of filling in for me, the absolute disappointment on Coach's face, or the concern on Dad's.

I don't have to care about these things because I've got a trapdoor out of reality, a button I can push that will take me somewhere that none of it matters. As soon as I get home there's a box under my bed that will take away what everyone thinks and how they all feel about me right now.

Even me.

Especially me.

CHAPTER FORTY-FOUR

healed: *sound or whole; cured of a disease, wound, or other derangement; restored to soundness or health*

When you've been seriously injured no one lets you forget it. Not your parents, your friends, your coaches, and definitely not receptionists at doctors' offices. I get a text reminder about my last checkup as we're unloading equipment from the bus after an away game that I made it through without falling over or getting hit by anything.

"Shit," I say under my breath, thumbing away the text.

"Booty call cancel?" Carolina asks. She's in a good mood because she struck out the first nine batters against Franklintown.

"More like I've got a definite date with some radiation," I tell her, hoisting my bag over my shoulder as we cross the parking lot to our cars.

"X-ray?"

"Yeah, last one. I hope," I say as I throw my stuff in the trunk. The school let us have senior parking spaces, and we could paint them however we wanted if we paid fifteen bucks. Carolina and I bought side-by-side spots and stenciled in our team record from freshman year on, leaving an area blank for this season. That's in my spot, and we never got around to filling it in, not even the first win. After spending a whole week of the summer on our hands and knees on boiling blacktop, neither one of us has even mentioned it to each other. Right now my bumper hangs over that part, our neglect neatly hidden.

Carolina shuts her trunk and I lean against my car and we look at each other for a second. It's late enough into the spring that it's warm even though it's almost dark out. Moths flitter around the lights in the parking lot, out of control, bashing themselves senseless.

"Three games left," she says.

I open my mouth to say "yeah" or "I know" or "crazy, right?" or something else stupid and instead I start crying. I don't know if it's the beginning of withdrawal or the fact that Carolina got streaks put in her hair without inviting me to go along or that stupid blank space under my car. I'm crying and I can't quit and Carolina crosses over to me but stops a little short, like maybe she was going to hug me and then thought better of it.

It's weird and uncomfortable and I have never been these things with her. A moth makes a miscalculation and ends up swooping into Carolina's hair. The tension is broken by a lot of screaming and hopping around and eventually I pick through her mane and assure her it's gone, and we both ignore the fact that I started crying for no reason.

I drive home sad.

But I go to bed happy.

Mom insists on coming with me to the doctor's office. I'm still really mellow in the morning so I'm okay with it, and don't even correct her when she keeps calling it my "moment of truth." If I did have one such moment, it was probably last week when I ended up facedown on the plate, mesmerized by a softball and overwhelmed by a mix of heroin, Benadryl, and Red Bull. That was ugly, but there was nothing dishonest about it.

We stop for coffee and doughnuts and have to wait forever in the drive-through because it's Saturday. Mom's thumbs keep tapping on the wheel and I'm try-ing to sort through all the bumper stickers on the car in front of us when she says, "I feel like we haven't talked much lately."

She's not wrong. Part of managing my heroin habit is

keeping my door closed.

"I've got a lot going on," I tell her.

"Yes, I get that," she says, handing over my coffee when we finally get to the window. "But you know you can talk to me, right?"

I do know. I know I can talk to Carolina, too. That last, unanswered text from her assuring me of that very thing has been pushed down toward the bottom of my messages, bumped by updates from Josie with Patrick's ever-changing number, and a few from Luther when he needed a ride to Edith's. There are a couple from him asking if I want to hang out, just me and him. I evade him with half lies about homework and being exhausted.

"Yes, Mom," I say, sounding bored. "But I'm fine."

Right now, I really am. It's hard to be anything else when you've still got a decent dose in you.

"Okay," she sighs. We drink our coffee, carefully popping our lids and blowing on it at a red light. I drink mine too fast, burning my tongue and the roof of my mouth. My tongue is fuzzy as I check in, my voice a little scratchy when I answer the few questions Mom tries to ask in the waiting room.

Even if I had something to say it's too hard to talk in here. All the parents trying to get through the week without taking off work have dragged their kids in on a Saturday morning. There are snotty noses and fevered cheeks everywhere and if I get out of here without contracting something it'll be a miracle. We've got Ridgeville on Monday and all my pistons have to be firing for that game.

"Mickey Catalan?"

I follow the nurse and Mom tails me through the halls. I am weighed, and I watch carefully as she taps something into her laptop, her face unreadable. My blood pressure is a little low—no surprise—and again the nurse makes a note in the laptop. I play with the cuffs of my long-sleeve shirt, trying to remember where all my bruises are at the moment.

A tech comes in to walk me down to the lab, and I leave Mom behind when I go to change into the little gown with blue and teal triangles all over it. It doesn't cover much, and there's no mirror in here to see if the holes in the back of my knee are healed, or if the vein I blew last week on my bicep is showing. I twist my head around to get a better idea, pulling something in my neck only to determine it's not showing, and I go to sit next to Mom on an uncomfortable chair, my tongue swollen and burnt in my mouth, my neck tight.

Another tech comes to get me and I walk down to the X-ray room with her, glad that Mom can't follow. I'm too aware of my skin, how the back of my gown slides up when I hop onto the table, tense as the tech positions me just right. She's not looking for bruises though; all her concerns are with my bones, almost as if she's looking straight through me and I don't even have skin at all.

I'm fine with that.

The familiar warning to hold still comes, along with a series of buzzes and a metallic taste in my mouth. I get to put my clothes back on and we're sent to a room to wait for Dr. Ferriman, where I see that someone has scratched an eye off one of the smiling teddy bears.

Mom keeps messing with her purse and I'm dangling my legs from the table, kicking them and letting them swing back so that my toes connect with the crossbars underneath, filling the room with a tiny *ding* every second or so. Dr. Ferriman finally shows up with a yellow folder under his armpit and a big smile on his face.

"Mickey," he says, giving my name a congratulatory edge, and Mom perks up immediately.

"Good news?" she asks.

"Very," he agrees, holding my X-rays up to the light so that everyone gets a good look at my pelvis.

The screws are so easy to spot, dense white fingers that hold me together. I lean in, curious about these things under my skin that I've managed to touch, which one I can feel boring into bone the most.

Ferriman talks to Mom about things like adequate fixation of the hardware and good reports from physical therapy, but the upshot is that I'm fine. I'm better. I'm healed. He says he's never seen anyone recover so quickly, and that I should be damn proud of myself. Ferriman blushes when he says *damn*, something I'm sure a pediatrician doesn't get away with very often.

I smile and say the right things, but the truth is that my gut just bottomed out. Because if there's nothing wrong with me anymore then there's no reason to text Josie, to update Patrick's number, to go to Edith's. Ferriman just took away any pretense I had, any excuse I could make to myself about what I'm doing and why. My tongue sticks to the roof of my mouth and it hurts to swallow. There's a sharp pain in my neck when I look down, focusing on my toes, no longer swinging my legs. I've got tears in my eyes and they both think it's for the wrong reason and nobody has any idea.

The thing is, I thought my hip didn't hurt because I wasn't going to let it, that I kept the pain at a distance as a form of self-care, preempting the agony with pills and then a needle. The thing is, I can't tell the difference between honest pain and withdrawal anymore.

I just know that I hate both and I've learned I don't have to feel either one.

Except now, if I keep using it's not because I'm fighting off an injury or for some noble self-sacrifice to keep the team going strong so Carolina can shine. If I keep using now, it's because I want to.

And yeah, I want to.

So when we go home I tell Mom I'm tired from the late game and I need a nap. She smiles at me and says that sounds great, like I just said I came up with a cure for cancer. I'm her golden child, the miraculous recovery, the strong one.

I shoot up and nod off, blissed out and warm in my bed.

Because if I'm an addict I might as well go ahead and just be one.

Fuck it.

CHAPTER FORTY-FIVE

abandoned: *forsaken, deserted—or—given up to vice*

It's easier after I embrace it.

There's still shame as I head over to Edith's on Friday night, but I've ditched any self-justification or rationalization, which makes room for anticipation. I spent all last Sunday cleaning up Mr. Henderson's half acre, dragging dead limbs, raking up yard waste, and burning it all before the sun set. Mom complained, saying that our neighbor has two grown children and a few grandchildren and there's no reason why his family couldn't help him out, instead of me volunteering my time. I don't tell her Henderson paid me sixty bucks.

That'll all be going up my arm.

I've developed affection for the process, my mind fixating on the spoon, the water, the flame. The end result is ecstasy, but getting there is part of the pleasure, the steps forming a ritual that I know will deliver me.

I get religious people now.

We're chatty when we're high, Edith still relying on her pills, not willing to make the leap with us but happy to be there to catch us when we come down. She brushes Josie's hair, my friend's pupils tiny as she stares at the TV, her words coming out in a never-ending stream.

"I can be smart and pretty," she says. "Everyone acts like their minds are totally blown when they find out I'm going to pharmacy school. Why is it surprising? I mean, Marie Curie was cute when she was younger and Ada Lovelace was flat-out hot."

Luther is on his back, staring at the ceiling.

"Try going to Baylor Springs without being rich, I mean just try it," he says. "I get free lunch. Did you guys know that? My little sister can't take it. She pays for hers anyway, doesn't want her friends to know. What I just shot up would cover her for a week. Fuck. What am I doing?"

Derrick itches. That's his thing.

"Guys, seriously. My skin is coming off. I want to unzip it and just step out of it right now, like a skin suit. A Derrick suit. It needs to happen. I can't take it. *Guys.*"

He is digging pretty hard, leaving red streaks up and

down his arms, dried skin flaking off. I borrow Josie's phone and call Jadine. She says to give him Benadryl. I find some in Edith's cabinet, expired. I give Derrick two and he washes them down. I tell him it'll make it better and whether it actually does or just because I said so, he stops itching.

"Betsy is dead," Edith says, her voice joining ours. "Bob and Helen and Betsy and Tom and Erin and Carter and Grant and Hayley." She names off her loved ones, destroyed by time and fire. "Everyone dies," she says. "Everyone leaves me."

"I don't fit," I tell them. "I'm not good at being a girl. I'm not actually my mom's daughter. My real parents are out there somewhere and if I saw them I might know what I am. If I was supposed to be smart or funny or strong or stupid or mean. I just don't know."

We're all talking and listening at the same time, one hundred percent dedicated to each other while simultaneously lost inside our own heads.

"Jane Goodall was pretty too, in that natural way."

"My coach paid for my shoes last season. Nobody knows that."

"I hate my skin. Not just when it itches."

"Don't ever be alone, kids. Die before your friends do."

"I don't know who I am."

The words come so easily here, in this place. Everyone else fades, Josie's head resting on Edith's knee, a half-finished braid abandoned in her hand as the older woman stares at a commercial for denture cleaner. Luther is pointing at the ceiling fan, his finger trying to follow its circular route. Derrick is out, unconsciousness delivering him from the torture of having skin.

I leave the others behind, no longer invested in their words, not interested in the warm hollow of Luther's arm. I'm restless and prowling, making Edith's house my own. The regular dose isn't taking me where it used to, and I'll have to pop another hole in my skin if I want to feel good tonight. But for now I'm wandering around, up the stairs to the second floor, somewhere I've never been.

It's tidy but unclean, beds neatly made with covers that smell musty when I sit on them. I picture Edith sleeping in her chair every night, the stairs a journey she can no longer make, osteoarthritis robbing her of half her home. I wonder when someone was up here last, and who it might have been. I go to another room, one with a larger bed and family photographs lined up on the dresser, a fine layer of dust covering them all. I swipe my finger across the glass of the largest one to see Edith's wedding picture, the same one used in Bob's obituary.

I rest on the bed and find a crossword puzzle book from 1992 next to the lamp. It's half finished, yellowed pages brittle under my fingers as I flip them. Bob's name is on the front cover, written in cursive. Under the crossword book is a dictionary—Bob, you cheater. It's huge and heavy, with an inscription inside from Helen, wishing them the best in their marriage.

Helen, you gave them a dictionary as a wedding gift? Weird.

Still, I pull it into my lap, fascinated by the heft of it, the tiny print inside and the seemingly endless, almost translucent pages. All the words must be in here, every single one I've ever said and a million I'll never use. In here is the right combination to tell Mom, to confess to Carolina, to come clean to Dad. If I knew all these words and could teach my tongue to say them, maybe I could make things right. I press it to me, hugging the book deep into my chest as I curl around it, willing the words inside of me.

CHAPTER FORTY-SIX

pride: *a sense of one's own worth; lofty self-respect; noble self-esteem*

I'm out.

The balloons have felt smaller since I had to up my dose, and I've found myself weighing them in my hand each time I get them from Josie. I did a shit job of rationing myself this week because I bobbled a perfect throw from Bella Left in the sixth inning when we played Radley. It's something we've done together a hundred times at least, since we were kids. She cleanly fielded a hard shot on the bounce, throwing it right down the third baseline so that I could peg the runner at home.

Left is a genius at this, winging it at a spin so that it bounces just right, timing it so that it hits directly behind the heels of the runner before she goes down into her slide, the ball hopping over her to my glove before her toes can touch the plate, my glove tapping her hip almost gently. No need to rub it in.

But this time I didn't do it. This time I flubbed the snag, my reflexes too slow. Coach practically dragged me behind the dugout and tore me a new one. I kept my eyes on the ground the whole time, thinking of nothing but the needle. That runner scored, and we would've lost the game if Nikki hadn't subbed in for me and punched a nice double in the bottom of the seventh, getting two RBIs and clinching the win.

Fucking Nikki.

I came home ready to forget about everything. Coach's eyes boring into me, Left ignoring my back slap when we came off the field, Carolina picking up Nikki and spinning her around when we won.

But what I have left in my shoebox isn't enough to make a kitten high. I call Josie but her mom is home and she doesn't want me just showing up. She gives me Patrick's new number, and he says he's close and will be over in five.

I haven't even showered and I'm still in my uniform. I strip down fast, pulling on sweats and a hoodie, but I don't have time to wash my face before I hear Patrick's polite knock on the door.

"Hey," I say, pulling it open. "Come on in. Mom's not here."

Patrick follows me inside and I'm all arms and legs, big and awkward in my own home. I'm so flustered I didn't even remember to get my cash around and there's a long moment of silence before I realize that's what he's waiting for.

"Shit," I say. "Sorry, hold on."

I run upstairs and rifle through my drawers, but I blew everything from Henderson last weekend, and Mom only carries cash in her purse, which is with her. I come back down the stairs, face red.

"So, I don't actually have any—"

Patrick waves me off, dropping two balloons on the kitchen table. "Pay me later," he says. "I trust you."

"Seriously?" I swipe them up fast, partly because I'm afraid he's teasing me, partly because I can't stand seeing them on Mom's table, or the rings of his spit that are left behind. I wipe them off with my sleeve.

"Yeah, you're a good customer. And we gotta keep you well. Last game of the season next week, right?"

"Right," I say, heart lifting. "You follow us?"

"I follow *you*," Patrick says. "There's a weird kind of pride in it for me."

"Huh," I say, curling the balloons in my fist.

His phone goes off, and he glances down. "Let me know what you need, when you need it," he says. "Catch you later, Catalan."

He leaves and I go upstairs, feeling oddly accomplished. I just did a whole drug deal on my own. My dealer even fronted me the stuff. Patrick's right, there is a weird sort of pride involved in it, and I imagine him following my stats in the newspaper. It sends its own sort of warmth through me, a pleasant precursor before the needle goes in.

I get a text from Josie before I nod off. Her mom's been suspicious lately, and she thinks she's been going through her phone. She deleted Patrick's last text with his new contact info, and needs his working number. I send it to her, pleased that I have it and she doesn't. I tell her he's close by because he was just at my place and she doesn't answer, and that makes me smile because her being jealous of me is something that would never happen in any situation except this one.

Mom comes home and sticks her head in my door to whisper good night. I'm with it just enough to answer, watching as the sliver of light fades into nothing at all as she closes the door and goes back downstairs. It's pitch-black and perfect in my room, an uninterrupted space for me to be whatever I want to be in the blank canvas of my mind.

My phone goes off, the screen bright and jarring.

It's a group message with the Bellas, Lydia, and Carolina, something about wearing our jerseys to school before the last game next week, and maybe even painting our faces too. Lydia says no, Coach would never be okay with that. Left says she would be if we wash it off before the game. Right says she's in if Center is. Carolina loops Nikki into the conversation.

A text from Luther comes in a few minutes later, asking me if I want to come over and watch some ESPN. I do, kind of, but there's no way I can drive and I don't want Luther to know that I'm using outside of Edith's. That thought makes me feel bad, and I don't want to feel bad.

I want to feel good.

I turn my phone off.

CHAPTER FORTY-SEVEN

catastrophe: *an event producing a subversion of the order or system of things; a final event, usually of a calamitous or disastrous nature*

Coach busts our asses all week.

She keeps saying now is not the time to congratulate ourselves. We can't claim we're undefeated until we've stared down the last opponent. Mattix says that in the regular season each game is a battle determining who gets to walk into the war of the tournament wearing conference champion patches on their uniforms, and a better rating for tournament bracket placing. If we want that to be us, we've got to earn it, and our last game will be the proving ground.

After the pep talk on Friday I'm feeling good. We all walk out of the locker room with set faces, determined to make it happen tomorrow morning. Left has forgiven me for bobbling the play at home last week and Coach assured me I'm starting, but if I lose my edge I won't be finishing the game. I nod, knowing she's right. I almost blew our record for everyone. That won't be happening again.

Patrick's stuff is consistent in quality, and I've taken copious notes so that I know exactly how much I can have, and when I can have it. My tolerance has risen, so I've had to adjust to shooting up the day before a game instead of two days before. I'll give myself a nice dose tonight, sweeping away the soreness of a grueling practice, the lingering pain in my hip, and the sting on my inner thigh where I missed a curveball from Carolina. Like, I didn't even get the glove on it.

It hit right on the meat of my leg and dropped dead in front of me. I gritted my teeth and acted like it just clipped me, but the entire inside of my thigh is purple, and I get to carry the stitches that I was admiring so much with me for a while. They're imprinted on my leg, little indentations that I could feel if it didn't hurt so bad just to touch the skin, the broken vessels all around them spiraling outward like fireworks.

The leg itself is swollen and I'm wondering if it wouldn't hurt to give myself a little more of a boost than normal as I drive home. As soon as I think it I

feel the ache in my joints, my body choosing the pain
of withdrawal to goad me into giving it what it wants.
I check my box when I get in my room to see if I've got
enough to buy myself a buffer for tomorrow's big game.

I don't.

Mostly because I am the world's biggest idiot and I
fucked up and my blood pressure skyrockets and I can
feel the pulse beating in my neck as I look at the mess
that I've made. I didn't screw the lid onto my water tight
enough last time, and I didn't tie off my balloons either.
There's a puddle of shit where my heroin is supposed to
be and I don't know if it's salvageable.

I grab my whole kit and run to the bathroom, leaning
over the counter, face close to the opened balloon. The
light in here is way better and I'm using the end of my
spoon to scrape together what I can from inside the balloon when Mom yells up the staircase.

"Mickey? You home?"

I kick the bathroom door shut. It's instinctive and
stupid and suspicious as hell, but it's the only reaction
my body allows for. I'm standing there with a heroin-
caked spoon in one hand and a shoebox full of needles
and there's no way to make this better.

"Mickey?" Mom knocks on the door. "What are you
doing?"

"What do people do in a bathroom, Mom?" I call

back, trying to keep my voice light. I toss my last balloon into the toilet and jam the spoon into Mom's makeup drawer. I bury my needles in the trash and shove the box into the bottom of the laundry basket.

"Mickey." Her voice is stern now, uncompromising. "Open this door."

I do the most impossible thing in this moment.

I take a piss.

I sit down on the toilet and think about nothing other than full bladders and running water and please, let me have to pee right now. I do. I pee as loud as I can and hope Mom can hear it through the door. But that's not an issue when she drops all pretense and walks right in because kicking a door shut doesn't lock it.

"Mom!" I yell squeezing my knees together. "What the hell?"

Please let me look innocent, even though I'm not. Please let her see her little girl, not what I actually am.

"Oh," she says, losing steam. She looks around. There's nothing to see. Some backsplash on the mirror and the hand towel I just used tossed on top of the hamper.

"Sorry," she says, shaking her head. "You just . . . scared me there."

"Why?" I'm tense, defensive, somehow righteously irritated that she thinks I was doing drugs in the bathroom even though I totally would have been, given another five minutes.

"Nothing, it's . . ." Mom waves her hands in the air, as if to clear it. "You know what? Never mind. You hungry?"

I really can't sit here much longer with a straight face. "Yeah," I say. "But do you mind?"

"Huh? Oh, yeah," she says. "Sorry."

She backs out, but she doesn't shut the door until I flush the toilet. I wash my hands, running the water long enough to cover the sounds as I dig through the makeup drawer, pulling out the spoon, which I jam into the waistband of my sweats.

"Big game tomorrow," I call. That's how it's done. Change the subject, remind her of something amazing I'm a part of that no junkie would ever possibly be able to accomplish. It works. She's smiling when I open the door.

"Let's get some food in you," she says, heading back down the stairs. "Steak? Lasagna?"

I hear her pop the freezer door when I'm halfway down the steps, my heart rate finally adjusting.

"I've got some corn dogs . . . ," Mom calls. "*Whoa.* Scratch that. Freezer burn."

My phone vibrates and I pull it out of my hoodie pocket to see a text from Josie.

You have anything?

I was just about to ask her the same thing. I go back to my room, dialing.

"No," I say as soon as she picks up. It's a white lie, but not much of one. There's only enough on this spoon to keep me well for a few hours. "You're out, too?"

"Down and out."

My ache increases, whether it's pain or want I don't know. But I can't feel this way tomorrow.

"Call Patrick," I tell her. "Get enough for me too and I'll pay you back . . ." I let my words trail off because I don't know how I'll pay her back, since I haven't squared up with Patrick over the dose I literally just pissed on and flushed down the toilet.

"Number's old," she says.

"I sent you his new one," I remind her.

"Yeah, but I deleted that text to cover my ass."

"Then we're screwed because I did too," I say. "You're not the only one with a mom."

Josie sighs like me having a mom is an annoyance.

"Just call Jadine. Get the new one. Then let me know," I tell her, and hang up.

When I get downstairs Mom is calling for a pizza. Apparently the sight of the freezer-burned corn dogs drove any inclination she had of making dinner out the window.

"Hope that's okay," she says when she hangs up. "I just didn't . . ."

"Feel like it," I finish for her. "Yeah, I get it."

And I do. I scared the shit out of her with that stunt in the bathroom, and while she's reassured now that I wasn't doing anything wrong, the adrenaline rush has left her drained. My phone goes off.

Jadine not answering.

I tuck it back into my hoodie, not bothering to reply. I offer to take the trash out while we wait for the pizza. Mom's thrilled to let me, and she smiles as she looks back at her laptop, one finger absentmindedly playing with the stem of her wineglass.

I dump the bathroom trash first, fishing out my last clean needle. I scrape a mess of tar off the spoon with my fingernail and put as much in the barrel as I can, topping it off with some water from the tap. There's not much in the syringe when I'm finished, but it's something. It goes into my waistband next to the spoon.

I dig my shoebox out of the laundry basket, toss it into my trash bag, and haul everything to the curb. Then I offer to meet the pizza guy at the door, and Mom hands me the cash. I keep the change. He gives me a shitty look when I don't tip, but his problems are not my problems.

I cram pepperoni and cheese and breadsticks with garlic butter in my mouth and down it all with Diet Coke, doing my best to appear normal. My mom knows the Mickey Catalan that eats like a horse, and I need to be that person for her right now.

I need to be who she thinks I am.

I eat until I might puke, my belly pushed tight against the band of my sweatpants, the dirty spoon and clean needle leaving impressions on my skin. We talk about plays and stats and things that happened at last week's game and what might happen tomorrow. My phone goes off twice more and I reach into my pocket to turn it off. I cannot be getting updates about heroin while I talk about softball.

By the time we're finished eating Mom has had a little too much wine and her eyelids are heavy. She groans when she stands and I tell her she's pregnant with a pizza baby and her face folds in a little and that was a stupid fucking thing to say to a woman who can't conceive. She goes into the living room and curls up with a blanket and a book, and I'm pissed at myself for being such a dumbass. Of all the words in the dictionary those are the ones I chose to say to her.

I take our plates to the kitchen and add the spoon from my pants to the dishes in the sink, then power my phone back on to find four texts from Josie.

Jadine still not answering.

Seriously do you have Patrick's number?

I am not doing so grassroots over here.

Lol weird autocorrect. * great *

I'm not doing so great either, and when I hear a slight snore from the living room I take a chance and call Josie.

"Where the fuck are you?" she demands.

"Nice," I say. "I'm at home."

"You seriously don't have Patrick's number?"

"No, I seriously don't."

I hear a tiny popping noise over the phone, and I think she just bit into one of her nails. I imagine nail polish cracking, Josie scraping away at what's left.

"Okay, look," she says. "Get over here, and we'll figure something out with Edith's guy. She gave me his number."

I glance into the living room. Mom is out.

"I thought she said he'd deliver, like Patrick?" I argue. "Why can't I just meet you at Edith's?"

"Because she doesn't want us over there right now," Josie tells me. "That neighbor, Mr. Suspicious Dick, told her that next time he sees more than just her car in the driveway he's calling the cops."

"He can't do that," I say. "It's not illegal for us to go to Edith's."

"Technically, no," she agrees. "But what we do there *is*

illegal, and she said to just chill for a little bit."

There's a rumble in my stomach, the pizza rolling uncomfortably. "Edith actually said *chill?*"

"No!" Josie yells at me. "And that is so not the point right now, anyway. Are you coming over or not? Mom's on a date with the new guy and she wore her expensive underwear so that means she's not coming home tonight."

"Ewww," I say.

"Try being me," she snipes back.

I glance back into the living room, where my mom is just being a mom. Tired and worn out on a Friday night, wrapped in a blanket with a book that'll take her a year to finish splayed across her chest. She's snoring louder, her chest rising up and down.

My stomach rolls again, and it feels like everything in there moves south.

"I'll be there in ten," I say.

CHAPTER FORTY-EIGHT

overdose: *an excessive amount; a lethal dosage of a drug*

"I can't hang out," I tell Josie as soon as she gets in my car. "I've got a game tomorrow and—"

"And softball is *everything*. Yeah, I know," she interrupts. "Head out to the truck stop on the freeway."

"Seriously? That's like twenty minutes."

"Yep," Josie confirms. "And we don't have Patrick's working number and Jadine isn't answering her phone and we can't go anywhere near Edith's. Now, either we make a new friend or we both have a long fucking night, and a real shitty day tomorrow, because I cannot *take this*, Mickey, and judging by the sweat that just popped up on your lip I'm guessing you don't feel so awesome, either."

I'm not exactly talkative, but I don't think I've ever

heard Josie say so much. She's in a bad way, her hands shaky and her nails torn, the tips just sticking out of the ends of her sleeves.

"No, I don't feel so awesome," I say. "And I've got—"

"A game tomorrow that decides the fate of the universe, I know, so can you fucking drive faster?"

"Being conference champs *is* important," I snap at her, remembering Coach's speech under locker-room lights, the set faces of my teammates. "It affects our ranking going into the tournament bracket. It matters, Josie. It really does."

"So does going into withdrawal," she says.

And I can't argue with that.

When we get to the truck stop, Josie checks her phone.

"Okay, he says drive over to where the dumpsters are."

"Classy," I say under my breath, breaking my silence, but I clam up again when we get behind the line of semis and a rusted-out S-10 flashes its lights at us.

"That's him," Josie says, tucking her phone into her pocket.

We get out together and walk over as the driver shuts his door. He's Edith's age, hair tied back in a ponytail, the seam on his flannel shirt blown out on the left shoulder.

"You Edith's girls?"

"Yeah," Josie says as we get closer.

"Let's make this quick," he says, glancing around. "I've got CVS, Zombie Eater, and a couple of Five-Toed Cat with me."

"Uh . . ." Josie's face goes blank. She looks to me for help.

"What are you even saying?" I ask him.

He cocks his head, like I'm the one not making sense. "You want heroin, right?"

"Yes," Josie and I say at the same time.

"So . . ." He pulls something out of his pocket, a little white baggie with a stamp of a cat's face on it.

"Black tar," Josie tells him. "That's what we want."

She says it like we have a preference or something, not like it's because we have no idea how to mix anything else.

He jams the bag back into his pocket, offended. "That Mexican shit?"

"Are you seriously trying to guilt me into buying American right now?" Josie snaps.

"Hey, girlie." He raises his voice, bringing his finger up to Josie's face. "I fought for this country and I don't need—"

"Fought for this country?" Josie repeats, cutting him off. "Against Mexico? Is one of your bags called Remember the Alamo?"

"Okay, okay." I step in between them. "This is not

helping. How much?"

Mentioning money brings the bag back out and improves his mood. "How much you need?"

The truth is, I have no idea. This is like me trying to play basketball, running up and down a court instead of in a diamond. I don't know how strong his stuff is or how much it'll take to put me in fighting shape tomorrow.

"I've got a hundred bucks," Josie says, pulling out cash.

I'm not an expert at buying drugs, but I do know she just fucked up. Now he knows what we've got, on top of knowing that we're out of our element. He can tell us that'll only get us one bag and we're in no position to argue. In the end, he hands over five bags—two with the cat face, one with a zombie on it, and two—bizarrely—stamped with the Starbucks logo.

"Let me know when you need me," he says, getting back in the car. "Have fun, kids."

I don't like this. I don't like him and his stamp bags and how he told us to have fun rather than telling us to be safe, the way Patrick does. But Josie doesn't share my reservations, is already texting Luther and Derrick, letting them know to come to her place instead of Edith's. I'm highly aware of the syringe I brought from home, loaded with something I'm familiar with. We get to

Josie's and she takes me straight downstairs to a den, where we dump the bags on the coffee table and Google for advice on how to shoot powder.

It really shouldn't be this easy.

Josie is drawing up a needle for herself when Derrick and Luther come busting down the stairs, bringing with them the smell of clear, cool outside air.

"What's up, ladies?" Derrick asks, polite enough to make it plural but too transparent to look at anyone but Josie.

"Yeah, what *is* up?" Luther echoes, but his eyes are on the table and the different setup going on there.

"Trying something new," Josie says breezily. "Couldn't get ahold of Patrick."

"Cool, cool," Derrick says, flopping onto the couch next to her. "I'm in."

Luther looks at me before answering, but I avoid his eyes, focusing on my phone. By the time they get their own needles together I'm stifling a yawn as I pull my own syringe out of my hoodie.

"The fuck?" Josie gives me a dirty look. "You said you were out?"

"This is nothing," I say, then tell everyone about taking a piss on my last balloon.

"Fuuuuuuuck," Derrick says, tying off his arm. "I would've fished that out, piss or no piss."

I definitely thought about it, but Mom made sure I flushed, any last suspicions she had circling the septic tank along with my heroin.

Derrick nods off, then Luther, and Josie asks me to dim the lights. I do it, yawning as I go, the massive load of food in my belly dragging me into sleepiness. My phone goes off. A text from Mom.

Where are you?

At Carolina's—last game, senior year, getting together.

Home soon.

I send along a selfie of me with Carolina and Lydia, faces crammed together. It's from a party at her place months ago.

K. Have fun. Don't stay out too late!

"I can't hang out," I remind Josie as she ties off and I sit down next to her.

"You going to do that here?" she asks, nodding toward my syringe.

I consider it. Taking anything back home would be stupid after such a close call with Mom, and what little is in the dose I scraped together will only take the edge off the withdrawal, not put me anywhere I can't function.

"Yeah, sure," I say, rolling up my own sleeve.

"I still say you were holding out on me," Josie says, pouting.

"Seriously?" I ask, searching my bicep for a good spot.

I find one and shoot, the warmth inside now matching the basement, my breath slowing, my heart relaxing.

"Whatever," Josie says, plunging her syringe. Her head rolls back. "Bitch." She smiles as she nods out.

It's the last thing she ever says to me.

CHAPTER FORTY-NINE

panic: *sudden, overpowering fright, especially when out of proportion to actual danger*

I'm headed home, my mouth in a tight line.

I will not think about the cooling bodies of my friends, even though I keep wiping my hands on the steering wheel, trying to rid them of the feel of Josie's neck, slick and chilly, with no pulse. I will not think about how Derrick finally escaped his skin, how Josie doesn't have to compete with Jadine anymore, or that Luther won't have to patiently smile through yet another basketball story, someone else reenacting his life.

My phone goes off, the screen flashing brightly in the cup holder. I snatch it, hoping I was wrong, hoping it's Josie and she wants to know where I went. It's a text from Patrick, from his new number.

Need anything?

Yes, I fucking do. I need every balloon he's got and I need it right now so that I don't have to think about what just happened. But I've pulled into the garage already and shut the door, the clatter undoubtedly alerting Mom that I'm home. If I leave again I don't think another old selfie will cover my ass, and I'm sure as shit not inviting Patrick over for a house call when Mom's there.

I turn off my car but stay inside, tapping my phone to dial Patrick's new number.

"Whatcha need?" he answers, and he's so cool and calm, so under control that it's like I finally have permission to lose it. Everything I clamped down on in Josie's basement and on the drive home is out, rolling from my mouth and down my face in a mess, loosely strung words and hot tears.

"They're dead, Patrick. They're all dead. I left them there. I didn't know what to do and I just left and I don't know."

"Whoa, whoa, whoa . . ." His voice is low and soothing. "Where you at?"

I wipe my nose and hiccup. "At home."

"And what happened? *Slowly.*"

"We couldn't get ahold of you, so Josie and I went out and got some from Edith's guy, but—"

"Out at the truck stop?"

"Yeah."

"No good. That's some bad shit they sling out there."

"You think?" I snap at him, my voice cracking. "So Josie and Derrick and Luther, they all shot it, but I still had some of your stuff so I did that instead so I'm okay, but they're not. They're all dead."

"Uh-huh," Patrick says, like the reiteration of the fact is mildly boring. Josie would be so pissed if she knew.

"So what do I do?" I ask, sniffing.

"Nobody knows you were there, right?"

"No," I agree.

"Then you're fine. Cops'll just say, look, bunch of kids OD'd. Another Friday."

And it kind of sounds like that's how Patrick feels about it too, like "stay safe" was just his catchphrase, not actually a motto.

"But what do *I do*?" I ask again.

"Shit, I don't know, Mickey. You're shooting heroin. People die. That's it."

"That's *not* it," I argue, useless words that only make his more powerful.

"Look, do you want anything or not? I missed three calls talking about this."

"*FUCK YOU!*" I shout so loudly my spine vibrates. "My friends are fucking dead!"

"Yeah, but you're not," Patrick says, calm as ever. "So call me when you need something."

I throw my phone and it bounces off the windshield into the passenger seat as I hunch over the steering wheel, sobbing. Patrick said to call him if I needed something but he wasn't talking about comfort. All he wants to do is sell me heroin to get me through this and if I had any cash on me at all right now I would call him back. I'm reaching for the phone anyway, wondering if we can work something out about what I still owe and how far my credit extends when the overhead light in the garage comes on.

"Mickey?" Mom's standing in the doorway, still wearing her clothes but with a crease in the side of her face from falling asleep on the couch. "What's going on?"

I grab my phone and wipe my eyes before I get out, even though I know I can't hide the fact that I've been crying.

"Honey." Mom comes to me when she sees, arms open. I collapse into her, smelling her shampoo and her overly sweet wine breath and a little whiff of the pizza from dinner. She pats my back.

"I know it's hard," she says. "Senior year. Last game of the season. But think about everything ahead of you. You've still got tournaments and you girls are going to go so far this year. Focus on that, honey," she says, pulling back and pushing a strand of hair out of my face. "Focus on the good things."

I would love to.

But I don't have any heroin.

CHAPTER FIFTY

hysterical: *feeling or showing loss of control over one's emotions*

I am a fucking mess.

My hands can't hold on to anything and my bones feel alive under my skin, zinging with an energy that doesn't extend to my brain. That's dead, dormant, unable to do anything other than spew out images of Josie with gray lips, Derrick slumped slightly against Luther, the only warm places left on their bodies where their skin touched, holding on to that last sliver of life. It's all I can think about, and the small measure of comfort that rested in that last syringe has long since lost any potency, overcome by panic—and guilt. My shaken mind keeps producing the word *if*, followed by an emphatic *I*, squarely placing blame.

If I hadn't ruined my last balloon.

If I hadn't deleted that text with Patrick's number.

If I hadn't driven Josie to the truck stop.

If I hadn't wrecked the car in the first place, shattering my hip and Carolina's arm.

It's one in the morning and this line of thinking is not doing me any favors as I pace in my room. I've got to be on a bus in five hours, headed to Dandridge. I've got to look rested and ready to go, not like a girl who was making time with her friends' corpses the night before. Nobody even knows Josie and Derrick *were* my friends, except Edith.

Edith.

Fuck.

My stomach rolls, everything I ate for dinner anxious to make an exit, one way or another. I collapse onto my bed, hugging my middle as if I can coerce it all into settling. My joints ache as I curl into a ball, the pervasive pain back again. My hip feels like it has more nerve endings in it than any other spot on my body, every hole I ever punched through my skin alerting me to its existence.

I can't play a game like this. My friends are dead and that sucks but like Patrick said—I'm not. I'm alive and if I'm going to get through tomorrow or the next day or the goddamn rest of my life I need something. I voluntarily pissed on my stash, and I'm sure as hell not going back to the truck stop because that shit killed everyone I know that uses.

Except Edith.

Shit, Edith again. I don't want to think of her right now, dozed off in her chair, the blue light of the TV playing off her face, unaware that Josie is dead. I can't imagine how she'll react, what the blow will do to her. But what I *can* imagine is the hallway leading from the living room, where she's probably sleeping right now, the bedroom it leads to, and the safe in the closet.

She might have Oxy. It might be enough to get me through the game. Urged on by the thought, my mind comes alive, reeling off scenarios that get me what I need. I can't get out of the house again tonight, but if I leave early enough in the morning I could stop at her place first. But she said to *chill* because of the neighbor, so maybe I can talk her into meeting up somewhere. All I have on me is the change from the pizza and that's not even enough to get a 20 off her but maybe she'll be desperate enough with her cash flow drying up that she'll go for it.

It's flimsy, but it's logic that puts something in my body other than agony. I'm calling her before I think about the time, unconcerned about waking her, or if I sound unhinged. Even Josie and Derrick and Luther are

gone from my thoughts, past tense. I'm in the present
and all I can think of is myself, and what I need.

"Hello? Mickey?" She's groggy and off, her tongue
thick with sleep and—if I'm not mistaken—a little bit
of Oxy.

"Edes, hey," I say, using Josie's affectionate name.
"You selling?"

I hear her sit up in her chair, the soft sounds of the
television in the background barely audible, an ecstatic
woman trying to sell me jewelry.

"What time is it?" she asks.

"I don't need it now," I tell her, trying to sound reassuring while not answering the question. "I just need to
know what you've got."

She's quiet again, and I hear her fumbling for the
remote, QVC mercifully muted a few seconds later.

"You can't come here," she says. "Mr.—"

"Yeah, I know. Josie told me all about that." I say it
like she's still alive, like I expect to talk to her again
someday. "But I could meet you somewhere in the
morning."

"Hold on," Edith says, and I hear the foot of her
recliner flip down, the springs grinding together. I
know the process so well, can picture her rocking back
and forth a little to build up momentum to get out of
the chair, leaning against the wall for support as her bad

knee resists straightening out. She's out of breath when she brings the phone to her mouth again.

"Done with the needle?"

No. God, no. Not ever.

"Yes," I say.

"It's dirty," Edith says, and I hear the indistinct hum of the police scanner in the kitchen as she passes it. "I told Josie—"

She cuts off, my friend's name a dead thing in her mouth.

"Edith?" I ask. "Edes?"

She doesn't answer, but I can hear the scanner clearly now, like Edith either leaned down next to it or turned the volume up.

7300 to 45 . . . Go ahead 7300 . . .
report to 2500 Baylor Hill Drive . . .

"Josie?" Edith says.

"No—" I say, the only word I can come up with.

"That's Josie's address," she says. "Mickey . . . Mickey . . ."

She's saying my name now, like I'm supposed to make it okay. Like I can fix everything.

. . . possible 16, 29 en route . . .

They're calling the squad, but I can tell them they don't need to be in a hurry. Because it's too late and it doesn't matter anymore and goddammit Edith is falling apart, her breath coming in huge gasps.

"Josie? Is it Josie? What happened? What's a sixteen?" she asks.

I hear a thump like Edith just hit the ground and I swear to God if she has a heart attack right now I've got to get the combination for the safe out of her before she dies.

```
45 to 7300 . . . Go ahead 45 . . . Call
in a 16f . . . three victims . . .
```

"Three?" The number and the coroner's code takes what wind she has left right out of her, all of it adding up to one thing. I'm alive. They're not.

"*Mickey!*" She screams my name like it's tearing her throat open, the most painful combination of letters she's ever spoken.

"Why not you?" She's screaming. "Why couldn't it be you? She was going to go to school and get out of here and do something with herself. She was a beautiful girl and a good girl and a smart girl."

"*And a junkie!*" I yell back, anger erupting. "She was a fucking junkie."

"So are you!" Edith screams.

"SO ARE YOU!" I shoot back.

"She never liked the needle," Edith babbles. "I had to do it for her that first time. She wouldn't have even *tried* it if it wasn't for you."

"Bullshit, that's bullshit." I seethe. "It was Josie's idea—"

"Josie would never—"

"She did, Edith!" I yell. "She sure as shit did."

"No," Edith insists, rearranging the world so that everything is the way she likes it—beautiful, golden Josie the victim, me the blunderer who wandered into her life and ruined it. And maybe she's not all wrong.

No, fuck that.

"Who gave her pills in the first place? Huh, *Edes?*"

"Shut your mouth. You shut your ugly mouth, you . . . you . . ."

"She was fucked the moment she met you," I say, tears running down my face, and I don't know if I'm talking to Edith or myself.

"Don't talk to me like that," Edith snaps. "Don't call me. Don't talk to me and don't call me. You're . . . you're dead to me."

"Yeah, just like everybody else you ever knew," I snap.

There's a strangled gasp and she hangs up. I throw my phone and it cracks against the wall, screen splintering.

I'm on the floor in a second, swiping my finger across the blank face, ignoring the scrape of broken glass. I hold down the power button, plug it in, shake it, beg it, throw it again.

Nothing works. It's dead and I'm dying and I can't even call Patrick and beg.

Fuck. Fuck. Fuck.

It's the middle of the night and I have nothing and I am nothing and every cell I have is exploding and sweat is pouring out of me and I'm shaking and I'm going to puke and shit myself at the same time.

Like Patrick said—I'm not dead.

I'm alive.

Hoo—fucking—ray.

CHAPTER FIFTY-ONE

endgame: *the final stage of an ongoing process*

Every time the bus hits a pothole I think my intestines will slide out and pool around my spikes. No one else seems to notice. We're all quiet this early in the morning, faces stuck to the windows. We'll be a team the second the doors slide open, but right now, Coach wants us to think. She made us sit alone, no doubling up, and took our phones away, not commenting when I had none to surrender.

"Focus," she'd said, standing like a sentinel at the front of the bus. "Focus on winning. Focus on being district champions."

I'm focusing on not dying, which right now is a form of winning.

It's a long ride to Dandridge and I've got plenty to

think about, but misery has an iron grip on my mind and soon I'm not focused on winning or dying or anything other than how shitty I feel. My plan was to rely on Imodium again, but the dollar store wasn't open that early and the credit card machine at the gas station was down. I had my change from the pizza, but it was barely enough to cover what I put in the tank of my car, let alone something to keep my own tank from emptying.

Sheer willpower has gotten me through many things; it can get me through this. I grit my teeth and grab my bag when the bus parks next to the field, digging deep to pull up my game face. I get through stretches and warm-ups, even though the slow jog to center field and back makes me very conscious of the liquid weight in my belly, last night's pizza converted into something unrecognizable.

The Dandridge girls are trickling in by twos and threes, the sun shining impossibly bright off their windshields as they pull into the parking lot. I slide my shades on, flinching even at the little bit of pressure as they pinch above my ears. Every inch of skin I have is screaming, letting me know it exists and has nerve endings in it. I think of Derrick.

Then I don't.

Somehow already the bleachers are full and the umpires are here, talking to each other and the coaches over home plate. Hands are shaken. Gear goes on. The Dandridge girls take the field and Coach still has enough faith in me that I'm batting cleanup. Carolina does her thing, lays down a bunt and beats the throw. I'm on deck, picking at the rubber grip of my bat, when I hear Dad's voice, and Mom answering, hers pitched a little higher so she can be heard over a baby's crying. Chad's crying.

My little half-adopted-something-or-other brother and Devra sit nestled neatly in between Mom and Dad like they actually belong there, and somehow Mom is smiling and Chad's little hand is wrapped around her finger and it's like nobody in the bleachers has ever accused me of being an addict and they're all friends again.

"Batter. Let's have a batter."

The ump is looking at me and I'm up without having taken any practice swings. The bat in my hands couldn't possibly be mine. It's too heavy. Too shiny. Too much. The first pitch sails past me, impossibly fast. She's not Carolina but she's not fresh meat either, and maybe I could've hit off her last year but right now I couldn't hit off a fourth grader in a church league.

The pitch is wide and outside, a small mercy. The next pitch is high, the third in the dirt. Coach is looking at me like why am I just now suddenly listening to her about taking until you get a strike? But then the pitcher throws the fourth ball and I'm in the clear, jogging down to first base like I'm totally fine with the walk, even though I could've put a bat on at least two of those pitches, and judging from the polite— but muted—clapping from the bleachers, I'm guessing everybody knows it.

Lydia comes on hard after me, ready to make something happen. She cranks it and it's on the ground and I don't even get a second to get ahold of everything inside me from the jog to first when I've got to go again, and faster this time. I've never been quick and Lydia could outrun me even on my best days, but this is far from one of those and she's practically on my heels as I round third.

"Get the lead out, Catalan!" Coach screams at me, because she has no way of knowing there's no lead in my pants but there might be shit in a second if things don't go well.

Coach tells us to hear only her when we run, but when you're coming down third baseline the batter on deck is the one telling you whether to slide and Bella Left is telling me to get *down, down, down.*

I hear her, along with the sound of the ball zipping through the air, right past my ear. If it's a good throw it's going to beat me to the plate and if it's a bad one then maybe there is a God. Either way if I don't get dirty Coach will have my ass, so I sink as I slide, right leg stretched, long and tight, left one folded under me, knee biting into the ground and tearing up the spot on my kneecap that's been ugly since fifth grade, scars healing over scars.

I might be fucked up right now but I know how to slide.

The catcher is over me, ball in her glove resting on my hip, the ump hovering behind her, arms straight out on either side of him, calling me safe. Everyone goes nuts and I might be safe but anyone near me is in danger of getting puked on in two seconds.

The Dandridge catcher hauls me up, but I don't even have time to thank her, bolting for the porta-potty beside our dugout, which is mercifully unoccupied. Even if I didn't have to vomit, the smell in here would make me. I'm guessing it's been sitting here all season, collecting everyone's hot dogs and Skittles once their body is done with them. For whatever reason it's the thought of Skittles that pushes me over the edge.

Carolina is standing outside when I crack the door, a bottle of water in her hand.

"What the shit?" she asks, but I only shake my head.

There aren't words for this. Even if I'd absorbed that entire dictionary at Edith's house I wouldn't know them. They don't exist. I take the water and go to the dugout, and put on my shin guards. Coach kneels in front of me as the other girls pull on gloves, the infielders adjusting face masks.

"Mickey," she says. "You look like shit."

"I'm fine," I tell her, strapping on my chest protector like if I can just get the gear on she won't be able to stop me from taking the field.

She reaches out, hand swiping my forehead, cool and dry. It comes back dripping. My own sweat looks sickly to me, heroin leaking out of my pores. Suddenly I want to cry, my mouth pulling down at the corners.

"Let me play, Coach."

I sound sad and pathetic, a little girl asking for a chance. I don't sound confident. I don't sound like a first-string catcher on a team everyone expects to win state. I don't sound like Mickey Catalan. I yank my helmet on, afraid to let her see me cry. Mattix reaches out again, her hand resting on top of my helmet.

"All right, Mickey," she says. She sounds sad, like she knows this won't end well. I shake it off and make my way to home plate.

"You okay, catch?" the umpire asks. I give him a curt nod, and ignore the searching look the Dandridge coach gives me. It's bleak and assessing, like he hopes I'm going to crash and burn right here so they've got a chance.

Fuck that.

I crouch, everything inside of me shifting together. I'm aware of all my organs and can feel each one touching the next, all of it putting pressure right where I don't want it.

Carolina throws out the first girl in three pitches, all of them perfect, right down the pipe. There might as well not even be a batter in the box. The ball zips between the two of us, almost too fast for anyone else to see. I stay as I am, the only thing moving my arm. If she can keep this up, I can too.

But the second batter gets the ball on one and it pops up. Pure reflex gets me on my feet and I flip off my helmet, looking to Carolina for a cue. She's pointing straight up and I see the ball, falling back down to the ground just a little to my left. I barely have to sidestep and it falls, neatly, in my glove.

I can do this.

Everyone's clapping and even Carolina has a smile for me as I toss the ball back to her, but Dandridge's coach is creeping on me again, eyes raking over my face before I get the chance to pull the mask back on.

I crouch again, and this time my stomach protests. Not upward, but down, and I have to grit my teeth and tell myself that I am absolutely *not* going to shit my pants. Not here. Not now. Not ever. Mind over matter.

We're three pitches in on the next batter—two balls, one strike—when I realize that I can't will myself out of this. My insides are pure liquid, and as I jump to snag the next pitch—one that got away from Carolina on the release—I know that something just shifted inside of me. I clench everything I have and call time, choosing to walk the ball out to the mound, like I've got something to say to Carolina about the count, when really I'm just delaying going back down into a crouch.

I push my face mask up, the cool air touching every bead of sweat on my face, ignoring the heavy eye of the Dandridge coach as I cross the space between home and my friend.

"Hey," I say, when I make it out to her. "Two down, you got this."

"I do." She nods. "What about you?"

I shrug, trying to be cool. "You don't want me behind the plate? Tell Coach to put Nikki in."

Carolina shakes her head. "She's not Mickey Catalan." I hand her the ball, our fingers touching for a brief second. "But you're not really Mickey Catalan anymore either, are you?"

I'd already half turned when she says it, so I don't see her face. But it's a knife in the gut all the same, the last place I needed it. Her words twist and burn, and everything inside of me goes with it and willpower couldn't keep me from the needle and it isn't going to keep anything out of my pants, either. So I'm running for the porta-potty, gear slowing me down, legs awkward in my guards. Somehow I make it in time and the smell of rotten shit is almost welcome as I tear off everything I can before it all comes out.

I swear there can't be anything left but somehow I'm still going, doubled over and half conscious and puking now too. The shin guards are splattered and my spikes will never smell like leather again and there's snot and tears and vomit on the chest protector and thank God I threw off the helmet before I got in here because I would've puked right through the face mask.

There's a knock on the door, timid at first but then insistent. Coach tells me if I can't come out that's fine, but they need the gear for Nikki. The entire game is held up because of me and everyone is looking when I crack the door, sliding out the gear piece by piece, giving over everything to my replacement, with a little something special smeared all over it.

I don't come out.

Not in the fourth inning. Not in the seventh.

I stay there, ignoring the occasional knocks, insisting to anyone who asks that I am fine. I stay there, and I hear the last game of my senior year unfold. I stay there, sweat trickling down my skin, filling needle holes. I stay there, listening to my team win the league title without me, the smell of shit in my nose, and the taste of vomit in my mouth.

CHAPTER FIFTY-TWO

empathy: *the action of being sensitive to, and experiencing the feelings of another*

They're playing "We Are the Champions." They do that on the bus ride home when we win. Or *they* win, I guess. I can hardly claim a part of this victory. I don't come out until I know the bus is loaded, my teammates' accusing faces safely separated from mine by glass and metal. Mom coaxes me out with the reassurance that no one is there but her, and I crack the door, not meeting her eyes. I slide out and close it behind me so she can't see the vomit on the floor, but I know she can smell it.

I keep my head down and she guides me across the parking lot, the sound of Queen and my friends' voices following as we get into Dad's minivan, bought new to go with his fresh start. Dad's behind the wheel, Chad and Devra in the middle row. The back has been reserved for me, covered in trash bags they must have rushed to buy when I had shouted somewhere around the sixth inning that I wasn't riding the bus back to the school.

I crawl to the back, collapsing onto the seat. Devra unbuckles and disentangles her hair from Chad's grip to join me.

"You really don't want to do that," I tell her.

She props me up, reaches across my chest and buckles my seat belt. I'm too weak to tell her no, and I don't care enough to fight her when she grabs my chin and makes me look her in the face, despite the smell of my breath. I can't resist when she pushes up my sleeves, going past the elbow to my bicep, cool index finger running over the broken vein there. Next she pushes up the leg of my pants, heading right for the crook of my knee.

Devra does it all in silence, touching each injection spot lightly.

"What's this from?" she asks only when she spots the trailing bruise from where Carolina's pitch got me in the thigh, the first two imprinted stitches of the ball showing past where she rolled up my pants leg.

"Didn't get my glove on it," I tell her, my voice weak. I can't hold my head up anymore, instead resting it on the back of the seat.

"Okay, Mickey," Devra says, covering everything

again as she puts my clothes back in place.

My head rolls to the side and I see that Mom is talk-ing to Coach over by the dugout. They both have their arms crossed and no one looks happy. Mom is crying. Coach might be close. I might be too, if I had anything left in me. But it's all out now. Snot, tears, shit, vomit, and the pretense of caring. Nothing matters anymore.

Mom walks away from Mattix, carrying my gear, impossibly small under the load. Dad opens the liftgate and she dumps it there before she climbs into the pas-senger seat. Apparently they all came together to my last game of the season in a big show of solidarity and all I did was hide in a porta-potty.

"Everybody buckled?" Dad asks when Mom shuts her door, like everything is fine and I don't smell like vomit and his ex-wife sitting shotgun while his baby sits alone and his new wife holds my hand in the back is perfectly normal.

I thought everything was out but I was wrong because I'm crying again and Devra is quietly reaching over and cleaning my face every now and then with a wet wipe from the diaper bag. Nobody talks, but Mom and Dad are having a conversation with their eyes, a trick that doesn't leave with a divorce.

Dad drives to our house and everyone comes in, like it was decided beforehand. Devra hands Chad off to

Dad and he gives me a sad smile over that chubby, perfect shoulder. "Go upstairs, Mickey," he says. "Go with your mom and Devra."

I don't have the energy to disobey.

They strip me in the bathroom, Mom shaking her head and crying while Devra peels my clothes off, the broken holes and burst veins nothing she hasn't seen already. I don't say anything. My teeth have melded together as I watch Mom, only able to look at her reflection in the mirror, unable to meet her eyes.

They make a pile of my stinking uniform, Mom actually folding it as if to restore some dignity, vomit-splattered spikes resting on top. Devra hands me a towel and I wrap myself in it, covering my body but no longer hiding my skin, every hole I ever put in myself on display as I sink to the floor, back resting against the tub.

"Mickey," Mom says, her voice small. "The Dandridge coach suggested to Mattix that you be drug tested."

Fuck. Fuck. Fuck. *Fuck.*

I thought I was empty but again I was wrong. I have screams in me. They come out, angry and belligerent, righteously offended even though my very skin brands me. I'm screaming and I can't stop, even though I taste blood in my throat. I've never been good with words but it turns out I don't need them. A primal sound is erupting from inside, tearing me apart at the seams, and

I won't ever be put back together again. Not the way I was before.

Dad's pounding on the bathroom door and Chad is crying and I see the baby in his arms for one second, the fear on Dad's face as Mom goes to the hallway to try to explain, as if there are sentences that make this okay.

I'm still screaming, unintelligible, my forehead resting on my knees and the towel the only thing between me and the cold floor and I just want to sink through it, just want to be gone. I want to go somewhere there's a rope swing and I get more than three pushes and all I want is my hair blowing behind me and the weight removed from my heart and the darkness out of my soul. That can't happen here, not in this bathroom where I'm practically naked and my dad's second wife is staring at me.

"*What?*" I shriek at her, my swollen throat distorting the word.

"Mickey," she says calmly, a stark counterpoint to my rage. "I'm not your mom and I'm not your dad, okay? All I am right now is a recovered addict, and you can talk to me."

But that one exclamation is all she's going to get out of me. I grind my teeth together, barely leaving enough room for breath. I can't deny what they've seen, but I won't confirm it either. So I just sit. Sullen. Silent.

"Your coach said she can't just ignore the suggestion from the Dandridge guy. So what will that mean, for you?"

My face crumples again, but there are no tears left, so I just sob, big, hitching breaths that send me into a dry heave. I go for the toilet, towel puddling around me, but nothing comes out. Devra cracks the door, asks Mom to bring me some comfortable clothes, then shuts it again. Devra leans against the wall and waits for Mom's quiet knock, then tosses me a pair of sweats and a hoodie. I put them on, wash my face, and rinse out my mouth.

"Want to get out of the bathroom?" Devra asks, but I shake my head. I can't look at my parents just yet.

"Okay," she says agreeably, sinking to the floor beside me. "So can they *make* you get tested?"

"No, they can't legally make me get tested," I say. "But now that it's been brought to her attention she'll have to report it to the school, and they have to tell the cops."

My voice breaks on the last word, one that never used to apply to me and now has terrifying connotations.

"Right," Devra says. "And what does it mean for you athletically, if they find something?"

She has the grace to say *if* they find something, even though she just saw my skin.

"First offense, you're barred from competition for

half the season," I say.

"So . . . no tournament games?"

No. No tournament games. No ticking off the wins through sectionals, districts, and regionals as we rise through the ranks. No state tournament run.

Not for me, anyway.

I shake my head and wipe my nose. The sweatshirt Mom grabbed for me is bright orange, bought so that I could run in the evenings and still be visible. Right now it looks like a prison jumpsuit.

"I don't want to go to jail," I say.

Devra laughs. It's light and soft, weirdly out of place in this room where I was just screaming so loud my ears popped. "Honey, you're not going to jail."

I think of Bella Left and *NCIS* and people being thrown against cars and handcuffed, metal bars striping their faces as their cells close. "Why not?"

"It's your first offense, and you were only using, not selling. Unless there's something else you need to tell me?"

I think of three dead bodies in a basement in Baylor Springs.

"No," I say.

"Okay," she says. "You're a minor. You'll get a slap on the wrist. Group counseling and some therapy."

We're quiet for a second, and she reaches out, fingers

entwining with mine. There's a small scar on her hand, a circular dot right above the big vein at her wrist.

"How long am I going to feel like this?" I ask her.

"Depends," she says. "How long have you been using heroin?"

Forever. Always. Since I was born.

"A month. Month and a half," I tell her.

"Okay," she says, and I notice she's been using that word a lot to start her sentences, like anything about this is actually *okay*. "You can try to go cold turkey, or I can take you to a methadone clinic. There's a good one on Broad and—"

I start crying again at the thought that I might need a methadone clinic.

Devra breaks off, hand moving from mine to go around my shoulders. "Maybe a week," she finally answers me. "When's the last time you used?"

I think of an empty needle on a coffee table, next to a bag with a cat's face stamped on it, the stuff I didn't use. "Had a little last night," I tell her. "Hardly anything."

She sighs. "Okay, well, you don't want to hear this, but you're going to feel worse before you feel better."

I nod, wipe my nose again. Devra's answering my question, but she thought I was only asking about withdrawal. I'm not.

"When do I stop wanting it?" I ask her.

"Never," she says.

My eyes are so swollen I don't think anything can get through them, but more tears do and I'm falling to the side, collapsing against Devra, who is so small her arm can barely reach the length of my shoulders. I've got no strength left and she can't possibly hold me up, her tiny bones could never prop up my own.

But somehow, she does.

CHAPTER FIFTY-THREE

support: *that which upholds, sustains, or keeps from falling, as a prop, or pillar*

I admit to using.

Once the accusation is out there, Coach can't ignore it, and I can't hide from it. There are many muted phone calls, Dad and Devra and Chad more or less shacked up with us for the weekend, everyone with dark circles under their eyes and more text messages than they can keep up with. Dad talks to the athletic director at the school, Mom takes a leave of absence, Devra secures a place for me in a recovery group. Everyone else is in control of my life now; I'm only riding the waves of their actions, a piece of trash in the ocean of their movements.

Devra's right. It gets worse.

The pain fades, but I alternate between wanting to be

held like a baby and wanting to kill anyone who touches
me. I scream at my dad that he should have never left us
and I tell Mom she never wanted me. Devra calmly joins
me in my bedroom and shuts us both in.

"Do you know what you're doing to your family?" she
asks.

"Do you know what YOU did to my family?" I scream,
and that—finally—is something that drives her away.
She takes Chad and goes back to Dad's new house, and
Mom yells at me for yelling at Devra, and I crawl under
my bedspread and refuse to come out.

Dad lets himself in and sits on the edge of my bed,
hand resting on my shoulder. I can feel the weight of
him on the mattress, the warmth of his hand through
the bedspread. I haven't looked him in the face yet.

He doesn't say anything.

I don't say anything.

Mom and Devra tossed my room before I was allowed
any privacy. They went through every pocket in every
piece of clothing, emptied my drawers and even pulled
them out of the dresser to check underneath. Dad
hauled my mattress into the hallway and everyone went
over it with their phone flashlights, looking for slits.
Devra found my shoebox, cardboard dry but mottled.
She carried it away and I almost followed her, nearly
ripped it from her hands to check for residue.

Something.

Anything.

Devra comes back the next day, keys jingling in her hands. "Time to get up, Mickey," she says. She's smart enough not to try to sound bright and cheery, just making a statement of fact.

I don't have to go to jail, that's the deal.

I do have to go to hell.

My team is getting on a bus to go to Medina and begin their tournament run. I am getting in a minivan and going to a methadone clinic.

It's not what I expect.

Mom fills out the paperwork. Devra sits on my other side. The people in the waiting room are not rocking back and forth. They're not scratching at their arms or talking to themselves. A mother waits her turn while her toddler plays with a set of scratched blocks from the bin in the corner. A clean-cut guy a little older than me goes outside to smoke a cigarette, the shake of his hand as he lights up the only thing betraying him. There's one older man who slumps in the corner, empty eyes on the TV.

I think of Edith.

My name is called and a lot of people want to talk to me, want to know what I used and how I did it, what's gone up my nose or in my mouth or in my veins or up my ass. I make a face on that last one and the nurse only shrugs.

"People do it."

They weigh me and check all my injection sites and ask me questions I don't want to answer. My teeth go together again, tight, but Devra comes back with me and she puts her hand on my knee, and I see that little needle-prick of a scar on the same hand as her wedding ring. Mom wanted to come back, too, but Devra said it might be easier for me to be honest if she didn't. So I've got this woman with me instead.

And I'm glad.

They ask how I started.

I talk about my hip and the wreck, how Carolina tried to pull me to my feet with her good arm and we both ended up falling in the snow. I tell the doctor about therapy and Kyleigh being the good cop and Jolene being the bad cop and how I cried every night from the pain. I get to the Oxy, explaining how it not only took the pain away, but how I could find words when it was in my system, how I said things to Josie that made her my friend.

I talk about Oxy as a pill I'd throw back, then as a sticky grit between my teeth, and finally as something I popped into a vein. I tell them about the almost economical choice to switch to heroin, and rope days in gym class. I confess to stealing Mom's wedding ring, cash from under Devra's jewelry box, to not knowing when to stop or even if I wanted to.

Devra assured me that anything I say is covered by doctor-patient confidentiality, so I talk about Josie and Luther and Derrick, dead in a basement. I talk about leaving them there. I tell them about Edith and how everyone leaves her. I talk until all the words I've ever known have been used, most more than once, and my throat is swollen and sore.

I say so much, all of it true.

Coming clean feels almost as good as heroin.

Almost—but it'll have to do.

CHAPTER FIFTY-FOUR

shame: *a painful sensation excited by a consciousness of guilt or impropriety, or of having done something that injures reputation*

I find their obituaries.

Luther *died unexpectedly.*

Derrick *passed away suddenly.*

According to the paper, only Josie overdosed.

Their senior pictures look odd next to an obituary, what was supposed to be the documenting of celebration now used as commemoration. I hardly recognize Derrick, and I realize it's because he looks confident. With Josie around he was either unsure or compensating, talking not at all or too loudly. In his picture, he looks like his skin fits.

Luther has a basketball on his hip, lanky arm hanging low. I have to zoom in to really see his face because

Luther was so tall the photographer had backed way up to get the basketball in the shot. I can't get a good look at his eyes without the image pixelating, but he's there, staring back at me. I wonder if I'd loved heroin a little less, what could have happened between us.

Josie looks perfect, of course. Her hair is a pale sheet, smooth and glossy. Her nails match her sweater. She's got one hip cocked and a look on her face that says she hasn't decided if she likes you yet or not.

Her mom starts a nonprofit. The news interviews her and Jadine as they sit, perfectly poised on a leather couch in their front room, a place I passed through approximately once, on the way up to Josie's bedroom, where she showed me the molecular structure of heroin. Jadine is wearing long sleeves.

There are certain things I can't have. Not right now, anyway. My laptop is long gone and my phone hasn't been replaced. Mom texts her number to all my friends so they can get in touch with her if they want to talk to me. No one does.

Coach Mattix does call, to make sure Mom knows I'm invited to the spring sports banquet.

I don't go.

Mattix texts the date, time, and location of the next tournament game.

I don't go.

We win districts.

I'm not there.

We win the first two regional games.

I'm not there.

My classmates graduate. Technically, I do too. But I don't walk. I ask the school not to put my name in the program so there isn't an awkward pause when they announce the graduates in alphabetical order, everyone noting my conspicuous absence in between Brady Castor and Jeanette Catawba.

Mom put parental locks on her iPad. I can use it as a calculator or to watch Netflix. That's about it. Mom makes me chili as a joke and we eat it all. It doesn't sit well and I lose most of in a fantastic fashion.

Dad talks to Vencella. They say I'm welcome to attend and play ball after a voluntary drug test, but Devra says it'll be easy to get drugs there, and I won't have my family as a support system, so it may be smarter to wait a year, until I'm a little stronger.

I agree.

Mom helps me fill out an application for the branch college twenty minutes away. My hand only shakes a little. She has to go back to work, but I go to Dad and Devra's, or one of them comes over and stays with me. It feels like closeness and family, but it also means I'm not trusted by myself.

There is no longer a knob on my door, just a hole where Dad removed it.

The same is true of the bathroom.

I'm not allowed to drive, either. Someone takes me to my group sessions, which I thought I would hate, but they actually make me feel less shitty. There are people here who have done worse things than I have, and more that haven't. We talk, and we listen, and when a new girl introduces herself as Jodie I almost smile.

Jodie from therapy is real.

I get my methadone pill after group and Devra takes me home. It settles my stomach and makes me think about heroin less. I could use a spoon to eat chili the other night and not curl my hand around an imaginary lighter. I don't hurt nearly as much, and I've stopped attacking my own pain, digging fingernails into old wounds.

What it doesn't help with is the guilt. I print out their obituaries and hang them around my mirror. Josie, Luther, and Derrick stare at me every morning. I let them.

I wake up from one of my many midafternoon naps to find Mom sitting at my dresser, looking at the obits.

"I recognize Luther," she says. "Did you know the others?"

"Yeah, they all went to Baylor," I say, sitting up and pulling sweaty hair out of my face.

"She was really beautiful," Mom says, reaching out to touch Josie's face.

"Supersmart too," I tell her. "And Derrick . . . he had all this energy."

"Did he play any sports?" Mom asks. "What did he like?"

"Fashion shows," I say stupidly, and cry. "They were my friends. Luther maybe something more than that. I don't know. I fucked it all up."

Mom stays where she is, folding her hands. "They weren't really your friends, Mickey. Not if they let you do what you did. Real friends would've stopped you."

Anger soars from a familiar place, the violence of withdrawal still skulking inside me. "And what would a real mom have done, huh? Maybe a real mom would've known. Maybe a real mom would've stopped me."

It's the lowest I can go, one of the worst things I've ever said.

"That's unfair, Mickey," she says, using the measured tone she's picked up since going to a support group for parents of addicts. I hate it. I throw myself back down on the bed and cover my head with a pillow.

"Leave me alone," I say.

I hear her get up and move to the door, but she falters there, and when her words come they're dulled by the pillow.

"Carolina never got an abortion, did she?" Mom asks. "You used that money for drugs and used a lie about your best friend—a real friend—to cover your ass, didn't you?"

"Yes," I say.

"Jesus Christ, Mickey," Mom says, her voice fading as she leaves my room. "Jesus Christ."

I cry some more, my tears soaking into the pillow, my breath coming back at me, hot and wet.

Sometimes it's hard to decide what's the worst thing I ever did.

I don't leave the house except to go to the clinic.

My team sweeps regionals. Coach texts Mom the time and date of the first state tournament game in Akron. I don't go.

Twenty minutes after the first pitch Mom comes in my room and hands me her phone with a little smile. I hold it awkwardly, like I've forgotten how.

"Hello?" I say.

"Top of the first," Nikki says. "We won the coin toss. Carolina put down a nice single. Bella Right is up with a full count—"

I hear a collective groan.

"Scratch that. She struck out."

I listen to the announcer, his voice heavy and strong as

it carries. Bella Left—he actually says her real name—steps into the box.

"Oooh, damn, that one was moving," Nikki says. "He's going to call it inside though . . . yep. Ball one."

"You're not seriously going to narrate the entire game to me?" I ask.

"Don't you want me to?"

Nikki's quiet for a second, and I hear the click of spikes on concrete, a helmet dropping, the ding of a bat hitting another one as someone gets theirs from their rack, Lydia ranking the other team by their attractiveness.

"Yes," I say.

"Okay. My dad's in rehab for the third time," Nikki says, like it's part of the conversation. "And that's a walk for Bella Left . . . nice. Runners on first and third. Carolina stole."

Of course she did.

"Coach'll send the one on first," I say. "Try to get the catcher to throw on her, then send the runner on third."

I hear Nikki spit out a sunflower seed. "Their catcher isn't fast enough. She's no Mickey Catalan."

"Neither am I," I say.

"Crap, I'm in the hole. I'm handing you off to Lydia, okay?"

"Um, yeah, sure," I say. I don't know if Lydia wants to

talk to me or if the phone is shoved on her, but suddenly she's there on the other end.

"Catalan," she says. "Aw, shit, their catcher just threw on the runner and the second baseman totally fucked it up."

There's indiscriminate screaming. Lydia doesn't bother taking the phone away from her mouth. My eardrum is blasted with the dugout going insane and I know that our runner on third just scored. When she speaks again she's out of breath.

"Carolina made it in!" she says. "She's got dirt all the way to the back of her neck. Perfect backdoor slide."

"I'm sure it was," I say.

I hear Carolina come into the dugout, can make out the sounds of everyone smacking her on the back, or the ass, whatever they can reach. The sound goes muffled for a minute and I know Lydia is telling her I'm on the phone, but I already know Carolina doesn't have any-thing to say to me.

"You're still my hero, Mickey Catalan," Lydia says.

"Heroine," I correct her.

"Yeah, fucking irony, right?"

Something impossible happens. I smile.

CHAPTER FIFTY-FIVE

bittersweet: *a feeling of happiness accompanied by regret*

They win state.

There is a parade and a bonfire even though it's eighty degrees out. I imagine the team sitting on straw bales and throwing candy at everyone as they're hauled through town on a flatbed trailer, most people throwing the candy right back at them. Last year when we won regionals Bella Left said we should throw out condoms instead and those probably wouldn't get thrown back, and her mom was mortified.

They're on the front of the newspaper and Carolina even gets a spot on the local news, talking about the free ride she got into college. The news reporter makes sure to mention that three other members of the team will be playing at the college level—Lydia Zoloff, as well as

Bella Carter and Bella Graham. I will never get used to hearing their last names.

Nobody mentions Mickey Catalan.

A month later I'm off methadone and Devra is making me take morning runs with her, before the sun is too hot. She says the heroin blew the dopamine receptors in my brain, which is why nothing is interesting anymore and it's almost impossible for me to be happy. Just like weaning off the drugs, now I have to build up my natural dopamine levels so that small things like seeing a puppy or watching a funny movie will feel good again.

I know better than anyone that exercise is a natural high, so I agree to go with her, shaking off the stiffness of my hip at seven in the morning when Devra shows up on the doorstep, looking perky in a bright-pink shirt.

She looks cute as hell, but she can't run for shit.

I beat her to the park and she waves at me from half a mile back, walking, arms above her head so she can get her breath. I'm sitting on a bench stretching my leg when someone comes up behind me.

"Hey," Carolina says.

She's strong and tan in an electric-blue tank that shows off her muscles.

"Hey," I say back, shading my eyes against the sun, all

too aware that I look pale and sickly next to her.

"Can I sit down?" she asks.

"Sure," I say. She does, but not too close. "I saw you on the news," I tell her.

"Yeah, that was pretty cool." She scuffs the toe of her shoe against the concrete. In the distance, Devra's pink shirt comes closer.

"Can I ask you something?" Carolina says.

"Yeah, anything." I've been answering intensely personal questions from so many people that nothing bothers me anymore.

"Why?"

Except maybe that one.

"What do you mean, *why*?" There's an edge in my tone, defensiveness I didn't mean to put there.

"I hurt too, you know," Carolina says, her voice lifting in response. "My arm was busted all to hell, and I went through therapy and took Oxy just like you did. But I listened when my prescription ran out and Mom and Dad said no more. I spent the winter scared shitless that I wasn't going to be able to throw all season and I'd lose my scholarship, but I didn't jam a needle in my arm. I didn't lie to my friends. I didn't fuck myself up. So why did you? Why you and not me?"

It's a hard question, one that gets passed around in group sessions and sticks in my head at night, while I lie staring at the ceiling, thinking about heroin. I've asked myself and we've asked each other and our parents have blamed themselves and our therapists have tried harder and our doctors have written articles.

What it boils down to is simple, and terrifying.

"I don't know," I tell Carolina.

Her face twists. She doesn't like the answer any more than I do.

Devra is at the edge of the park now and she waves at me. I wave back to let her know I'm okay, but when I turn to say more to Carolina she's gone. I watch her ponytail sway between her shoulder blades as she walks away from me.

I still had things to say, and I could call her back and give it a shot. Try to find the words—in any language— to tell her that I fucked everything up between us and that I know it. That she's the best friend I've ever had and I set her aside for something that almost killed me. But even those words don't feel like enough, and I can't get them out anyway. They're too stuck inside, tangles of guilt not letting them escape.

So I stand silently, and watch her go.

Maybe in ten years we can go to our reunion and I'll have a better answer than *I don't know*. Maybe she'll have seen someone else she loves go through it and realize it wasn't entirely in my control. Maybe I'll be a decade clean and know more by then and I'll have the words to explain it. Maybe she won't even come to the reunion. Maybe I'll relapse and be dead.

I don't know.

CHAPTER FIFTY-SIX

renew: *to make new again; to restore to freshness, perfection, or vigor; to give new life to; to rejuvenate*

Leaves are falling, and I decide to go for a walk when I get home from my first class at the branch, a nutrition class that should transfer easily if I decide to take Vencella up on the scholarship that still stands and finish my physical education degree.

I'm allowed to drive myself places now, and I have a phone. Mom has the passcode to open it and I know she checks my location occasionally because last week she texted me asking if everything was okay when I stopped to get gas without alerting her ahead of time. It's annoying, and sometimes we fight about it. Mostly though, I get it. Trust has to be earned, and I'm trying.

I text her to let her know I'm going to the park, and

grab a jacket. There's just enough of a chill in the air that I need it. Kids getting out of school rush past me on their bikes, and I pull my hood up to cover my face as the upperclassmen start driving past. I leave the sidewalk and cut into the grass, going down the hill to where the softball fields are. They're unkempt this time of year, and I've started to come here when I can, pulling up clumps of crabgrass with my bare hands. It feels good to have dirt under my fingernails again.

Today I'm not alone.

There's a Pokémon backpack resting against the fence, and a little girl is trying to toss her own ball in the air, then get both hands on her bat and hit it into the fence. It's not going well. Her face is red with frustration as she tosses it either too close or too far away from her, and she can't get her hands back on the bat quick enough.

I pull my hood down.

"Plant your back foot," I say.

She jumps, alarmed, and the ball falls to the ground at her feet.

"Sorry," I say. "Didn't mean to scare you."

She doesn't answer, only bites her lower lip.

"Want me to toss for you?" I ask her. "It's really hard to do it by yourself."

She looks around, sees that there are other people in

the park and we're not alone. Taking comfort in this, she nods, still not speaking. I crouch down next to her, ignoring the familiar twinge in my hip. She turns to face me, ready to clean my head from my shoulders. No one's ever done this for her before.

"Nope," I say, getting back up. "The way you were before, facing the fence. See, I'll be down here and I'll toss it, you hit it into the fence. Don't swing on this one, just watch."

I toss it and it falls in between us. Her fingers twitch on the barrel. She really wanted to swing.

I pick up the ball. "Ready?"

She nods, but her swing is a mess. Her shoulder dips, back foot sliding all over the place, trying to pull all her power from her arms, not using her hips. I stand back up.

"What's your name?"

"Angie," she says.

"Okay, Angie," I tell her. "I know you really want to hit the ball, but that's not going to happen until we fix your swing. Will you let me show you how to do it right?"

She nods, but there's a second of hesitation before she hands the bat over to me.

"All right, look."

I show her how to stand, how to plant her back foot

and follow through, how to use her hips and move everything except her head.

"That stays still. Keep it pointed at Carolina," I tell her.

"At who?"

"At the pitcher," I correct myself.

"'Kay," she says, holding her hand out for the bat. I give it to her.

She's wearing cheap flip-flops, so her back foot keeps wanting to slide when she pivots, but she gets the bat on the third one I toss, and gives a little yelp of surprise. The next two she whiffs and her face goes dark with concentration when she tries again. She's under it a little, but makes contact. It sails over the fence and into the weeds, her face sinking as it lands out of sight.

"That's my only ball," she says.

"I'll get it," I tell her. "There's poison ivy."

I pick my way through the tall grass, looking for the telltale flash of white. I spot it, but it's not her ball. It's a syringe, used and tossed, waiting here in the grass for Angie or some other kid in sandals to step on it, proof that Patrick couldn't care less about the message I asked him to pass along.

Fuck him.

I pick it up carefully and throw it into the short grass where I can grab it later and dump it in a trash can.

"You find it?" Angie calls.

"One sec," I say, spotting another needle. It joins the first, and then I do find a softball, not Angie's white one but a bright yellow one.

"Cool," she says when I hand it to her. She wipes the sweat from her forehead, then asks me what time it is. I check my phone and tell her.

"I gotta get home," she says, slinging her backpack over one shoulder, her bat over the other. "Think you could toss for me tomorrow after school, maybe?"

"Yes," I say.

"Cool," she says again. "What's your name?"

"Mickey," I tell her, and she makes a face. My heart sinks because she knows who I am and she's about to tell me she can't be here tomorrow after all because I'm a junkie.

"That's a weird name," she says instead. "See you later."

I go back into the grass. I find three more needles, and two more softballs. One of them is Angie's, worn to gray, the stitches frayed.

The needles I throw away.

The softballs, I keep.

Those I'm going to need.

AUTHOR'S NOTE

I've been in pain. I'm guessing you have, as well.

In the summer of 2012, I underwent advanced surface ablation. In short, a doctor scrapes the epithelium off your corneas and treats the surface of your eyes with a laser to improve your vision. This is an option for patients who want LASIK but whose corneas are too thin for that treatment.

Also, it hurts.

Imagine that initial sting of being poked in the eye lasting for three days while your epithelium grows back.

To alleviate my pain, my doctor gave me three Oxy-Contin—one for each day. I took the first one believing that nothing would ever make a dent in my misery, but twenty minutes later I was fine.

More than fine. I felt *amazing*.

I woke up the next day in pain again but aware that I could easily be out of it . . . and I freely admit, very much looking forward to recapturing the feeling of lightness and peace that Oxy had bestowed upon me.

I didn't get it the second day. I felt fine, quite good in fact, but not equal to how I had the day before. I took my third—and last—pill the next day and was once again disappointed in the results.

Yep—out of pain, but . . . disappointed.

I later learned that this is what's called *chasing the dragon*, an attempt to replicate the initial experience of opiates. People who are chasing the dragon raise their dosages in that pursuit, and while I had a very limited supply—three pills—I understood how habit-forming it could be after taking just one.

Opioids treat pain, yes, but they also allow the user a sense of relief and peace, something that people suffering from mental and emotional trauma are in deep need of. The ease of a trapdoor out of a sometimes cruel reality proves too tempting for many.

Do all opioid users abuse them? No. Plenty of people use opioids daily to treat pain, never sliding down the slippery slope.

The exact formula of what it takes to create an addict is unknown, but the debate includes factors such as environment, genetic predispositions, and childhood trauma.

I chose to write *Heroine* from the point of view of an addict because addiction begins with a single pill prescribed by a doctor, carrying no hint of illegality or allusions of shame. Many of us have been written that prescription or given those pills by hands we trust.

It could be you. It could be me. It could be any of us.

If you or someone you know struggles with addiction, please be sure to check out the resources section at the back of the book.

—Mindy McGinnis

RESOURCES

There are many resources available for those struggling with addiction. Below is a short list of some of the well-recognized programs that can offer help.

Substance Abuse and Mental Health Services Administration (SAMHSA): www.samhsa.gov

The Substance Abuse and Mental Health Services Administration (SAMHSA) is an agency within the US Department of Health and Human Services. SAMHSA devotes its resources, including programs, information, and data, to help people act on the knowledge that behavioral health is essential to health, that prevention works, that treatment is effective, and that people recover from mental and substance-use disorders.

SAMHSA's site features a treatment locator, a helpline (800-662-HELP), and a suicide prevention hotline (800-273-TALK), as well as educational materials spanning prevention, treatment, and recovery.

National Institute on Drug Abuse (NIDA): www.drugabuse.gov

NIDA is a federal scientific research institute under the National Institutes of Health, US Department of Health and Human Services. Their mission is to advance science on the causes and consequences of drug use and addiction and to apply that knowledge to improve individual and public health.

NIDA's site features educational resources for parents, teachers, kids and teens, and family and friends of addicts, as well as resources for those struggling with drug abuse themselves.

NIDA for Teens (www.teens.drugabuse.gov) has the latest on how drugs affect the brain and body, featuring videos, games, and blog posts relevant to teens.

Narcotics Anonymous (NA): www.na.org

NA is a nonprofit society of people for whom drugs have become a major problem. Recovering addicts meet regularly to help each other stay clean.

NA's site features literature about the program as well as a meeting locator.

Alcoholics Anonymous (AA): www.aa.org

AA is an international fellowship for people who have had a drinking problem. It is nonprofessional, self-supporting, multiracial, apolitical, and available almost everywhere. There are no age or education requirements. Membership is open to anyone who wants to do something about their drinking problem.

AA's site features program information, video and audio PSAs, as well as a meeting locator.

Al-Anon & Alateen: www.al-anon.org

These groups offer help and hope for families and friends of alcoholics. Al-Anon and Alateen members are people who have been affected by someone else's drinking. They are parents, children, spouses, partners, brothers, sisters, other family members, friends, employers, employees, and coworkers of alcoholics.

The site offers an FAQ, a First Steps podcast, member resources, and locators for both Al-Anon and Alateen meetings.

Self-Management and Recovery Training (SMART Recovery): www.smartrecovery.org

SMART Recovery is an abstinence-based, not-for-profit organization with a sensible self-help program for people having problems with drinking and using. It includes ideas and techniques to help change lives from self-destructive and unhappy to constructive and satisfying. It teaches commonsense self-help procedures designed to empower users to abstain and to develop a more positive lifestyle.

The extensive site offers information about treatment programs, a providers locator, a suggested reading list, and urgent help resources, as well as an online community forum and a message board.

ACKNOWLEDGMENTS

No book is easy to write; this one was even more difficult.

For their continuous and unwavering support, huge thanks goes to my editor, Ben Rosenthal, and my agent, Adriann Ranta Zurhellen. The entire team at Katherine Tegen Books deserves a nod from me as well. This is my sixth book with them and I can easily say they are one of the best imprints to work with.

To my steady and reliable critique partners, R.C. Lewis, Kate Karyus Quinn, and Demitria Lunetta, go my unending thanks, as well as to Lydia Kang, who answers all my emails about wounds without flinching. I also need to thank Jay Willis, who answered my legal questions.

Lastly, I relied heavily on my friend John Nash, an addiction counselor, for resources and information regarding addiction in general and opioids specifically. His clients are lucky to have him.